Glow

ALSO BY STEVE GANNON

STEPPING STONES

A SONG FOR THE ASKING

KANE

ALLISON

L.A. SNIPER

INFIDEL

KANE: BLOOD MOON

GLOW

Steve Gannon

A
KANE
BOOK

Library of Congress Cataloging-in-Publication Data
Gannon, Steve.
Glow / Steve Gannon.
p.   cm.
ISBN 978-0-9849881-7-4

Printed in the United States of America
10 9 8 7 6 5 4 3 2 1

For Dex, who stayed up all night reading it.

Once upon this same earth, in an age long forgotten, monsters walked the face of the land. Not beings of legend or myth, or creatures of tooth and claw, but men, ordinary in every respect save one. Though years have passed and the world has changed, these monsters are with us still . . .

~ Unknown

He who fights with monsters might take care lest he thereby becomes a monster. For when you gaze long into an abyss, the abyss also gazes into you.

~ Friedrich Nietzsche

Who has not asked himself at one time or another: Am I a monster, or is this what it means to be a person?

~ Clarice Lispector

Glow

Prologue

Vinnie Scala watched the woman as she drifted out of the Troubadour Club and started up Santa Monica Boulevard. Two things about her caught his attention. The first was the skintight dress that clung to every curve of her body— black leather, cut low in the back and taut around her thighs, short enough to expose plenty of leg. Second, and more important: She was alone.

Without turning, Vinnie followed her with his eyes as she made her way up the deserted boulevard. A real looker, he thought to himself. And all by her lonesome too, this late at night.

Vinnie hesitated, trying to decide whether to follow her. From the door of the music club behind him came the sounds of a vintage rock band that had been booked for the entire weekend. From where he stood in the shadows, Vinnie could make out the thrum of the bass and an intermittent snatch of vocals. Ignoring the music, he continued to watch the woman as she retreated up the street. Her handbag looked expensive and hung from a temptingly thin strap slung over her right shoulder. Her calves seemed to wink at him as she walked, beckoning. Without glancing back, she turned into a dimly lit side street.

Unconsciously, Vinnie's hand moved to the handle of his Buck hunting knife. Six inches of stainless steel, the razor-sharp weapon hung in a leather sheath looped through his belt—in plain sight and perfectly legal. Vinnie was proud of his knife. He liked the way it made people act when they saw it.

Vinnie came to a decision. He stepped from the shadows and headed up the street, rounding the corner in time to see the woman disappearing into an alley farther on. Not wanting to alarm her, he kept his pace to a fast walk, but he knew he had to catch her before she arrived at her car.

Vinnie broke into a lope when he reached the alley, rapidly closing the distance to the woman. Even so, by the time he caught up with her she was standing beside a white Mercedes convertible, plucking a parking ticket from her windshield. When Vinnie arrived, the woman turned to stare at him. Then, with a smile, she ripped the ticket in half and dropped the pieces to the pavement.

Grinning, Vinnie leaned against her driver's side door. "Littering's against the law, lady," he said, feeling clever.

The woman's smile turned cold. "Please get off my car."

Vinnie's pulse quickened. In one quick motion he pulled his knife from its sheath. He watched the woman, waiting for her first flicker of fear. Strangely, she seemed calm. A faint alarm began sounding in Vinnie's mind. Sometimes women carried mace in their purses, occasionally a gun. He'd even had a few try some karate moves they'd learned in one of those Beverly Hills defense classes. Vinnie was prepared for any and all of the above. In fact, he almost hoped that she tried something.

The woman glanced up the alley, making no attempt to escape. Her arms hung loosely at her sides, hands away from her purse. For the first time Vinnie looked at her face. As he had initially thought, she was beautiful, although a bit too wholesome for his taste. Nevertheless, Vinnie hated being ignored, and right then he decided to do a lot more to her than simply take her money—even if he had to use the knife.

"Lookin' for somebody to save you?" he asked mockingly.

"Actually, I was checking to see whether anyone was coming to save *you*," the woman replied, her eyes turning hard as diamonds.

Vinnie felt a renewed surge of irritation. It wasn't supposed to go this way. There was something about this woman, something he couldn't quite place . . .

"Hand over the purse," he ordered.

The woman shook her head. "I don't think so."

Vinnie stepped closer. Flashing his knife, he snarled and grabbed for the handbag.

With a movement almost too fast to follow, the woman avoided Vinnie's grasp. "That's an awfully big knife," she observed calmly, as if this sort of thing happened to her every day.

Vinnie was again struck by the impression that something about the woman was *wrong*. And how had she moved so fast?

"I'll bet it's sharp," the woman continued, her voice turning silky. "Why don't you cut yourself with it?"

Vinnie glanced up and down the alley. Did the woman have a friend he hadn't noticed? He saw no one. Nevertheless, things didn't feel right, and the thought occurred to him that a guy could catch pneumonia hanging around this bitch. He was deliberating on whether to cut the woman to teach her a lesson, or simply to snatch her purse and get the hell out of there when suddenly he felt an overwhelming *push* inside his head.

Cut yourself.

Although the woman's words had been spoken softly, almost whispered, they struck Vinnie like a sledgehammer. He experienced a surge of confusion. A moment later he felt a terrible burning in his arm.

He looked down. Somehow his knife had become embedded in his left forearm. It was stuck in all the way to the hilt, the glistening blade protruding from his skin on the other side. Blood gushed from the wound, dripping to the asphalt at his feet.

"Wha—" Vinnie gasped, trying to back away. For some reason his legs wouldn't work. In fact, nothing worked. He couldn't move.

The woman stepped closer, gently placing her hands on Vinnie's shoulders. He could smell her perfume, something that reminded him of the lilac that had grown behind his trailer park when he was a kid. Moving even closer, the woman stared at him for a long moment. Then, in a low, sensuous voice, she told him what she wanted him to do.

First your eyes. Then your throat.

Once more Vinnie felt a terrible *push* inside his skull.

The woman stepped back, studying him intently.

During the seconds that followed, Vinnie felt as if he were watching a movie—one of the gory ones he liked in which the camera didn't shift away when things got bloody—except he was *in* this one and couldn't get out. He saw the blade rising in his

3

hand, the tip blurring as it neared his face. He tried to turn his head. He tried to stop his hand. He tried to scream.

He couldn't.

Vinnie Scala felt the tip of the knife touch his right eye, followed by a flash of light and a stab of pain as the cold steel popped through. His hand twisted, then moved the blade to his other eye.

The woman was no longer smiling. Had Vinnie been able to see her, he would have been puzzled by the expression on her face. But now Vinnie couldn't see anything. Lost in a world of darkness, he tipped back his head and ripped the razor-edged blade across his throat.

As Vinnie's life slipped away, somewhere deep in his terrified mind he saw the woman one last time, her face maddeningly beautiful, her lips parted in ecstasy. It was then that he realized what was wrong with her.

Her eyes . . . it was her eyes.

Part One

Tercio de Varas

Chapter One

Thinking back on these past days and weeks and wondering how I got from there to here, I often wish I had done just one thing differently—not returned a phone call, skipped a newspaper assignment, disappointed a friend. I keep thinking that if I had made just one small change, my life might have gone on as before. If so, maybe those I lost would still live, maybe the world I thought existed would still exist, maybe my life would still be as it was. Maybe *I* would still be as I was, not knowing who I truly am. Not knowing *what* I truly am.

Maybe.

Have you ever awakened in the middle of the night, shaken and sweaty from a dream you can't quite remember, yet plagued by the knowledge that you've done something unforgivable, that you've committed some unthinkable crime, and in doing so you've discovered a hideous secret about yourself, something you never suspected? And now, as much as you wish you could change things, you can't . . . and nothing will ever again be the same.

Ever.

That's the way these past days and weeks have been for me. Except for one difference. Hard as it is to believe, even for me, what happened to me wasn't a dream.

Where to begin? Well, as I suppose is true of most things, the best way to begin is at the beginning. Okay, here goes. My name is Mike Callahan. I'm thirty-three years old, divorced, and a newspaper reporter for the *Los Angeles Times*.

Earlier that morning I had picked up my thirteen-year-old daughter, Jamie, from her mother's house in Pacific Palisades. Upon hearing my motorcycle pull to the curb behind her mother's Jaguar, Jamie had opened the front door and bounded down the flagstone walkway to greet me. We planned to take a ride up Pacific Coast Highway to Neptune's Net Restaurant that day, and I saw that she had already dressed for the trip, wearing a faded pair of jeans, hiking boots, backpack, and a leather jacket I had given her the on previous Christmas. Her long dark hair was clasped in a ponytail, but her exuberant run from the house had loosened the tie. As she hugged me, disheveled wisps of hair framing her face and a parade of freckles traversing the bridge of her nose gave her an appealing, almost tomboyish appearance.

It was an impression that was for the most part accurate, but Jamie was growing up. With a mix of both pride and regret, I had watched it happen. Over the past year she had shot up several inches in height, last November her orthodontic braces had come off, and recently her slim figure had begun to show hints of the emerging curves of a young woman, mostly hidden beneath the sweatshirts and loose clothes she still preferred to skirts and blouses. Nevertheless, it was obvious to anyone with eyes that, like her mother, Jamie was going to be a beauty.

Traffic was light on the ride up the coast to Neptune's Net, a casual outdoor dining spot on the beach near the Ventura/Los Angeles County line. Located just off Pacific Coast Highway, Neptune's Net serves a wide assortment of fresh fish, shrimp, live lobsters and crabs, mussels and clams, seafood chowder, and the like. Heading up PCH on a sunny day for lunch there was one of our favorite weekend motorcycle rides, and Jamie and I had continued to make the journey even after Susan and I were divorced.

An hour later, as we eased to a stop in front of Neptune's Net, I noticed a line of surfers bobbing on the waves across the highway, waiting for the next set. Most of those in the water were wearing wet suits, even though it was late summer and one of the hottest days of the year—the unseasonable mid-September heat having been compounded over the past few days by offshore Santa Ana winds ushering in hot, dry air from the desert. A surfer myself, upon returning from my final tour in Afghanistan I had tried to get back into my old sport, but somehow it hadn't been the same.

Leaving the Harley in a dirt lot around back, Jamie and I headed into the restaurant. It was still early and there wasn't much of a line at the order counter. Fifteen minutes later we picked up our food, headed to an outside picnic table, spread out a makeshift newspaper tablecloth, and dug in. Before long a mound of shrimp hulls, clam shells, and discarded crab parts lay piled on the table between us. I had just about given up on the clumsy dissection I was making of a Dungeness crab—wishing I had skipped the crab and ordered more shrimp—when Jamie broached a subject that took me completely off-guard.

"So what happened between you and Mom? Why did you two get divorced?" she asked, seemingly out of the blue.

Surprised, I looked up to find Jamie's clear, inquisitive eyes regarding me from across the table. Though she had kept her tone casual, I knew her question hadn't been asked lightly. I had never talked with her about my breakup with Susan. To be fair, I knew that our divorce had affected Jamie nearly as much as it had her mother and me. Now that Jamie was older, I conceded that maybe she deserved to know some of the details. On the other hand, there are some things you don't discuss with your kid. "I assume you've already talked with your mom about this," I hedged, attempting to put off answering.

"Of course," Jamie replied. Noting the difficulty I was having with the crab, she reached across the table, slid my mutilated crustacean in front of her, and began working on it. "Mom and I talk about everything. So give me your version. C'mon, I'm curious to know why two people who seem so perfect for each other couldn't make it."

I watched as Jamie's clever fingers began teasing out morsels I had missed. "What did your mother say?" I asked.

Jamie concentrated on the crab. "Not much," she answered, not looking up. "Just that something happened to you when you were in Afghanistan. And when you came back, you were . . . different, somehow. Changed." She hesitated, then added, "She still loves you, you know."

"I know," I said quietly. I glanced out at the ocean, noticing that the swells had begun to build. Many of the surfers offshore were paddling for deeper water as a particularly large set began marching toward the sand. "Jeez, how did we get on this?" I sighed. "Today is supposed to be our day to have fun."

Jamie regarded me for a long moment. "Sorry," she said finally. Done with her salvage work on the crab, she slid the crustacean back in front of me, along with a pile of crabmeat I had missed. Clearly making an effort to change the subject, she added with a smile, "That's about the best I can do, Dad, considering the mess you had already made of it. Next time you order crab, instead of using your hands, why not just run over it with the motorcycle?"

"Thanks. I'll consider that," I said. I finished the crabmeat, cleaned my seafood chowder bowl with a hunk of French bread, and washed down the remainder of my fries with a swig of Coke. Then, leaning forward, "Listen, Jamie, about your mom and me—"

"It's okay, Dad," Jamie interrupted. "You don't have to explain now. But maybe, if you want, we could talk about it sometime. You know, when you feel like it."

"Okay. Thanks."

Jamie looked away. Again making an effort to change the subject, she pulled a small digital camera from her backpack, which she had set beside her on the bench atop her leather jacket. "How about a picture of you and me?" she asked, sliding around the table to sit beside me.

"Sure," I agreed with an absent shrug, still thinking of my failed marriage.

"And try to smile, Dad," Jamie said. "I know you're not much for photos, but you'll thank me someday. Pictures are moments we can look back on and remember. You know, remind ourselves of the good things, the things that matter."

She held the camera at arm's length and pressed the button. After checking the image in the display screen, she grinned and handed me the camera. "Carry this for me, will you? Maybe we can take some more shots on the way home."

"No problem." I shoved Jamie's camera into my pocket, resolving to put aside thoughts of Susan and make the most of the rest of the afternoon with my daughter. Checking my watch, I reluctantly added, "Speaking of home, I promised your mom I would have you back early. We should probably get rolling."

"I suppose so," Jamie agreed with a sigh.

Together we folded up our newspaper tablecloth, enclosing paper plates, shrimp hulls, crab parts, drink cups, and breadcrumbs—depositing the entire wad of trash into a plastic bin near the rear of the deck. That done, we headed for the parking area where we'd left the bike. As we rounded the corner into the dirt lot, I noticed a group of youngsters crowded around my motorcycle. Black lacquer and shining chrome, the bike sat gleaming in the afternoon sun—a vintage Harley-Davidson, a collector's dream that routinely drew admiring glances. I'd spent hundreds of hours restoring it in my garage. Jamie had helped, and both of us were justifiably proud of it.

When we arrived, all the kids drew back—all but a small boy with a crew cut and bright blue eyes. "This your bike, mister?" he asked.

"Yep," I replied, retrieving my jacket and helmet from the handlebars. "Like it?"

The boy nodded somberly. "It's an old knucklehead, right?"

"Right," I answered, surprised. "A '36EL. You know your motorcycles, kid."

"Is it an original?"

"Mostly. We had to machine a few parts, but everything's been restored to the original specs," I answered. I pulled on my jacket and handed Jamie her helmet, which she had left perched atop a chrome sissy bar mounted behind the rear seat—one of the few modifications I had made to the bike for safety.

"Can I have a ride?"

I laughed. "I don't think your mother would go for that," I answered, spotting a woman watching from the deck. "Tell you what, though. If it's okay with your mom, you can sit on it for a minute, okay?"

"Yeah!"

After waving to the boy's mother and getting a smile in return, I hoisted the youngster onto the motorcycle. The delighted child grabbed the throttle and goosed it several times, making a roaring noise with his mouth as he did. A grin lit his face as I set him back down on the ground.

Donning my helmet, I straddled the heavy bike. Hands on the grips, I kicked the starter several times without success. Following a few more tries, the motor coughed once and died.

"Hold on," said Jamie, leaning down to tinker with the carburetor. "There. Now try."

The Harley caught on the next boot, its deep, throaty bellow filling the parking lot with a guttural growl as distinctive as a fingerprint.

"As soon as that kid's old enough, I'll bet he's going to be riding a motorcycle of his own," Jamie remarked as we watched the youngster running to rejoin his mother.

"You've got that right," I said with a chuckle as Jamie slid onto the seat behind me.

As soon as a slot opened in traffic, I exited the parking lot and swung left onto Pacific Coast Highway. Seconds later we were speeding along the coast, the Harley purring steadily beneath us, a blast of ocean air cool on our faces. We passed Broad Beach, with its wide expanse of sand and multimillion-dollar residences, then Zuma Beach, finally ascending the steep grade to Point Dumé.

As usual, weekend traffic began to build as we approached Malibu Canyon, just south of Pepperdine University. We made good time nevertheless by riding the line between stopped and slowing vehicles, and despite the traffic, I found myself enjoying the sunny afternoon. And as we progressed south, my mind drifted back to the first time I had taken this same ride with Jamie's mother, many years before.

Susan and I had been attending Santa Monica College at the time. Susan, a straight-A student, had been enrolled in a pre-architecture curriculum. I, somewhat less of a student, was barely maintaining a passing average and not too sure what I wanted to do with my life. We met in a grassy park at the west end of campus, an open area that has long since been replaced by parking structures and a maintenance building. Susan had been eating lunch on the lawn between classes, and I thought she was undoubtedly the most beautiful girl I had ever seen. Somehow I got up the nerve to approach her. When I did, she looked up and

12

smiled, and that was it for me. To my surprise, I later learned that she had felt the same about me. Like interlocking pieces of a puzzle, love at first sight does happen, at least sometimes. That's the way it was for Susan and me.

The following Sunday we took a motorcycle ride up the coast to Neptune's Net, though at the time I had owned a 650 Triumph instead of the Harley-Davidson. Later we returned to Susan's apartment in West Los Angeles to share a meal of barbecued chicken, artichokes, potato salad, and wine. I stayed the night. I smiled thinking back on it, recalling our first time together. We had made love twice, then fallen asleep happily tangled together on Susan's tiny bed. Twice, and again the next morning.

After that we were inseparable, and by the end of the school year Susan had moved into a small house I was renting near campus. Six months later we married. We continued our studies at Santa Monica College, both of us working at part-time restaurant jobs in the evening. Although I had never been happier, eventually my slipshod study habits caught up with me, and at the end of one particularly party-packed semester I received three F's, one D, and an incomplete. Not surprisingly, the college registrar politely asked me not to return. To make matters worse, I had joined the National Guard several summers earlier to help with school tuition, and the abrupt end of my college career, at least for the moment, coincided with Susan becoming pregnant and my Guard unit being deployed.

Susan decided to continue her education in my absence, at least for as long as her pregnancy allowed. I arranged to have my military paychecks sent directly to our joint bank account. Between that and a savings account I put in Susan's name, I felt she would be financially secure until my return. Susan's dad had died some years back, and Susan's mother, Carol, offered to fly out from Chicago to help when the baby came. Until then the plan was for Susan to pursue her studies, and when I returned we would begin our life together anew.

That was the plan. There's an old Yiddish saying that goes something like: Man plans, and God laughs. I'm not certain that God, if there is a God, laughed about this, but over the weeks and months following my arrival in Afghanistan, something happened to me. In retrospect, I've never been able to pinpoint the exact moment I realized I was different from those around me, different in some deep and fundamental way, but I was.

And over time, that difference became obvious to everyone in my unit as well. Simply put, I had an inexplicable ability to sense danger. Several times I *knew* that we were approaching a roadside explosive device, even before we were near. On another occasion I *knew* that an enemy sniper lay in ambush, well before we entered his field of fire. Somehow I could feel impending danger with a sense as real to me as any of my other five. I don't know how, but it was a newfound ability that I grew to trust. It saved my life and the lives of friends more than once.

If only that had been the end of it.

Unfortunately, it was only the beginning. Word of my ability spread. Eventually I was asked to accompany a Special Forces unit as an observer on a low-risk mission. Given the insular nature of Special Forces, it was an extremely unusual request, to say the least. But those were unusual times, and given the circumstances, I accepted. That first mission proved uneventful, but other missions followed.

During my initial time spent with the small, tight-knit special operations unit, I was marginally helpful on several occasions, but for the most part I was simply an outsider along for the ride, a temporary presence in the elite group. Though initially dubious, several men in the group eventually grew to trust my odd ability, but I was still an outsider.

Several weeks later things changed. Following a report that a senior Al Qaeda leader was present in one of the tribal areas, I accompanied the Special Forces unit on a foray across the border into Pakistan. We were inserted by air in the dead of night. Once on the ground, I didn't need an intelligence report to know the enemy position. I could feel their presence. Worse, I knew they were aware of us. They were searching for us. I sensed their number. I knew how they would approach. I even knew when they would arrive.

Instead of immediately proceeding to our planned objective, at my repeated suggestion our unit leader decided to set up an ambush, not certain about my strange ability, but not willing to discount it, either. We finished preparations just before dawn. As the sun began a slow ascent into the clear morning sky, we waited. Tension filled the air. An hour later when the enemy force drew near, a curious sensation gripped the base of my spine, presaging the death to come. To my surprise, I found myself trembling with anticipation, feeling more alive than ever before. Deep inside, I *hungered* for the slaughter that I knew would follow. And when it did, when our claymores and intersecting fields of fire ripped the unsuspecting enemy force to shreds, I secretly reveled in the carnage, though it left me feeling strangely . . . empty.

Upon returning to base the next day, I lay awake long into the night contemplating aspects of myself that I didn't want to consider. Nevertheless, drawn by the killing, I volunteered for the next Special Forces mission, and the next, and the next. And they took me. I'm unable to describe the compulsion that drew me after that first taste of death, but it was more than a morbid fascination, more than an obsession, more than an addiction. That first experience awakened something inside me that I hadn't known existed, something that couldn't be ignored. And as time went on and the missions piled up, I began to wonder what sort of man I was.

A short, emotional reunion with Susan followed the completion of my first tour. It was then that I met my new baby daughter, Jamie Reid Callahan. Though overjoyed to be holding my child for the first time and to be reunited with Susan, I also knew that I would be returning to Afghanistan. I had no choice.

Weeks later Susan was totally bewildered when I announced that I had signed on for a second tour of duty. To my shame, I let her believe that my decision was motivated solely by patriotism and love of country. Nothing could have been further from the truth. Despite the guilt and self-contempt I felt for leaving Susan alone with our daughter, I had to go back. I had unfinished

15

business there, things I needed to know. Things I couldn't leave unresolved.

That spring, to my wife's amazement but to the surprise of no one who knew her, Susan was accepted to the University of Southern California School of Architecture—an offer that included a partial scholarship. Susan's mother, delighted to be spending so much time with her granddaughter, agreed to extend her stay in Los Angeles and continue to help with Jamie, at least until I returned. Carol also offered to pay the remainder of Susan's tuition, and in September Susan began classes at USC, dividing her time between raising our daughter and continuing her education.

Near the end of my second tour I was wounded during a mortar attack, a danger that even my sixth sense couldn't help me avoid. I took shrapnel in my left hip in what turned out to be a serious but not life-threatening injury. After a short stay in a military hospital in Germany, I was shipped back to the States, where I spent what seemed like endless weeks in a rehabilitation clinic near San Diego.

The shrapnel injury eventually healed, but there was a deeper wound that didn't. When I finally returned home the nightmares began, every night without fail, and always the same dream. After almost a year the dream left me, but the terrible memory never faded—the flickering torch in the forest, the strange unsettling melody, the hooded stranger, the horrible screams . . .

Though Susan begged me to get professional help for what she was sure was posttraumatic stress, I refused, certain that neither medical treatment nor psychiatric counseling would cure what was wrong with me. In time I learned to smile once more, to joke at parties, to interact with friends. But though I tried, I never forgot the darkness I had discovered growing inside me, a hunger I was certain no one could ever condone, much less comprehend.

Of course, Susan sensed the change in me. She was hurt at my withdrawal, wounded that I wouldn't share my problems with her. But what could I tell her? How could she understand, when I didn't understand myself? I knew that Susan hoped raising a child together would reunite us as a family. I wanted for that to happen with all my heart, but it never did. And in the end, hating myself but unable to change, feeling progressively more disillusioned and alone, I watched as Susan began pouring all the love she had once felt for me into our daughter.

After earning her architecture degree, Susan took an apprentice position with an up-and-coming Los Angeles architectural firm. With Susan now making a decent salary and Susan's mother thrilled to be caring for Jamie during the day, I quit a temporary restaurant job I'd taken and returned to Santa Monica College on the Post-9/11 G.I. Bill, retaking courses I had formerly failed. In the process I astounded a few of my past instructors by making the Dean's List semester after semester. I surprised myself, too. Not because I was excelling in class—I'd always thought I could if I really tried—but because since last being a student I had somehow developed a near-photographic memory, a talent that enabled me to breeze through the didactic portions of my courses. Two years later I transferred to UCLA, graduating cum laude with a degree in English.

In my college writing courses I demonstrated an ability to portray people, places, and events with the dispassion of someone on the outside looking in. Which, in retrospect, I suppose I was. Capitalizing on this, the summer after graduating I took an entry-level job at the *Los Angeles Times*, over the next several years working my way up to a top position on the L.A. crime desk.

Though our respective careers were flourishing, my relationship with Susan continued its downward spiral, and shortly after Jamie's tenth birthday Susan filed for divorce. I didn't contest it. And in all fairness, I didn't blame her. I, not Susan, was the one who had betrayed our marriage. It had started on that day in Afghanistan when I had looked deep inside myself and to my horror discovered a darkness growing there—a malignancy that neither prayers nor tears nor denial would ever change. And with that discovery came the realization that, for me, the feelings that make life both bearable and worthwhile—hope, and trust, and love—had all turned to dust, leaving me with nothing but a hollow, overwhelming, unspeakable sense of isolation and shame.

Isolation, shame, and a persistent, gnawing *hunger.*

Chapter Two

Fitfully, she tossed upon the sweat-soaked sheets. The Ritz-Carlton's overworked air conditioning system had failed earlier that afternoon, pushed to the maximum by the unseasonably hot weekend weather. Unable to book new accommodations on short notice, she had thrown open her balcony doors in the hopes of capturing a breeze from the ocean. Instead, rising from the pool deck below, superheated air shimmered in the afternoon sun. From the adjacent room came the sound of arguing.

You would think a first-rate Marina del Rey hotel could afford to properly soundproof their walls, she thought petulantly. Increasingly vexed, she listened to the quarrelsome voices next door, finally realizing that the racket was coming through her open balcony doors, not the wall.

With an irritated sweep of her hand, she brushed back a dark strand of hair from her forehead. Though diverting, the events of the previous evening had tired her. She had hoped to nap for part of the afternoon before the black-tie dinner she would be attending that night in Century City. The Los Angeles fundraiser promised to be an engaging outing, and she wanted to be refreshed when she arrived.

Nude except for a black thong, she swung her long legs from the bed, smiling with satisfaction at her reflection in the mirror above the dresser. Arching her back, she cupped her breasts, pleased by what she saw. As she pinched her nipples to erection, a bead of sweat trickled down her chest, leaving a glistening trail from throat to navel. Carrying the scent of the ocean, an errant breeze wafted in from the marina, billowing the drapes. The brief current of air made her skin prickle with a delicious sensation not unlike the one she had felt when taking the boy in the alley. Shuddering with remembered pleasure, she moved a hand to her thigh, thinking it was a pity she hadn't had more time to enjoy him.

"Charlie, I don't care *what* you say, I'm not going to ride in that goddamn car one more minute!" a corrosive voice whined from the next room. "Why didn't you get one with air conditioning?"

"Agnes, they didn't have any with air conditioning," another voice explained. "They had all been rented!"

"That's so like you. Always an excuse. Well, if you think I'm going to the Davidson's party sweating like a trucker, you're wrong!"

"What do you want me to do?" the other voice replied. "Just tell me and I'll do it, for chrissake."

She had to get some sleep. Tonight would bring to fruition a critical element of her plans, and she wanted to enjoy the evening to its fullest. She strode across the room and closed the balcony doors. Then, upon returning to her bed, she lay on the rumpled sheets and covered her ears with pillows. She could *still* hear them bickering, their strident voices rising as their squabbling intensified. Sighing, she draped an arm across her eyes.

Enough.

"Hertz isn't the only rental place in town," Agnes hollered, her voice penetrating the wall like a saber.

"I checked Budget, Alamo, and Avis," Charlie yelled back. "In case you haven't noticed, there's a convention in town. Jesus, Agnes—"

"Don't you take that tone with me, Charlie Parker! And another thing. If you think you can—"

At that precise instant she took possession of the one called Charlie, brushing aside his consciousness as easily as clearing cobwebs from a corner. He recoiled in shock as she entered, scurrying to some dark recess inside his own skull.

"—keep me from coming on these so-called business trips of yours by making me miserable, you're sadly mistaken!"

"Be quiet," she ordered, glancing around Charlie and Agnes's room. With the exception of several pieces of simulated artwork and a tawdry collection of clothes strewn across the bed, the room was identical to her own. Curious, she walked to the mirror above the dresser, examining the body she'd taken. Looking

20

comical in a pair of flowered undershorts, Charlie Parker was middle-aged and balding, with a flabby paunch and white, skinny legs. Agnes was no better.

"Don't tell me to be quiet, you *momzer*," Agnes spat, her face mottling with rage. "And don't walk away from me. Where do you think you're going?"

Ignoring the woman, she marched the one named Charlie into the bathroom and locked the door. Like the bedroom, the bathroom was identical to her own: sink, toilet, a tub and shower with retractable clothesline above the curtain. After sweeping back the shower curtain, she closed the drain and began filling the tub, turning both valves on full.

"You're taking a bath?" Agnes shouted through the door. "Now? We have to leave soon!"

"It's for you," she replied in Charlie's hacking voice.

Agnes pounded on the door. "I don't want a bath. I want you to get us another car! You hear me, Charlie?"

"I hear you," she said. When the water in the tub began gurgling down the overflow, she reached out with Charlie's knotted fingers and twisted off the valves. Then she threw open the door. Agnes stood outside, her chubby hands perched indignantly on her hips. "What do you mean by—"

The first blow drove Agnes to her knees. The second snapped back her head, sending her toppling to the floor. "What are you doing . . . ?" she blubbered through smashed lips, choking on a flood of blood.

Without a word, she dragged Agnes into the bathroom and lifted her into the tub. The shock of the water seemed to drive the confusion from Agnes's eyes. She began to fight with all her strength, staring goggle-eyed through the churning water, thrashing like a gaffed fish. Several times she almost brought her lips to the surface. Almost, but not quite.

It was over in a few minutes.

How disappointingly little of life's essence had the one called Agnes possessed. She took it nevertheless, leaving the woman's plump carcass floating in the tub. Next she walked Charlie out to the balcony. Through his eyes, she peered over the edge.

21

Fourteen stories below lay the hotel patio, its tables and umbrellas appearing toylike in the afternoon sun. Without hesitation she swung Charlie's legs over the railing. Thinking that now she might be able to get a few minutes of peace, at least until the police arrived, she stepped out into space.

She stayed with him all the way down.

Chapter Three

Weekend beach traffic grew progressively worse. By the time Jamie and I reached Sunset Boulevard, the coast highway had ground to a state of near-gridlock. Thankful finally to be out of it, we turned left at the light onto Sunset and began a short climb into Pacific Palisades.

Nestled at the foot of the Santa Monica Mountains, the community of Pacific Palisades lay on a coastal plateau a few miles from the shoreline. After our divorce Susan had bought a modest, Tudor-style cottage there, despite my opinion that she was overpaying for the property. Eventually I had to eat my words, for after a tasteful remodel that she completed the following year, the value of Susan's home now exceeded more than many earn in a lifetime.

Three miles up the canyon we slowed as we passed through the center of town, passing a procession of boutiques, restaurants, and real estate offices. Six blocks east of Via de la Paz we swung left on Hartzell, proceeded a half mile north, and pulled to a stop behind Susan's Jaguar, which was still collecting leaves on the tree-lined street in front of her house. As I killed the engine, Jamie hopped off the motorcycle and removed her helmet, kneeling to greet a scruffy mongrel who had bounded across the lawn to greet her. "Hi, Georgie," she crooned. "Miss me?"

All whiskers and eyebrows, Georgie was a three-year-old terrier mix—short on looks but long on personality. Without words, Georgie did his best to inform his young mistress that he had indeed missed her, and that he sincerely hoped she never made the mistake of leaving him again.

"I missed you too, boy," Jamie said, scratching the dog's ears. "Oh, Dad, I almost forgot," she added, glancing up at me. "Mom said to ask you if you'd like to stay for dinner. We're having pasta, so there'll be plenty."

Regretfully, I shook my head. "I'd love to, Jamie, but I'm kind of tired. I think I'll go home, grab a shower, and make it an early evening. Tell your mom thanks, though. Maybe we can all go out to dinner next week."

Jamie forced a smile, disappointed. "Sure. Same time next Sunday?"

"Count on it. I'll call later this week."

Jamie gave Georgie one last pat. "Okay. Well, thanks for a great day," she said, rising on her toes to kiss me on the cheek. Then with a final look back, she ran to the house, taking the steps to the front door two at a time, Georgie at her heels.

I waited until Jamie had disappeared inside. I remained at the curb for a moment longer, attempting to quiet the storm of memories that had revisited me on the ride back. Finally, with a despondent sigh, I kicked the motorcycle to life and headed for my home in Venice, a seaside city several miles south of Santa Monica.

For years my town of Venice had boasted the dubious reputation of being the Santa Monica Bay's foremost low-end beach community. The original development had started off well enough, subdivided at the turn of the previous century by a builder whose grand scheme had envisioned creating a sister city for the Italian town of the same name. Canals designed to be flooded and flushed daily with seawater were laid out, streets and building sites platted, bridges constructed. Though initially a success, as years passed the new community had hit hard times. Sea locks fell into disrepair. Canals filled with mud. Water stagnated. And in the end, the developer went bankrupt.

After I returned from Afghanistan, Susan and I had rented a rundown, ranch-style house tucked far back on a side street paralleling one of the canals. Later when I began working at the *Times*, we had purchased the property. Now, following years of real estate development in nearby Marina del Rey, a spirit of rejuvenation had seized the entire area, including Venice. Like weeds sprouting after a rain, classy malls and trendy restaurants were popping up everywhere, and my dilapidated house was rapidly becoming an anachronism. Despite skyrocketing land values, however, the old Venice had suited me just fine, and I regretted seeing it go.

Afternoon shadows were draping my driveway as I eased the Harley past a thirty-foot-tall stand of beach cane that had taken over my front yard. The air seemed unnaturally still as I cut the engine. Seconds later the sounds of the neighborhood gradually reasserted themselves: wind gusting through the trees, neighborhood kids playing in a nearby vacant lot, ducks on the canal behind my house fussing through their final meal of the day.

I raised my garage door and rolled the bike inside, parking it beside a partially restored Mustang convertible—my alternate means of transportation and another renovation project I had been working on for years. Letting the garage door close with a bang, I walked past a well-used workbench to a door leading into the kitchen. I stood in the doorway for a moment, removing my leather jacket. Then I flipped on a light, hung my coat on a hook beside the pantry, crossed the kitchen, and grabbed a beer from the fridge.

Although from the street my ramshackle home looked like a set from *Gilligan's Island*, the interior was open and spacious. After we'd purchased the house, Susan had drawn plans for a remodel and I had done most of the carpentry—removing over half of the interior walls and picking up the roof load with exposed trusses and Glulam beams. A maple bar ran between the kitchen and living room, serving as an eating counter and work surface. At the far end of the main room a pair of French doors opened onto a deck overlooking a canal out back, and to the left of the kitchen a stone fireplace fronted a leather couch and matching armchair. Above the fireplace an oak mantle displayed several journalism awards, pictures of Jamie and Susan, and a shot of me standing beside a military helicopter with several other soldiers. To the right lay a bedroom and bath, beyond which was a small study. The overall effect of the redesigned interior was one of wood and glass, high ceilings, and interesting angles.

Beer in hand, I decided to shower later. Instead I headed for the living room couch, detouring on the way to check my answering machine. I often don't carry my cell phone on weekends, and friends knew to leave messages on my home phone. Three calls. Taking a pull on my Red Hook, I hit the play button.

The first message was from Nelson Long, a Los Angeles Police Department lieutenant whom I had first met while reporting for the *Times*. Nelson had been an LAPD patrol officer at the time; he had since worked his way up to the rank of lieutenant II and was now the detectives' commanding officer for the West L.A. Division. "I'm free tomorrow night," Nelson's voice announced, sounding raspy from too many cigarettes. "Rochelle's going out with the girls. Gimme a call if you want to grab a couple beers."

Jamie's voice came next. "Dad, I forgot to get my camera back from you. Can you drop it off at Mom's sometime? If you change your mind and come over tonight, we could still have dinner together," she added hopefully. I knew that Jamie would like nothing better than for Susan and me to get back together, but that wasn't going to happen, as much as I might have wanted it. Susan had moved on with her life. Even though it was painful for me to watch, I was glad to see her happy, even if it meant her being with someone else. Still, late at night, I sometimes tortured myself with the thought that if I could somehow go back in time and do things over, we might still be together.

But of course life doesn't work like that.

Anyway, with a regretful sigh, I again decided that my plans for the evening went no further than the beer already in hand, a light dinner, maybe some TV, and bed.

The final message changed that.

"Callahan, where the hell are you? We have to be at that Republican shindig in Century City by six-thirty. You haven't forgotten, have you?"

I recognized the voice of Taryn Bentley, a reporter friend who worked the political desk at the *Times*.

"You'd better not stand me up again," Taryn warned. "You owe me. I went to that awful wedding with you last month, remember? I swear, I've had more fun at the dentist. I'm not attending this thing alone, Mike. Six-thirty, Century City. Be there."

I glanced at a clock above the bar. I had agreed to accompany Taryn to a fundraiser for Arthur Bellamy, Republican nominee in the upcoming California gubernatorial election. Like most events of its kind, the fundraising dinner promised to be an excruciating night of hearty handshaking and political back-thumping. Taryn, obligated to attend, had asked me along to ease the boredom. Like many things I didn't want to do, I had somehow let it slip my mind. I briefly considered calling Taryn and attempting to cancel. But if I didn't show, I would really owe her, and Taryn wasn't one to be easily bought off.

Deciding to face the music, I shrugged in resignation and headed for the shower. If I hurried I could just make it.

Chapter Four

Seventeen feet below the street-level lobby of the Century City Hotel, the subterranean conference room bustled with activity. After riding an elevator up from the hotel's underground parking garage several levels down, I spotted Taryn near a check-in table by the conference room door.

As I waded through the crowd, I noticed Taryn glancing impatiently at her watch. For tonight's event she had her sun-streaked blond hair in a French braid, complementing a simple skirt and gray silk blouse that tastefully revealed enough of her trim figure to make her a distraction for any male under ninety. Taryn stood a trace over five-foot-ten, her girl-next-door good looks marred only slightly by a small scar tracing the angle of her jaw—the thin white line the result of a childhood accident. Over the years, despite the advice of friends to get it fixed, Taryn had refused to have the blemish surgically corrected, joking that it gave her character. As I got to know her, I had grown to like the small imperfection, not that Taryn needed character.

Despite her stunning appearance, Taryn seemed unaware of the effect she had on men, a trait I attributed to her having grown up in a large family with several older brothers. Whatever the case, something about Taryn reminded me of a student nurse I had once seen in a movie. In the opening minutes of the film, the young starlet in question had been impeccably prim and suitably proper—long blond hair tightly coifed in a bun, too-large glasses perched on the bridge of her nose, starched white uniform straining to conceal her voluptuous curves. By the end of the first reel she had predictably succumbed to the effects of an ethanol punch, and hair down, glasses and blouse removed, she was dancing atop a table to the whistles and cheers of the entire male medical staff.

When I'd first met Taryn, I had idly wondered what it would be like, metaphorically speaking, to remove her glasses and let down her hair. That was not to be, for Taryn had an inviolable rule about not dating anyone at work. In time I decided that her proscription was a blessing, for over the years Taryn had become a trusted friend. Lovers came and went, but friends were hard to find.

"So you actually made it," Taryn said when I arrived, her blue eyes regarding me appraisingly.

I grinned. "You know me. Never forget a promise."

"I know you, all right. It's a miracle you're here." Reaching up, Taryn smoothed my hair, which the motorcycle trip from Venice had rearranged into a thick, dark tangle. "Left the Mustang and rode the bike, huh?"

"Yeah. I was, uh, running late."

"I'll bet you were." Taryn stepped back, inspecting me critically. "This is a black-tie affair, you know."

I had on an open-necked shirt, tan sport coat, jeans, and loafers. "Monkey suits are for suckers paying a grand apiece for a chicken-and-rice dinner," I replied. Taking Taryn's arm, I started toward the reception table, adding, "We're just working stiffs. C'mon, let's head in before we miss all the fun."

Upon reaching the check-in table, Taryn and I showed our press passes to an off-duty LAPD patrol officer moonlighting that evening as a security guard, then drifted into the banquet hall. To the left of the speakers' table, a small enclave had been set up for the media, affording a good view of the room. After making our way over, we joined a surprisingly large group of other press-corps members already present.

Once seated, I leaned back and let my eyes roam the room. Like similar conference halls everywhere, sliding-partition tracks traversed the ceiling, allowing the huge space to be subdivided as necessary. Tonight all the partitions had been folded back, and a quick estimate of seating in the room exceeded twelve hundred. Doing the math, I whistled softly, calculating that the evening's function would buy Arthur Bellamy plenty of air-time for the glossy TV spots he'd been running over the past weeks—clips of him shaking hands, listening attentively, and in general acting gubernatorial. Lately it seemed as if the irritating ads had been running incessantly. Even I, a talented channel surfer, had been unable to avoid them completely.

Restlessly, I glanced at the time. Almost seven. Waiters were beginning to drift among the tables, pouring white wine and ushering in late-arriving guests. Arthur Bellamy was already seated at the speakers' table, conversing with a heavyset man near the lectern. If the evening ran true to form, I expected Bellamy to deliver his speech before dinner, leaving guests free to sneak out prior to the obligatory self-serving remarks from other political dignitaries preceding dessert. "Fill me in on this guy, Taryn," I said, attempting to show some interest. "Think he'll be our next governor?"

Taryn, who had been scanning a sheaf of notes she'd pulled from her purse, looked up. "You don't follow politics much, do you, Callahan?"

"Not if I can help it."

Taryn frowned. "Well, until a month ago it was a one-sided race in favor of Bellamy," she explained. "But recently Lyle Exner, the dark-horse Democratic candidate, has been coming on strong. You've been tracking the race enough to know who Exner is, right?"

I nodded. "Lyle Exner is a businessman with deep pockets and no political experience. He was formerly a board member of the Elysian Foundation, a closely held international corporation with investments in real estate, banking, and telecommunications."

"Correct so far," Taryn conceded.

"Exner divested himself of his business interests before declaring his candidacy," I continued. "He became the Democratic nominee for governor by default a few months back when his main competitor, Senator Jason Wainwright, got embroiled in a nasty sex scandal. At present the polls have Exner trailing by nineteen points, but gaining."

Taryn eyed me speculatively. "I keep forgetting that memory of yours. You don't forget much, do you?"

I shrugged. "It's one of the traits that separates a professional journalist such as myself from someone with a real job."

Taryn shook her head, ignoring my attempt at humor. "Anyway, the jury's still out on Exner. He's gaining, but the problem is that he relies almost solely on direct voter appeal, with very few TV ads. Instead of using a media blitz like Bellamy does, Exner has been speaking at rallies all across the state, but doing little else. Yet against all odds, he's raised a groundswell of support. I went to one of his meetings, Mike. Exner is . . . I don't know how to describe it. He made a big impression on me."

"So he's got your vote?"

"Absolutely. If you had heard him, he would have yours, too. He spoke so convincingly, I . . . I've never felt anything like it." A faraway expression came over Taryn's face, as though she were recalling some pivotal moment in her life. Then, returning to the present, "I doubt he'll win, though. The polls have him lagging too far behind."

"So why doesn't Exner go to saturation TV advertising like Bellamy? He certainly has the money."

Taryn lifted her shoulders. "I caught one of the few television commercials Exner's run. It just wasn't the same. I don't know why, but for some reason he doesn't come across on TV."

Seconds later the heavyset man who had been talking with Arthur Bellamy moved to a thicket of microphones at the speakers' lectern. Following a brief round of applause, he raised his hands for silence and opened the evening with a series of introductory comments. I made little effort to follow, letting my mind drift until Bellamy took his turn at the podium.

A tall man with a golf-course tan and a leonine head of silver-white hair, Arthur Bellamy spoke in a direct, homespun manner, using his large hands to punctuate whatever point he was making. I suspected that the candidate's good-old-boy demeanor concealed a highly perceptive mind, and as I listened, I tried to picture him as the state's next governor. As I did, a shiver crept up my spine—the same presentiment of danger that had saved me many times in combat. My feeling of danger continued to grow. I glanced around the room, fighting an ominous sense of panic.

Unable to spot anything out of the ordinary, I returned my attention to the podium just as the off-duty LAPD officer whom I had noticed at the check-in table stepped forward. Covering the microphone with his hand, the officer spoke to Bellamy in a low voice. Bellamy nodded. The policeman withdrew his service weapon and extended it butt-first to Bellamy. A hush fell over the room, every eye focused on Bellamy as he reached for the weapon.

With a surge of dread, I realized this was no publicity stunt. Bellamy's conservative views on gun control were well known, but this had nothing to do with that. My internal alarm was telling me something was wrong.

Strangely, at that point not a person in the room had moved, not even Bellamy's security men, who were stationed a dozen yards away near one of the exits. Puzzled, I glanced around, noting that everyone present, including Taryn, was sitting immobile, as if frozen in shock.

Silence.

More convinced now than ever that something terrible was about to happen, I stood. Whatever it was, someone had to stop it. I ducked under a ribbon circling the press tables and strode quickly toward the speakers' podium, not sure what I was going to do, but certain I had to do something. Still, no one else in the room had moved.

I arrived at the podium just as Bellamy began placing the gun to his temple. As if in a nightmare, I grabbed Bellamy's arm and pulled the weapon from his head just as he pulled the trigger.

A deafening explosion rocked the room as the gun in Bellamy's hand belched fire, sending a round into the ceiling. Released by the sound, the room abruptly erupted in motion. Amid a chaos of screams and a general rush for the exits, Bellamy's grim-faced security men surged forward.

Bellamy whirled, leveling his pistol at them. Confused, his security team hesitated, clearly unprepared for the situation confronting them. Again I forced the gun in Bellamy's hand toward the ceiling.

At that point Bellamy suddenly slumped, collapsing beside the podium. Still holding his arm, I wrenched the pistol from his grasp and slid the weapon across the floor, well out of his reach.

Hands open at shoulder height, I backed away as Bellamy's security team again rushed forward, weapons drawn.

The LAPD patrol officer, who had been positioned nearby, arrived first. Bellamy still lay sprawled beside the podium, apparently unconscious. Kneeling, the policeman retrieved the weapon that I'd taken from Bellamy.

Continuing to back away, I reached into my coat and withdrew Jamie's camera. I had slipped it into my jacket pocket before leaving for Century City—intending, if I had time, to drop it off at Susan's house on the way home.

I raised the camera, watching in shock as the patrol officer jammed the gun to Bellamy's head and pulled the trigger. I snapped a picture just as the pistol's concussive blast once more rocked the room. A crimson spurt fountained from Bellamy's temple. It pulsed once . . . twice . . . then died to a dribble.

A moment later, like an automaton acting out the final scenes of a chilling drama, the patrol officer stuck the gun barrel into his own mouth and again pulled the trigger.

In the pandemonium that followed, I attempted to get a picture of the fallen patrol officer. By then Bellamy's security team had surrounded both bodies, obscuring my view. I hesitated, then turned and took two rapid shots of the panicked crowd. My internal alarm was still ringing on full. Though I didn't understand how, I was certain someone in the room had engineered the deaths of both Bellamy and the policeman—*controlling* them somehow.

As I scanned the panicked crowd, I noticed a tall woman wearing a broad-brimmed hat conversing with two men near one of the exits. Abruptly, the woman turned in my direction. I had the impression she was staring directly at me. On impulse I snapped a picture of her. As I did, a blinding shaft of light lanced from her eyes, glittering with the brilliance of the sun. Instinctively I lowered my gaze.

When I looked up again she was gone.

"Damn, Callahan," said Taryn, her voice trembling. Around us the room was roiling in confusion. "Do you have a death wish or something?"

"I . . . I can't explain it," I mumbled, starting to shake. The emotional numbness that had enveloped me during the shootings was beginning to wear off. "I knew something was about to happen. I had to do something . . ."

Pale with shock, Taryn stared at me in disbelief. "You could have been killed."

"I know. It just seemed like I was the only one who could help."

Taryn took a deep breath, then let it out. "Well, you were right about something happening. But . . . how did you know? Has anything like this ever happened to you before?"

"No," I lied, recalling my experiences in Afghanistan. My mind reeled, both drawn and sickened by the violence I had just witnessed. My hands began to tremble. With an effort of will, I clenched my fists to still them.

"Well, I'm just glad you're okay," Taryn said, raising her voice to be heard above the roar in the room.

"Me, too," I agreed, still fighting to quiet my shaking.

"You took pictures?"

I nodded. "One of the patrol officer shooting Bellamy, a few of the crowd."

"Why shots on the crowd?"

I considered relating my suspicion that someone in the room had engineered the killings, but decided against it. Taryn would never believe me. For that matter, I was having trouble believing it myself.

I thought a moment, then came to a decision. Later there would be time to ponder what had happened. Right now there was a story to get to the paper. Instead of answering Taryn's question, I popped the memory card from Jamie's camera. "I need you to get these photos back to the *Times*," I said, handing the memory card to Taryn.

"But—"

"We can talk later," I interrupted. "This place will be crawling with cops before long. I'll phone in the story, then hang around and find out whatever I can from the police. They will probably want a statement from me, too," I added. "Oh, and I need the memory card back. It's Jamie's. She has some shots on it."

"Okay," Taryn said uncertainly. She glanced around the rapidly emptying room and started to say something else, then changed her mind. "I . . . I guess I'll see you back at the paper," she stammered, turning for the exit.

After Taryn had left, I lingered for a few minutes in the dining hall, trying to make sense of what had just happened. No answers came. Ultimately I gave up, resolving that *whatever* had taken place, I still had a job to do. I could sort things out tomorrow.

Avoiding a crowd jamming the hall by the elevators, I took the stairs up to the lobby, stepped outside, and used my cell phone to call the *Times*. As I waited for someone in the newsroom to answer, the first of the LAPD black-and-whites began arriving, sirens blaring, lights blazing. Before long a dozen police vehicles were parked haphazardly out front, completely blocking traffic on Avenue of the Stars.

Someone at the *Times* finally answered. "Crime desk. Allender."

"Jay? This is Callahan. The chief in?"

"Nope. He went home an hour ago."

"Have someone patch me through, okay? It's important."

A long pause. Then the voice of my editor, Hank McCaffery, came on the line. "What is it, Callahan?" he demanded irritably.

Not bothering to apologize for calling him at home, I hurriedly told him what had happened at the fundraiser. I added that I was going to stick around and get whatever I could, and that Taryn was on her way to the *Times* with the pictures I'd taken. "Damn," Hank muttered when I finished. "There's still time to make tomorrow's edition. When you're done at Century City, get over to the paper ASAP."

"Right," I said. But by then the line had gone dead.

Again avoiding the elevators, I reentered the stairwell and headed back down to the conference room, intending to interview as many security personnel, members of Bellamy's staff, and police investigators as possible. Partway down I slowed, for the second time that evening sensing danger. Someone had entered the stairwell behind me. I glanced back.

I saw no one.

After a moment I resumed my descent. On impulse I continued past the conference level, descending all the way to the subterranean parking garage where I had left my motorcycle. By the time I reached a metal door accessing parking level C, the sound of footsteps again echoed in the stairwell above me. My internal alarm was still ringing on full.

I entered the garage and slipped into the shadows behind a concrete column. Seconds later a large, powerful-looking man slammed through the door, the tuxedo he wore looking incongruous on his thick-muscled body. In the distance, a car engine coughed to life. Otherwise we were alone.

The man glanced around the garage, then walked unerringly to where I stood behind the column. A glint of light seemed to spring from his eyes. An instant later a jolt exploded inside my skull, as though someone had reached inside my head and *shoved.*

Come out.

Without willing it, I stepped into the open.

The man moved closer. "You're a big one, ain't you," he sneered, his face inches from mine, spittle spraying my cheek.

I felt another enormous *push* inside my head.

Don't move.

Taking his time, the man backhanded me, rocking me onto my heels. My mouth filled with the coppery taste of blood. Anger flooded up inside me. Though I wanted to strike back, I couldn't.

"Where's the camera?" the man demanded. Another *push.*

Tell me.

"In my coat," I heard myself answer.

Give it to me.

36

My hand reached into my jacket and withdrew Jamie's camera.

The man grabbed the camera and turned it on. He examined it briefly, then delivered another backhanded blow, cutting me with a ring on his middle finger. "Where's the memory card?" he demanded. A wound had opened under my eye. I felt a trickle of blood flowing down my cheek. Still, I was unable to move.

Tell me.

I felt the answer rising in my throat. *Taryn.* My mouth opened to say her name. What will happen to her if I tell? I wondered. I clenched my teeth, waging a battle to remain silent.

"Holding out on me?" the man said.

Stick out your hand.

Obediently, my arm extended from my body. Smiling, the man withdrew a cigarette lighter, sparked it to life, adjusted the flame to high, and placed it beneath my outstretched palm. "Where's the memory card?" he repeated with a humorless grin, exposing a mouthful of yellowed teeth.

The nerves in my hand began sizzling in agony. Sweat streamed down my face. I could smell the stink of my own charring flesh. Still I said nothing. Abruptly, something *clicked* inside my head. And as easily as one can sometimes solve a puzzle with a flash of insight rather than hours of deduction, I knew what to do. Until then I had been disconnected somehow, displaced within my own skull. With a sideways, sliding jolt, I rejoined mind and body.

The man sensed the change. His eyes grew large. "Wha—"

My fist closed on the lighter, trapping the man's hand. Pain from my burned palm shot up my arm. Ignoring it, I yanked my assailant toward me. At the same instant I threw my other fist, putting all my weight behind the blow. I connected, but the man didn't go down. I hit him again. This time something in his face broke under my knuckles with a satisfying crunch.

The man's knees buckled. He slumped to the floor unconscious, blood gushing from his nose and mouth. I leaned down to retrieve Jamie's camera. As I did, I sensed another presence rushing me from behind.

I knew I was too late, but I tried anyway. Whirling, I lowered my shoulder and lunged at the second man . . .

The thunk of something hard against my head sent me spiraling down a long, dark tunnel into oblivion.

* * *

Six levels down in the subterranean garage, she waited. Seething with frustration, she gripped the steering wheel of her white Mercedes, her knuckles bone-white against the leather covering. Though longing to vent her fury, she knew that any further bloodletting, however satisfying, would surely prove ruinous.

What's taking those two so long? she wondered.

With an effort of will, she struggled to control her anger. Revenge would come later; right now she needed to think. The latent's resistance had been incredibly strong. She had caught a glimpse of his mind, and in other circumstances she might have been intrigued. But his actions, intentional or otherwise, had nearly derailed her plans. Nevertheless, she briefly considered recruiting him. Scowling, she decided against it. Though he might have eventually proved useful, the fact remained that he had defied her.

Her!

No, he would pay . . . but not until she had examined him. Latents were rare, and there were questions to be answered. How, for instance, had he lived so long without realizing his powers? How, for that matter, could he even exist, denying his own true nature?

She would wait. Soon he would be hers, and she would have her answers.

Then he would die.

Chapter Five

". . . really strong for a latent, huh, Roscoe?"

"Shut up."

Slowly, my mind rose from the fog. I lay without moving, face pressed against the cold concrete floor, cheek resting in a sticky puddle of blood.

"I felt you pushing for all you were worth," the first voice observed, sounding amused. "He shook it off like it was nothing. Guess this ain't your day."

"Screw you, Tyler. Where the hell were *you*, anyway?"

"Right here, pal. I was the one who put his lights out, remember?"

"Yeah. Well, I'm gonna be the one who puts 'em out permanently. Gimme the gun."

"Did you get the picture?"

A hesitation. "No."

"And now you're gonna pop him? Good thinking. She's already pissed off about what happened upstairs. Her instructions were to retrieve the picture he took of her, then bring him in. Alive. You wanna explain why you didn't follow orders?"

Apparently Roscoe couldn't come up with an answer, which didn't improve his mood. As the two men continued to argue, I risked opening an eye. My attackers were standing about six feet away—Tyler tall and angular, holding a pistol; thick-necked Roscoe glancing nervously around the garage. "Okay, now what?" I heard him say.

"It may take some time to find out what he did with the picture," Tyler replied, rubbing his chin. "Let's get him someplace where we can work on him together. Someplace private. The rear of the van should do." He handed Roscoe the pistol, a snub-nosed revolver. "Keep an eye on him. I'll be back in a minute."

I heard the sound of receding footsteps. If I were going to escape, I knew I had to make my move before Tyler returned.

But what could I do? Roscoe had a gun, and in his present mood, he probably wouldn't hesitate to use it.

A moment later I heard him approaching, grunting something under his breath. I felt a stab of pain as his boot tore into my ribs. The blow partially rolled me over. Suddenly I saw a glimmer of hope.

I fought to keep from moaning, still feigning unconsciousness. Through slitted eyes I saw Roscoe looming over me, his nose caked with blood, his shirt spattered with red. He hawked a bloody gob of phlegm on me, then raised his foot for another shot, this time a stomp at my face. At the last instant I grabbed his foot. Caught off balance, Roscoe hopped awkwardly on one leg, arms windmilling as he tried to maintain his balance. His eyes hardened with rage.

Still holding his foot, I rolled to my knees, hooking Roscoe's other ankle as I rose to my feet. Jerking upward, I pulled both his legs out from under him. For a long moment Roscoe hung suspended in air, his mouth opening in astonishment, his legs rising . . .

The back of Roscoe's head touched down first, followed by a gut-wrenching crack as the weight of his body drove his skull into the concrete, snapping his neck.

I knelt beside him. His head lay twisted at an unnatural angle, eyes open and unseeing. His lips were curled back from his teeth in a final paroxysm of pain, making him appear even more menacing in death than he had in life. Resisting an odd compulsion to touch the body, I stood, absently thinking that Tyler had been right. This definitely wasn't Roscoe's day. For the second time that evening finding myself in the presence of death, I felt both fascination and revulsion warring within. Forcing myself to turn from the body, I glanced around the garage. No sign of Tyler.

Yet.

I hesitated, trying to decide what to do. I didn't know whether Tyler would be returning alone or coming back with others. Worse, he might have another gun in the van. Though I wanted to question him, I decided my best course was to get out of there. Fast. After prying the revolver from Roscoe's lifeless fingers, I headed for my motorcycle. Keeping low between rows of cars and avoiding open areas as much as possible, I arrived at my Harley without being seen.

For once the engine caught on the first kick. After shifting into gear, I raced up a curved exit ramp to the street, thrust my parking slip at the gate attendant, impatiently paid the fee, and roared out into the darkness.

Outside, the Santa Ana winds had finally diminished for the evening. The cool night air felt good on my battered face as I rode west on Pico Boulevard. Still shaking from my encounter with Tyler and Roscoe, I turned north at the light on Beverly Glen Boulevard. Minutes later, after crossing Santa Monica Boulevard and putting some distance between me and Century City, I pulled into a gas station and killed the engine.

An attendant regarded me strangely when I asked for the restroom key. When I inspected myself in the bathroom mirror, I understood why. I used most of the towels in the dispenser cleaning my wounds. I still looked ragged when I finished—my right eye was closing and the gash on my cheek from Roscoe's ring probably needed stitches—but at least the bleeding had stopped. For some reason, my burned palm had already stopped throbbing.

Outside, I used my cell phone to call Taryn at the newsroom. She answered almost immediately. "Did you get anything more from the police?" she asked before I could say anything.

"No," I answered, attempting to keep my voice steady. "I had to leave. I didn't get a chance to talk with anyone. I'm at a gas station a few miles from the hotel. Can you handle things till I get there? Speaking of which, did you deliver the pictures?"

"As soon as I got here. The prints are on McCaffery's desk. But why—"

"Good," I interrupted. "Listen, Taryn. Be careful. I don't know why, but after you left, two guys wanted the shots on that memory card bad enough to rough me up trying to get them."

"Are you okay?"

"Yeah. One of them wasn't as lucky." I quickly brought Taryn up to date, leaving out the part about Roscoe's strange commands that had held me frozen, realizing that including those details would only confuse matters. Besides, I still didn't understand what had happened myself. At any rate, when I finished, Taryn remained silent for a long moment. Finally she spoke. "This is too weird, Mike," she said. "Bellamy, and the police officer, and now this. What's going on?"

"I don't know," I answered. "But I intend to find out."

Next I dialed the home of my LAPD friend, Lieutenant Nelson Long. Nelson's wife, Rochelle, answered.

"Roe? Mike here. Is Nelson around?"

"Hi, Mike," Rochelle replied, sounding sleepy. "Nelson just got an emergency call and had to leave."

"He say where he was going?"

"Century City, I think," Rochelle yawned. "Some ruckus over there has the chief up in arms. He's setting up a task force. Nelson's supposed to head it."

"Thanks, Roe. If you hear from Nelson, please ask him to call me on my cell."

After hanging up, I tried reaching Nelson at work, dialing the police station number from memory.

After several rings, a night duty officer answered. "West L.A. Police Station."

"Connect me with Lieutenant Long, please. This is Mike Callahan, L.A. Times." Upon saying the latter, I mentally kicked myself for mentioning the paper. Though it sometimes opened doors, with the LAPD it generally had the opposite effect.

"He's not here," came the duty officer's curt reply. "Wanna leave a message?"

"No, I need to speak with him right now. I just witnessed a homicide in Century City. Please patch me through."

A pause followed, after which I went through a similar routine with someone else. At last Nelson came on the line. "I'm kinda busy right now, Mike," he said, his voice sounding distant. "What's up?"

I hesitated, wondering how much to say. Nelson and I were friends, but first and foremost Nelson was a cop, and a skeptical one at that. "I was at Century City tonight," I finally answered. "I saw Bellamy's murder, and the patrol officer shooting himself—all of it. Believe me, Nelson, there's more to that situation than meets the eye."

"Like what?"

"I don't want to talk over the phone. Can you meet me someplace when you're done?"

"Where?"

I thought a moment. Westwood wasn't far. I hadn't eaten since lunch with Jamie at Neptune's Net, and despite all that had happened, my stomach was rumbling. "How about Chuck's?" I said, suggesting a restaurant where we sometimes met for drinks.

"Fine. I'll see you there."

"One more thing, Nelson. Two goons jumped me in the garage. I'll tell you about it when I see you. In the meantime, you'll find what's left of one of them on parking level C."

Chapter Six

Avoiding the customary snarl of weekend traffic, I took Westholm Avenue and entered Westwood Village from the rear, arriving as a number of late movies were beginning to let out. After passing the Ronald Reagan UCLA Medical Center, I hung a U-turn on Le Conte, snagging a boulevard parking slot just as it opened up. A rare commodity in Westwood these days, I thought to myself as I backed against the curb and shut off the Harley's engine.

Maybe my luck was changing.

Originally a bedroom community for the newly established University of California, Los Angeles, Westwood Village had sprung up on the outskirts of the nascent campus during the early thirties. Over intervening years Westwood Village had grown, its once quaint streets now shadowed by high-rises, shopping malls, and entertainment complexes like the ones that were currently flooding the village with moviegoers exiting the theaters.

A short walk down the crowded sidewalk brought me to Chuck's Steak House, a few blocks from campus. I passed through Chuck's heavy brass doors and descended a flight of stairs to the restaurant below. A bar on the right was jammed with college kids, singles on the prowl, and couples enjoying late-night drinks. To the left lay the dining area, separated from the entrance by a lattice of rough-hewn timber and hanging ferns. The tables beyond appeared almost deserted, the few patrons still present finishing coffee and desserts.

I paused at the hostess station, my eyes taking in the early "Chart House" decor—sandblasted beams, construction-grade lumber accenting expanses of redwood and cedar, resin-covered tables. Black-and-white blowups of surfing beaches and racing schooners decorated the walls, and in the bar on an elevated platform near the back, a young musician playing jazz guitar was adding his laid-back contribution to the pleasant ambiance.

The hostess, an attractive young woman wearing a short plaid skirt, an open-necked blouse, and a dazzling smile hurried over.

She hesitated when she saw my battered face. "Can I help you, sir?" she inquired, her manner turning friendly again when she saw my smile, but her eyes plainly saying: "I hope you're not here for dinner."

"Too late to get something to eat?" I asked anyway. "I'm sure your kitchen is about to close, but I'm starving. I'll eat anything."

The hostess looked doubtful.

"Anything would be fine," I added before she could refuse. "Really. Leftover potatoes, stale bread, yesterday's clam chowder. Anything."

"I'll see what I can do," the young woman replied, her smile turning sympathetic. She disappeared into the kitchen. Moments later she returned. "Anything on the menu except seafood. That's already in the cold locker."

"Thanks," I said with a grin. I followed her past a double-sided grill to a table in the rear. As I seated myself, I added, "I'm supposed to meet a friend here. He's a big guy, about my height. Send him back when he shows up, okay?"

"Sure," said the hostess. "Your waitress will be here shortly. Enjoy your dinner."

After she left, I turned my attention to the menu, a large wooden paddle with the words "Bill o' Fare" inscribed at the top on both sides. Again, despite all that had happened, I was surprised to discover that I was famished, and when the waitress arrived—another attractive young woman whose nameplate read "Arleen,"—I ordered a fourteen-ounce baseball-cut sirloin with sautéed mushrooms, baked potato, asparagus with hollandaise sauce, a green salad with blue cheese dressing, and a basket of hot bread.

Fifty minutes later, as I was finishing my meal, Nelson arrived. An African American who'd ascended the ranks of the LAPD on ability alone, Lieutenant Nelson Long was an unusually large man, even for a police officer. A somewhat flattened nose he'd earned from four seasons as a college linebacker seemed appropriate on his square, friendly countenance, but his inquisitive brown eyes betrayed a razor-keen intelligence that many missed upon first meeting him. He had on a rumpled dark-gray suit, a white shirt, and a conservatively striped tie pulled down to the second button. Under his left arm I could make out the bulge of his service weapon.

Nelson paused at the hostess station, squinting into the room. After spotting me sitting near the back, he crossed the restaurant and dropped into a chair across the table. He studied my battered face without comment. Then, eyeing the remnants of my dinner, he pulled out a pack of Camels and shook one out. "Enlighten me, Callahan," he said, ignoring my questioning look at the cigarette. "How do you do it?"

"Do what?"

"Eat like a pig and still keep your girlish figure."

"Genes. Speaking of which, how's the diet going?"

"Terrible," Nelson muttered. Though he was still in passable shape, hours spent at a desk had gradually taken their toll, and recently Nelson's wife had gently suggested that Nelson cut down on his meals and get more exercise. Observing California's proscription against smoking in public places, Nelson toyed with his cigarette without lighting it. "The guys in the garage do that?" he asked, again studying my face.

"Yeah," I answered. For some reason, over the past hour my cuts and bruises had stopped bothering me. I had almost forgotten how I looked.

"Well, so much for your movie career," Nelson remarked dryly. Then, with a weary sigh, "It's past my bedtime, Mike. What's so important you couldn't tell me on the phone?"

I hesitated, not certain where to start. "How do you have the shootings figured?" I asked. I still hadn't decided how much to tell Nelson—or more to the point, how much he would believe—and I wanted to know where he stood on the killings before I started.

Impatiently, Nelson drummed his fingers on the table. "I didn't come here to give you my thoughts, Mike. You said you had something to tell me. Whatever it is, spill it."

"Bear with me, Nelson. Please. How do you have it figured?"

Nelson looked at me closely. Like most law enforcement personnel, he had a healthy distrust for all members of the media, especially print reporters. Nevertheless, unlike many of my associates, I had always treated the LAPD fairly in my articles, and over the years I had earned Nelson's trust. "Off the record?" he asked.

"Off the record."

"All right. But whatever you have for me better be good," Nelson grumbled. "You wanna know how I have things figured? Truth is, I don't. What, for instance, was Bellamy doing waving around a loaded pistol at his own fundraiser? He took the gun from an off-duty LAPD officer?"

"The patrol officer *gave* it to him."

"Just walked right up and handed it over? And Bellamy's security team stood by and watched?"

"Yep."

Nelson shook his head in disbelief. "So next Bellamy puts the pistol to his own head. Some guy from the press table runs up and stops him from shooting himself, the gun goes off, and Bellamy collapses like somebody hit him with a sledge hammer. Sounds like a publicity stunt so far. But next the off-duty cop, Officer Hidalgo, retrieves his service weapon, shoots Bellamy, and turns the gun on himself. Definitely not a publicity stunt."

Nelson cracked his knuckles and continued. "I checked on Hidalgo. He was a good officer—graduated the top third of his academy class, had a wife and kids, was in excellent health with no particular troubles at home. It doesn't add up."

"Is that how the department is going to see it?"

"Not likely. The brass wants this wrapped up as quickly as possible. At present there's no evidence that anyone else was involved, and no indication we'll find any."

"What about Bellamy putting the gun to his own head?"

"Not the actions of a gubernatorial hopeful," Nelson observed. "Perhaps he was trying to prove something—make a point about gun control or whatever. Maybe he didn't actually mean to shoot the gun. Speaking of which," he continued, looking at me curiously. "We still haven't found the guy who stopped Bellamy from shooting himself, or whatever the hell he was doing. That guy happens to match your description, Mike. You want to tell me about it?"

"I'll tell you," I said. "But you're not going to believe it."

"Try me."

"Okay," I sighed. "Like I said, you're not going to believe it, but here goes. When Bellamy first took the gun from the patrol officer, I *knew* something bad was going to happen. I don't know how. I just knew. As a result, I had a jump on everyone else and got there first."

"You just *knew*, huh? And nobody else made a move to help?"

"Nope."

Nelson grunted doubtfully. "Okay, go on."

"When Bellamy's security team finally started moving in, Bellamy acted like he was going to shoot them. I had to fight to stop him."

"Yeah, I heard that."

"Then Bellamy collapsed. I took his gun, placed it on the floor, and backed away."

"Right. And we know the rest," finished Nelson. "So what's the part I'm not going to believe?"

I hesitated a moment, then continued. "I think someone was trying to make Bellamy kill himself," I said. "And when the murder didn't come off as planned, I think they forced the cop to finish the job."

"Excuse me?" Nelson said dubiously. "I don't think I heard you correctly."

"I know it's hard to accept, but—"

"Hard to accept? I've got another way of putting it," Nelson growled. "It's bullshit."

I shook my head stubbornly. "I think somebody wanted Bellamy dead, and they wanted it done in a way that would disgrace him."

"Somebody? Who?"

48

I shrugged. "Who stands to gain from Bellamy's death? He was a career politician. He must have had enemies."

"Hold on, amigo. You're talking about a conspiracy here? Just supposing you're right and other people *are* involved, how did they do it? You can't hypnotize someone into committing murder, let alone suicide."

"It wasn't hypnotism."

"What, then?"

"I don't know," I admitted, deciding to tell Nelson the rest. "But whatever it was, I felt it. I don't know why no one else did, but there was something in that room, a force of some kind . . ."

"Jesus H. Christ," Nelson exploded. "If this is your idea of a joke—"

"It's no joke. I don't know how, but I'm certain Bellamy was being forced to do what he did. And the patrol officer, too. There's more," I added grimly. "I know it sounds crazy, but the two mugs who jumped me in the garage—"

"We searched the garage," Nelson interrupted. "Nothing."

I ran my fingers through my hair, realizing that my chances of convincing Nelson had just grown slimmer. Nevertheless, I started at the beginning and related everything that had happened that night. Nelson grunted impatiently when I got to my encounter with Tyler and Roscoe, but he was particularly attentive when I mentioned Jamie's camera.

"You took pictures?" he asked when I finished. "What happened to them?"

"Taryn took the memory card to the *Times*," I answered. "Among others, I got a shot of the patrol officer shooting Bellamy. Get tomorrow's paper. It'll be on page one."

"That picture is evidence, Callahan."

"It's news, too. Call my editor, Hank McCaffery. I'm sure you can pick up copies of all my shots. I got a couple of the crowd, too. Oh, there's something else," I added, remembering the pistol I had taken from Roscoe. I pulled the revolver from my belt and slid it across the table. "I took this from the dead guy you couldn't find in the garage. My prints are undoubtedly on it, but maybe you can lift a few from its previous owner."

"You touch the shell casings?"

"No."

Nelson eyed the gun. "We might be able to get something," he conceded. "We'll need your prints for elimination purposes. I suppose we can pull them off your army records," he added absently, still looking at the gun.

Just then our waitress returned, stopping short when she noticed the weapon on the table. Ignoring her, Nelson lifted the pistol by inserting a pen into the barrel, then deposited the gun into a plastic bag he pulled from his coat. "Would you care for anything else?" the waitress finally managed when the gun had disappeared into Nelson's pocket.

"No, thanks," I replied, reaching for my wallet. "Just bring the bill and I'll—damn!"

"What's wrong?" asked Nelson.

"They took my wallet."

"I should be home in bed," Nelson sighed, pulling out his own billfold and handing a credit card to the waitress. "Instead, I'm here listening to your horseshit story and buying you dinner to boot. You owe me, Mike."

"Does that mean you're not going to follow up on the conspiracy angle?"

"No, I'll follow up on it . . . unofficially," said Nelson. "There's no way I can present what you just me told me to the brass, but something about this case stinks. Officially, however," he added, "the preliminary task-force report will undoubtedly read that Bellamy died at the hands of an LAPD patrol officer, who then took his own life."

"But—"

"Mike, I said I would check into things, and I will. Speaking of which, we'll need you to come in tomorrow and give a formal statement. And when you do, I'd advise you to leave out the bull. In the meantime, go home and get some sleep. After the story you just told me, I think you need it."

After leaving the restaurant, I called Taryn again at the paper and told her I had just met with Nelson, adding that Nelson was spearheading an LAPD task-force investigation into Bellamy's murder and thus far the police had no comment on the case. At that point, as it was impossible for me to make it back to the *Times* before morning deadline, I decided to go home and grab a couple of hours rest. After retrieving my motorcycle, I took the San Diego Freeway south, exited onto the Santa Monica Freeway, and headed toward the beach.

My body ached, my head throbbed, and I longed for sleep, but as I rode through the night my mind kept returning to the events at the fundraiser. The deaths I'd witnessed there had stirred up emotions I hadn't experienced in years, not since my tours in Afghanistan. Shuddering, I attempted to turn my mind from memories better left forgotten, but as I roared through the darkness toward home, images of the murders kept returning. I had nearly reached my house in Venice when another thought occurred. I cursed myself for not realizing sooner, irritated that I'd overlooked it.

They had taken my wallet; they had my ID.

They knew where I lived.

I coasted onto my street, pulling up short at the far end of my block. I cut my light and killed the engine. Quietly, I rolled the Harley into a neighbor's driveway and left it there. With a shiver of foreboding, I walked the final distance to my house, moving stealthily past the thicket of beach cane that hid my home from the street.

I stood in the shadows for several minutes, listening. One block over, a dog barked. From a house down the way came the sound of a TV, mixing with the murmur of the canal lapping its banks. My house appeared dark and silent, the lights off just as I had left them. Nothing seemed out of place.

But the icy fingers clutching my spine for the third time that evening told me otherwise.

Someone was inside.

Chapter Seven

Heart pounding, I moved closer, staying in the shadows by the beach cane until I reached my garage. I stood for a moment, trying to decide what to do. Part of me wanted to turn and run. Another part was angry—first at what had happened at Century City, and now they had broken into my house. Clearly, whoever was behind this wanted something from me, and they weren't going to let the matter drop. Maybe the best course would be to meet them head-on. At least I was on home turf, and I had the advantage of knowing they were there. I also wanted answers to questions I was barely able to frame. Whoever was inside might have answers.

Silently, I moved to the garage door. Thankful I had never installed an automatic opener, I pried open the door a few feet, rolled underneath, and allowed it to descend gently behind me. Once inside I rose to my knees, every sense alert.

No sound came from inside the house, but I knew someone was there. I could sense his presence, stronger now than ever. When my eyes adjusted to the darkness, I rose to my feet.

I needed a weapon.

Regretting having given Roscoe's pistol to Nelson, I crept to my workbench. Careful not to make a sound, I groped through my tools. My hand closed on a twenty-two-ounce framing hammer. I hefted it. Not as good as a gun, but a weapon nevertheless. Hammer in hand, I made my way to the door into the kitchen. Holding my breath, I eased inside. Once there I stopped again and listened.

Still nothing.

Inching forward, I peered into the living room. Although I could only make out dim outlines, I detected the presence of someone there as surely as if I could see.

I moved swiftly then, entering the living room in a low crouch. I gripped the hammer tightly, the weapon heavy in my hand.

There.

A figure lay on the couch. From the darkness came the sound of soft, even breathing. I closed the distance to the couch in four quick strides and jammed my knee against the intruder's chest, grabbing his throat at the same time. The figure grunted in surprise and began struggling. I raised the hammer. For a furious instant I almost gave vent to my fear and anger. With effort I stayed my hand. "Don't move," I warned. "Don't even think about it."

The intruder stiffened, then lay still.

"Who are you?" I demanded. Beneath the crush of my fingers I felt the intruder's throat attempting to form words. I relaxed my grip, but only slightly.

"Don't hurt me," the intruder managed to choke, fighting for breath. "I'm here to help." Despite the strangling pressure of my fingers, the intruder's voice sounded surprisingly cultured and rich. The voice of a woman!

"What the . . . ?"

"Would you get your knee off me, please? I promise I won't move." The woman had a faint accent—English, or possibly Swiss.

"Not yet." Though suddenly unsure of myself, I didn't lower the hammer. "I'm going to turn on a light. Don't try to get up. Don't even twitch."

"I won't."

Releasing my grip on the woman's throat but still keeping her pinned with my knee, I leaned over and flipped on a lamp beside the couch. Narrowing my eyes against the glare, I stared at the intruder pinned beneath me. She was young—in her midtwenties or so—and undoubtedly one of the most hauntingly beautiful women I had ever seen. She had on tight-fitting jeans, sandals, and a light silk blouse. She didn't appear to be wearing a bra, and her breasts were pressed tight against the silky fabric of her shirt by the pressure of my knee. From the feel of her body, I suspected she had the wiry strength of an athlete.

The woman gazed up at me, brushing back a thicket of jet-black hair from her forehead. Her face looked open and innocent—high cheekbones, sensuous lips, and a fine, straight nose that gave her a slightly patrician air. But without question her arresting green eyes were her most striking feature. She glanced briefly at the hammer in my hand, then back at me. "Well?" she said with a note of impatience. "Are you going to let me up?"

Finally lowering the hammer, I removed my knee from her chest and stepped back. "What are you doing here?"

"I already told you," the woman replied. She sat up and adjusted her blouse, fastening several buttons that had come undone. "I was told to keep an eye on you. I'm here to help."

"What makes you think I need help?"

A rueful smile touched her lips. "Mike Callahan, if anyone in this city ever needed help, it's you."

"How do you know my name?" I demanded.

By way of reply, the woman started to reach into a small leather handbag beside her.

Warily, I stepped closer, hammer ready.

"Relax, Mike," she said. "I'm not here to hurt you." Gingerly, she withdrew a leather wallet from her purse and tossed onto the coffee table.

I scooped up the billfold. It was mine, everything still there—money, cards, ID. "Where did you get this?" I asked.

"I took it from the man you killed in the garage. Roscoe, I believe he called himself."

"You were there? No more games. What's going on?"

"I was present when Bellamy was killed. Afterward I followed you down to the parking garage," the woman replied evenly. "We knew something was going to happen at the fundraiser. We just didn't know what." She spread her hands. "Look, I'm sorry I wasn't able to help you. The agents who attacked you were both very strong. Against one of them I might have had a chance. I was definitely no match for both of them together. At any rate," she added with a nod of approval, "it appears you did just fine all by yourself."

"You're losing me. Exactly what happened at the fundraiser?"

"What happened?" The woman lowered her voice. "You challenged an extremely dangerous person and lived, that's what happened," she answered, her tone tinged with respect. She regarded me curiously. "You've never had any training?"

"I don't know what you're talking about," I answered, now more confused than ever. "You mean the woman?"

The intruder on the couch leaned forward, her eyes locking on mine. "How do you know it was a woman? Did you see her?"

"I think so," I answered, taken aback by her sudden intensity. "I noticed a tall woman staring at me from the exit. Her eyes were . . . I can't describe how they looked."

"Could you recognize her?"

"I don't know. I only saw her briefly, and a hat covered part of her face. Who is she?"

"As I said, someone extremely dangerous. If she even suspected you knew her identity . . ."

"You still haven't told me what's going on," I said impatiently.

Instead of answering, the woman glanced at her watch, then swore softly. "Damn. We don't have time for this. Look, Mike, for now please believe me when I say that you've interfered with an extremely powerful organization, and an extremely powerful individual as well. If you want to live, we have to get out of here. Now."

"I'm not going anywhere. Tell me what's going on."

Irritation flashed in the woman's eyes, but I also detected fear there as well. "I told you, there's no time!" she insisted. "And in any case, I can't simply tell you. You wouldn't believe me. I'll have to *show* you."

Exasperated, I crossed to the bar and placed my hammer on the counter. I considered for a moment. Maybe she was telling the truth. The men in the garage had definitely meant business, and it was more than likely that whoever had sent them was still looking for me. And if this woman had managed to find me . . .

The woman crossed the room. Placing a hand on my shoulder, she turned me to face her. "I want to help, Mike," she said earnestly. "And I will, I promise—but only if you come with me now. If you won't leave, I'm going alone. What's it going to be?"

I searched her face. She looked back at me, her expression direct and sincere. I found myself staring, almost losing myself in her near-hypnotic beauty. "Why should I trust you?" I asked, forcing myself to glance away.

"Because you have no other choice," she answered. "They're coming for you. Don't you feel it?"

I hesitated, realizing she was right. The premonition of danger I had first felt outside my house hadn't abated. If anything, it had grown stronger. How had she known?

"My car is parked one block over," the woman said. "Let's go."

I hesitated a moment more.

"Please, Mike. We have to leave now."

"Okay, we'll play it your way . . . for now," I agreed, deciding that getting out of my house, at least for the moment, made sense. I couldn't risk ignoring her warning. Something deadly was out there, and my sixth sense told me it was coming my way. "Give me a second to get my motorcycle into the garage."

"There's no time for that!"

I have never liked being rushed. Stubbornly, I moved to the door. "I'm making time."

"Then do it fast. Please."

Hand on the doorknob, I turned. "By the way, I didn't catch your name."

"Devon. Devon Summers. Now for God's sake, hurry up!"

"One more question. Where are we going?"

"The airport. We're leaving Los Angeles. Until my organization has time to get things under control, you don't stand a chance of surviving in this city. You have to disappear completely—at least for a few days. Possibly longer."

I shook my head. "I can't leave L.A. right now. Arthur Bellamy's murder is going to be the hottest story of the—"

"Last chance, Mike," Devon interrupted, now close to panic. "Come with me . . . or die."

Despite my reservations, I was chilled by the unmistakable terror I saw in Devon's eyes. "All right," I agreed, deciding that if worse came to worst, I could stay in touch with the *Times* online or by phone. Besides, Devon was my only lead to understanding what had happened at the fundraiser. A lot had taken place that didn't make sense, and until I learned whatever it was Devon had to "show" me, I had no intention of letting her out of my sight. "Are we going somewhere in particular?" I asked.

"Anywhere out of Los Angeles," Devon answered. "And the sooner, the better." Briefly, she seemed lost in thought. Then apparently coming to a decision, she added, "How does Mexico sound?"

Chapter Eight

I stared out the window of the aircraft, watching as the rugged Mexican coastline fell away beneath the wing. We had been descending for the past several minutes, and clusters of towns and villages dotting the landscape below were increasingly coming into view. Emerging from a bank of low-lying clouds to the east, jungle-covered mountains marched majestically to the Pacific, a thin ribbon of asphalt road at their base tracing the edge of the continent as the coastal range met the sea.

From the adjacent seat came the gentle sound of Devon's breathing. Her face was turned toward me in sleep, and I could smell a faint floral fragrance in her hair. I envied her feline ability to nap, something I had never been able to do on any moving vehicle except a ship, and even that was questionable. At any rate, I doubted I would be able to sleep before getting answers to questions that had plagued me since the previous evening. I had repeatedly queried Devon on our way to the airport, but she had steadfastly refused to answer any of my questions, reiterating that she would have to *show* me at the proper time, whatever that meant.

Upon arriving at LAX, we had left her car in short-term parking and walked to the Mexicana terminal. I had stood with Devon at the airline counter, wondering how she was going to manage to get tickets. I didn't have my passport with me, and neither did she. When I raised this point on the ride over, Devon had told me that they wouldn't be necessary. Puzzled, I listened as she informed the airline agent that we had prepaid reservations. Not locating our names on the computer screen, the man started to question her. At that point I sensed some sort of force *uncoiling* from Devon's mind. It flicked at the ticket agent, then withdrew. Something shifted in the agent's eyes. Again, Devon spoke to him briefly. His fingers flew across the keyboard. Moments later we were proceeding to the security gate, boarding passes in hand.

We spent the rest of the night in the airport. Devon slept. I did not. Once on the plane later that morning, Devon again deflected my questions with a patient smile, and shortly after takeoff she had again fallen asleep.

As I studied her now, I found her even more beautiful than I had first thought. More than her beauty, however, something else about her drew me, something I couldn't quite define. As I brushed back a strand of hair from her face, I remembered with a chill that only hours earlier I had come within a heartbeat of crushing her skull.

The aircraft lurched, beginning its final descent. Outside, beneath the stainless-steel nacelle of a jet engine, I watched as the city of Puerto Vallarta came into view, its streets and buildings showing signs of an urban area in transition. Wherever one looked, especially along the brilliant white beach running the length of the bay, construction cranes loomed like giant insects, towering over partially completed structures.

After my release from the hospital in San Diego and a subsequent honorary discharge from the service, Susan and I had left Jamie with Susan's mother and headed south for a few weeks in Mexico. More a belated honeymoon than a vacation, I realized that Susan had hoped that some time together, just the two of us alone, might heal the rift between us. It was something I desperately wanted, too.

We had borrowed a friend's VW camper and worked our way down the Baja coast, camping and fishing the beaches along the Sea of Cortez. Upon reaching La Paz we had taken a ferry to the Mexican mainland and driven south, eventually arriving in Mazatlán. Although we had originally envisioned continuing on to explore the Yucatan peninsula, by then it was clear that as a means of breaching the barrier between us, our trip was a failure. As a result we cut short our stay, but before returning home we made it as far south as Puerto Vallarta, a coastal village 150 miles west of Guadalajara that was originally made famous as the shooting location for the film *Night of the Iguana*. With regret, I looked down at the sprawling city that had subsumed the sleepy Mexican village I recalled.

"We will be arriving in a few minutes. Please fasten your seat belts and place your seats and tray tables in their upright position," a cabin attendant repeated in English and Spanish over a loudspeaker. "Please have your tourist cards filled out prior to disembarking. You will need them as you pass through Mexican immigration. Thank you."

I leaned forward, allowing my seat to click upright. "Devon, we're about to land," I said, giving her a gentle shake.

"Ummm," she purred, snuggling her head deeper into my shoulder.

"Wake up, Devon."

A look of near-panic filled Devon's face. She sat up and for an instant seemed lost, her eyes darting about the cabin. Then she smiled and relaxed, realizing where she was. "Good morning," she yawned. Placing a hand on my knee, she leaned across my lap to gaze out the window. "Oh, we're here. Isn't the bay fantastic? Look! There's someone down there being pulled behind a boat."

I glanced out the window. Near one of the luxury hotels below, a powerboat was trailing a parachute on a long tether, a tourist dangling beneath the parachute's multicolored canopy like a sack of potatoes. When I turned back to Devon, I found her eyes searching mine.

She said nothing for a moment. Then, without looking away, she took my hand in hers. "Thanks for being patient," she said. "I know things have been happening awfully fast for you, and I know you have a lot of questions. I promise you'll you're your answers soon. Although some of them you may not like," she added.

After exiting the plane and crossing a blistering expanse of tarmac, Devon and I stood in the heat for several minutes, waiting in a line of tourists to pass immigration. At the front of the queue, a Mexican official sat in a shaded portico stamping passports and tourist cards. When we reached his station, I shifted uncomfortably, wondering what would come next. I hadn't seen much point in completing our tourist cards, as we didn't even have passports. Before I could speak, Devon fired off a string of rapid-fire phrases in Spanish. Once again I felt her deliver a brief mental *push*, and we were through.

Passing a knot of departing travelers waiting for the next plane, we proceeded to the front of the airport and out onto the street. Though it was still early morning, the sun already sizzled overhead, reflecting with scorching intensity off a broad façade of glass and concrete fronting the air terminal. Cabs idled at the curb. We made our way to the lead vehicle, where Devon spoke to the driver as we slid into the rear seat. "Hotel Meliá, por favor."

"Sí, Señora," answered the driver with a grin, flashing more gold than teeth.

I remained silent on the short ride to the hotel, which turned out to be located near a marina north of the city. Over the past hours I had become progressively troubled by the casual manner in which Devon used her mysterious ability. In essence, she wielded the same power that Roscoe had used on me. Although she hadn't actually harmed anyone, it still seemed wrong. People weren't puppets to be manipulated, whether they were hurt in the process or not.

I shifted uncomfortably beside her in the backseat, wondering what had possessed me to travel a thousand miles with a woman I'd just met—especially considering that I had abandoned my newspaper job in the middle of what would undoubtedly be one of the biggest stories of the year. Granted, there was the unmistakable element of danger that had made leaving Los Angeles seem prudent—at least at the time. But for a moment I also considered the possibility that Devon had given me one of her mental "nudges" to convince me to leave. No, I finally decided. I would have known.

Or would I?

Sensing my withdrawal, Devon ignored me. Still in high spirits, she continued to converse in fluent Spanish with the driver—who for his part seemed pleased to have an American fare who spoke his language so well. I listened idly, catching a phrase here and there. I had taken Spanish in high school but rarely used it. Nonetheless, I understood enough to follow the conversation as Devon asked the driver about the market, the bullfight, and the best restaurants.

Upon reaching the Meliá Hotel, I paid the driver, then followed Devon through a pair of wide glass doors into the hotel. Joining Devon inside the entrance, I glanced around the lobby. The Meliá's architectural style was tasteful and inviting, with concrete columns supporting a high ceiling that displayed a series of interesting vaults and recesses. Beneath my feet, native stone laid in intricate designs led to a cheerfully lit bar where couples sat enjoying tall, fruit-laden drinks. To the left, an entire glass wall opened upon a seaside garden of palms and flowering plants, creating an effect of tropical elegance.

"Not bad, huh?" Devon remarked as we proceeded across the lobby.

"You've been here before?"

"Once."

I withdrew my wallet as we approached the reception counter, still wondering what I was doing there.

"One room, two beds, okay?" Devon suggested when we arrived at the desk, glancing at me shyly.

"Works for me," I agreed. I wasn't certain where things with Devon were headed, but if nothing else, it appeared she wanted to keep me on a short leash, even if it meant sharing a room. Remembering how she had acquired our airline tickets, I added, "Let me take care of registering *my* way, all right?"

Devon laughed. "You don't approve of my little tricks?" Then, her expression frosting slightly, she added, "There's much you don't understand yet, Mike. Don't be too quick to judge."

After registering, we followed a Mexican boy in a white uniform to a bank of elevators on the far side of the lobby. We rode up four floors and crossed a wide corridor overlooking a cluster of tennis courts below. A quarter mile to the north, past a vacant arc of sand, I could make out the monolithic outline of another hotel complex fronting the ocean.

When we reached our room, I found the accommodations there as pleasant as the Meliá's lobby. Two queen-sized beds stood against one wall, beside which a sliding glass door accessed a generous balcony overlooking the beach and the grounds below. I tipped the bellboy, then stepped out onto the balcony as he began explaining the workings of the television, room safe, and minibar to Devon.

From the balcony I could see that the Meliá's designers had constructed the hotel in the shape of a giant horseshoe, open side toward the Pacific. Separating the hotel from the beach was a huge, irregularly shaped pool with an aquatic bar, past which the sweep of the Pacific curved south toward the central section of Puerto Vallarta. Partway down the coast a luxury liner was lumbering into port, dwarfing a nearby fleet of local fishing boats. Absently, I followed the cruise ship's progress, trying to sort out my feelings about Devon and the casual manner in which she used her strange power.

Finally I gave up, deciding that whatever else Devon had done, she had probably saved my life by getting me out of town. Resolving to take her advice and reserve judgment until I had all the facts, I stepped back into the room. By then the bellboy had departed and Devon was sitting cross-legged on the bed playing with the TV remote control, surfing through the channels.

"Check it out," she said, skipping past several stations that were updating their coverage of Bellamy's murder. "Same programming you get in L.A. Even Showtime and HBO."

I walked to the television and turned it off. "The place is terrific, Devon. And the TV works fine. Now it's time for some answers. What the hell's going on?"

Devon smiled. "I thought I had made that clear. I can't simply tell you. I'll have to show you."

"And when is that going to be?"

"When you're ready. Soon."

I shook my head in frustration. "This is going nowhere," I grumbled. "I'm going to go clean up."

Devon wrinkled her nose. "Please do," she joked, impervious to my ill humor. Then, raising a quizzical eyebrow, "One question first. What did you do with the pictures you took at the fundraiser, the ones the men in the garage wanted so badly? I'm assuming they were shots of the murder?"

I hesitated, realizing Devon must have heard everything that happened in the garage. She must have been close. But where? "I'm a reporter," I finally answered. "I sent them to the newspaper."

Devon nodded. "That's what we assumed you would do."

"What you assumed . . . what's so important about those shots, anyway? Hundreds of people saw the patrol officer kill Bellamy. Other people undoubtedly took pictures, too. My shot of the murder won't change anything."

"Maybe the men wanted something else on your camera."

"Like what?" I asked, abruptly recalling the picture I had taken of the woman near the exit.

"I don't know."

"Then we're even," I retorted, having become progressively irritated by Devon's secrecy and perversely deciding not to share my thoughts. Scowling, I walked to the bathroom and closed the door.

After stripping off my clothes, I turned the water on full and stepped into the shower. With a bone-weary sigh, I stood under the showerhead and let the warm jets beat against my body, loosening the knots in my neck and back.

A few minutes later I heard the bathroom door open. Through the steamy shower glass I saw Devon enter the room and stand in front of the sink, regarding herself in the mirror. I watched as she unbuttoned her blouse. As I had surmised earlier, she wasn't wearing a bra. Lifting her shoulders, she let the silky garment slip to the floor, exposing her breasts. Next, after kicking off her sandals, she wiggled out of her jeans. Nude from the waist up, she stretched lazily, inspecting her trim, perfect figure in the mirror. Then, with a sweep of her palms, she rolled her underwear over her hips and smoothly down her legs. Last, from her neck she removed a delicate gold chain that held a small, curiously shaped key. Carefully, she set the chain and key on the counter.

64

I suddenly no longer felt tired. Devon opened the shower door and stepped in beside me. My mouth went dry. I tried to say something but couldn't. All I could do was stare.

Nude, Devon was even more beautiful than I had imagined—tall and slim, with just a trace of a bikini tan line on her flawless skin. Her long legs flowed to a lean, flat stomach, and as she moved under the stream of water to join me, her upturned breasts brushed lightly against my chest. "Hi," she said with a mischievous grin, glancing at a part of my anatomy that was rising in undeniable welcome.

I swallowed. "Uh, hi, yourself," I managed to reply. This wasn't what I had expected. Despite Devon's beauty, I have never been one for casual sex, and I wasn't certain I wanted things to proceed any further, at least not yet.

Before I could say anything more, Devon took my hands in hers, interlacing her fingers in mine. "This isn't what you think, at least not exactly," she said. Moving closer, she searched my eyes, her breasts nuzzling against me, her thighs pressing against mine. "This isn't about sex," she explained. "Last night I said I had something to show you. Now is the time."

"I don't know what you have in mind," I said, "but—"

Devon tightened her grip, keeping her fingers interlaced in mine. "Look into my eyes, Mike."

A warm spray from the shower splashed from my shoulders onto Devon, forming glistening beads on her skin and wetting her ebony hair so it shined like satin. Her small, dark nipples had grown hard and erect, and I felt my own excitement thrusting almost painfully against her.

"Look into my eyes, Mike."

I lifted my gaze from Devon's body, finding her eyes. Without warning, a tingling sensation began spreading through my limbs. Spellbound, I watched as the pupils of Devon's eyes appeared to grow larger—abruptly transforming into inky, bottomless pools. Next I sensed from somewhere within her a force uncoiling as it had earlier, flexing like a tentacle. Without words, she used it to touch my mind—not the whiplike flick she'd used on the Mexicana ticket agent and the customs official, but an intimate caress. Abruptly my flesh seemed to ignite, every nerve alive as never before, my entire being burning with sensation. Waves of ecstasy began building inside me, flowing through me like a fiery current. I groaned with pleasure. "Devon, what . . . what's happening?"

"Shhh. Relax," Devon instructed, her lips parting slightly, her breath coming more quickly now. She kissed me, softly at first, then with growing insistence. Finally, with a moan of desire, she whispered, "Touch me, Mike."

I tried to raise my hands, but she held them fast. "Not that way. Here, I'll show you."

What happened next shook me to my core. Something shifted in Devon's mental touch. Slowly, she began probing another part of my mind. Though I can't describe the sensation, I felt her presence inside my head, moving lightly from place to place, her explorations a gentle caress. Gradually, like a blind man regaining his sense of sight, I felt an alien part of me coming alive—slowly at first, then growing stronger as Devon increased her efforts. As if in a kaleidoscopic dream, my mind spun in confusion, fighting to make sense of what was happening.

"Don't fight it, Mike," she said. "Just let go. Do it for me."

Deep inside I sensed a barrier beginning to tear, crumbling like an ancient wall. A moment later, with a surge of hot, lusty satisfaction, I felt the bonds that had long held me give way. After a lifetime of suffocation, I was finally able to breathe. I was free!

"I knew it!" Devon whispered in awe. "But why—no, *how* have you kept your power hidden so long?"

Reeling in shock, I found myself unable to answer, much less accept what was happening to me. "I don't . . . I didn't—"

"Never mind," said Devon firmly, again coupling her mind with mine. "We can talk later. First touch me here . . . and then here . . ."

Devon still resolutely held my hands, but I made no further attempt to free them. Shaken and confused, I was powerless to break the mental bond Devon had forged between us. Instead I closed my eyes, surrendering to the waves of rapture welling within me. And with Devon's help, I used my mind to touch her pleasure nexus as well. Distantly aware of the hot spray of water on my back, and the sound of Devon's shuddering moans, and the warmth of her body on mine, I abandoned myself to a paralyzing storm of pleasure. Each surge of ecstasy seemed to last forever, followed by another, and yet another—each more intense than the previous, each building with inexorable, near unbearable intensity before subsiding, only to begin again, and again . . .

When I thought I could endure no more, Devon released my hands and placed her palms on my chest. "Enough," she gasped, pushing me away. "Enough!"

"Whatever you say," I agreed almost thankfully. A moment later I sensed Devon disengaging her mind from mine. To my surprise, I discovered it a simple task to withdraw back into myself as well.

Out of breath, Devon opened the glass enclosure door and stepped from the shower. "God, Mike," she laughed, reaching for a towel. "You certainly learn fast."

My heart racing, I remained silent. Still shaking with emotion, I stood under the warm spray, filled with an unsettling conviction that I had just crossed a line from which there would be no turning back. I now understood why Devon had insisted on "showing" me, but her demonstration had raised more questions than it answered.

I watched as Devon began to dry herself, admiring her lithe figure as she lifted her hair and refastened her gold chain around her neck. Then, as she began gathering her clothes, I turned off the water and moved to stand behind her. Encircling her with my arms, I kissed the nape of her neck, breathing in her fragrance. "That was . . . I don't know a word for what that was," I said. "I don't even know if there *is* a word. But whatever just happened between us, I'm now more confused than ever. What's going on?"

Without turning, Devon took my hands and placed them on her breasts. At my touch, I could feel her nipples starting to harden again. "Mike, that's just the beginning of what I have to show you," she said. Then she turned in my arms to face me, her nude body sleek and smooth against my skin. She started to kiss me but drew back, her mouth opening in mock surprise as she felt my need pressing against her. Although I was mentally exhausted, another part of me still remained unsatisfied.

"Why, Mike," she said playfully, reaching down to take me in her hand. She hesitated a moment, pursing her lips in thought. "Look, I know you're confused," she continued, her tone turning serious. "Don't worry, you'll know everything before long. I promise."

Then, with an impish smile, she gently began stroking me. "In the meantime," she added, "I think I know something that just might take your mind off things."

Chapter Nine

Jamie Callahan stood at her second-floor bedroom window, trying to decide what to do. Cell phone pressed to her ear, she stared out at a pair of giant sycamores that sprawled across her front yard, listening to the recorded message on her father's answering machine. She had tried to contact her dad once before school and twice since arriving home that afternoon. Still no luck. Dejectedly, she walked to her bed and sat, ending her call without leaving a message.

"Where is he, Georgie?" she asked the wiry mongrel who hopped up beside her on the bed.

Georgie thumped his tail at the sound of his master's voice, then sighed and settled in.

Jamie realized there could be any number of reasons why her father hadn't returned her calls. She could get her camera back from him anytime; maybe he had decided to wait until the following weekend to return it. For that matter, maybe he was on assignment and hadn't even received her messages.

So why can't I shake the feeling that something's wrong? she wondered.

Jamie heard the front door open, then the sound of footsteps on the hardwood floor below.

"Jamie?"

"Hi, Mom. I'm up in my room."

"How was school?"

"Fine," Jamie called back, trying to sound untroubled, and failing. Her mother's steps hesitated in the entry, then started up the stairs.

With a sweep of her hand, Jamie gently scooted Georgie from the bed. "Mom's coming, boy," she whispered. "You stay down for now." Georgie regarded her quizzically, then padded to his wicker bed by the closet. As he did, Jamie got up and crossed the room, again looking out her window. The sun had just descended into a rust-colored strata of smog overlying the ocean, painting a crescent of western sky in sickly hues of orange and red. To the north, marine fog shrouded the Santa Monica Mountains. As Jamie watched, a streetlight on the corner sputtered to life, sending cold, harsh shafts of light into the misty night.

"You okay?"

Jamie turned. Her mother was standing in the doorway, a hallway chandelier lighting her from behind. Shadow hid her face, but Jamie heard the concern in her voice.

"Yeah, Mom." Jamie returned her gaze to the street. "I'm just . . . I'm just worried about Dad."

"Jeez, why's it so dark in here?" Susan asked, flipping on a light. "There, that's better."

Jamie could see her mother's image reflected now in the window, superimposed on the gloomy scene outside. Her mother had on one of her "work outfits"—a short navy skirt and matching jacket, white monogrammed blouse open at the throat, and a single strand of pearls. Her auburn hair fell loose on her shoulders, in contrast to her otherwise conservative, professional appearance. Despite Jamie and her mother's difference in age, friends often observed that they looked more like sisters than mother and daughter.

Susan entered the room and sat on the bed. "Come here, honey," she said, patting the comforter beside her. "It's time you and I had a talk."

"About Dad?"

"Yes, about your father. Come sit by me. Please."

Jamie returned to the bed. Kicking off her shoes, she slumped down beside her mother. Georgie immediately bounded back up on the bed, laying his muzzle in Jamie's lap. Jamie glanced guiltily at her mother. "He'll get down in a minute, okay?"

Susan nodded and smiled, reaching over to touch her daughter's hair. Then, lowering her hand, she said, "I want you to listen to me, Jamie. There are some things about your dad we need to discuss. I just hope you're old enough to understand."

"If you mean what happened between you and Dad when you split up, I—"

"That's part of it, but not the real issue I want to discuss," Susan interrupted. "Not the heart of it, anyway. Let me get this out my own way, all right? This isn't easy for me, and a lot of it doesn't make sense . . ." Susan's voice trailed off.

"Mom, you don't have to do this."

"Yes, I do. I've thought about this for a long time, and I know we've talked about it a bit. But there's more." Susan took a deep breath, then slowly let it out. "You really love your father, don't you? Not just because he's your dad, but because he's who he is."

Jamie searched her mother's face, then lowered her eyes and nodded.

"This may be a hard lesson for you, Jamie, but just because Mike is your dad doesn't make him perfect. Aside from being your father, he's also a human being. And like everyone else, he has problems of his own. In his case, serious problems. Do you understand what I'm trying to say?"

"I think so. You mean what happened to Dad in Afghanistan."

Susan looked away and sighed. "Time goes so quickly. Sometimes it seems like you're growing up so fast that I can't keep up with you." She paused, then forged ahead. "I need to tell you how it was between your dad and me at the start. Maybe that will help you understand what I'm going to say next."

Jamie remained silent as her mother hesitated again, struggling for words. Finally Susan straightened her shoulders and continued. "When your dad and I first met, I couldn't get him out of my mind. I knew we were meant for each other, right from the beginning. I never doubted it. And neither did he. I loved your dad more than life itself, and he loved me the same way."

"And then he went to Afghanistan."

"Yes. And then he went to Afghanistan," Susan said bitterly. "Something happened there to change him, Jamie. I don't know what. He wouldn't talk about it with me, or with anyone—even the doctors. But when he came back from the hospital after his final tour, he had built a wall around himself. He went through

71

the motions, but something inside was missing. He seemed . . . *numb.* But in spite of that, there were so many good things about him that still remained, an essential kindness that still shone through, I knew the caring man I married was still in there somewhere. I just had to find him. I hoped sharing you with him would . . ." Again Susan lapsed into silence.

"You still love him, don't you, Mom?"

Susan nodded. "God help me," she said softly, "I do."

"Then why—"

"Haven't you been listening?" Susan asked, close to tears. "I don't know what the war did to your dad, but when he came back he wasn't the same man who had left. It wasn't so much that he couldn't love anyone anymore; it was more that he couldn't even love himself, and that has to come first. I think he lost faith in everything, especially himself. It's been years, but nothing has changed."

Susan paused, then took Jamie's hands in hers and continued. "Your father would give his life for us, Jamie. He would. I know that beyond a doubt. I also know that although you love him with all your heart, don't expect him to love you back in the same way you love him. Even though he wants to, he can't."

Sliding closer, Jamie put an arm around her mother. "Aw, Mom, don't worry about me," she said lightly. "Things will turn out okay. You'll see. Dad will come around sooner or later. After all, how could he resist two gorgeous women like us?"

"Right," Susan said, realizing with a touch of embarrassment that somehow things had reversed, with her daughter now attempting to raise *her* spirits. "I think you're one heck of a girl, Jamie," she added quietly. "I'm proud of you, you know that?"

"With good reason," said Jamie, grinning. Then, more seriously, "I'm proud of you too." She started to add something, then stopped. "Mom," she began again uncertainly. "All day long something has been telling me that Dad's in trouble. I've tried to call him repeatedly, but he's not answering. I even tried him at the paper. No one has seen him. I don't know what to do."

Susan regarded her daughter curiously. She knew from experience that Jamie's uncanny hunches often proved accurate, and she had learned not to dismiss them out of hand. "Well, whatever else your dad may be," she said, "he's a survivor. I'm sure he's fine. But if you want, I'll stop by the paper tomorrow. I have a meeting with the Planning Commission at ten. I'll drop by the *Times* on my way back. If he's not there, I'll swing by his house. Okay?"

Jamie nodded. "Thanks, Mom."

"No problem. That's what moms are for." Susan rose from the bed. "Hey, you hungry?"

"Always."

Susan glanced at her watch. "It's too late to cook. Feel like grabbing a pizza at Guido's in the Village?"

"Mushrooms, sausage, pepperoni, and pineapple?"

"Only if they keep the pineapple off my half."

"No spirit of adventure," Jamie laughed. "Okay, Mom. You're on."

Chapter Ten

I awoke to the smell of coffee and the sound of Devon's voice. I opened my eyes, squinting into bright shafts of sunlight streaming through the drapes. Wearing an oversized tee shirt and pair of thong underwear, Devon was sitting on the balcony outside, sipping coffee and talking on the hotel phone. "We can use him," I heard her say. "Chances like this don't come along every day." She paused, listening. Then, "I'm handling this. It's *my* decision." She turned toward the bed. Her eyes narrowed as she saw me watching her.

Forget what you just heard. Go back to sleep.

Instinctively, I blocked her thrust.

Devon's lips tightened. Then she smiled sheepishly. "Sorry," she mumbled, covering the receiver with her palm. "Sometimes I forget myself. You *do* catch on fast," she added, shaking her head. Returning her attention to the phone, she said, "I'll get back to you. For now my decision stands."

I raised up on one elbow. "Conferring with the head office?"

Devon hung up the telephone and stepped into the room, returning the phone to a table near the balcony door. Appearing preoccupied, she crossed to a dresser where a pile of her clothes lay in a heap. "Something like that," she answered vaguely.

Though curious about Devon's call, I decided not to pursue it. "What time is it?" I asked instead, watching as Devon began pulling on her jeans.

"A bit after ten. You were really out."

"Ten in the morning?" I said incredulously, realizing that I had to get in touch with the *Times*. I had meant to take a short nap after our lovemaking the previous day, not sleep the entire afternoon and straight through the night. "I can't believe I've been out since . . ."

"Yesterday afternoon," Devon said. "Like a light. Our experience in the shower must have tired you, not to mention our time together in bed," she added with a smile.

She finished wiggling into her jeans, then pulled off her tee shirt, stretched, and slipped on her blouse. Leaving the silky garment unbuttoned, she crossed to the bed and sat beside me. "Speaking of which," she continued, taking my hands in hers, "what we shared yesterday turned out to be a lot more than I bargained for. You really surprised me, Mike. I don't know what to say, except that . . . well, you're not what I expected."

"And what was that?" I asked, having a hard time pulling my eyes away from her open blouse.

"I don't know," she answered, apparently unaware of the effect her body was having on me. "Latents are extremely rare, to say the least. I've never met one before."

I recollected hearing Roscoe and Tyler use the same term. "'Latent?' Is that what you call someone like me?"

"Yes," Devon replied. "Anyone with the power usually discovers it by the time they reach puberty. To find someone of your strength who's never . . ."

". . . used it?" I finished, recalling the occasions in Afghanistan that my premonitions had saved me. "How do you know I haven't?"

"Oh, I know. Perhaps you've employed your powers a bit, but at best you've barely tapped a fraction of your potential." Devon seemed to consider her next words carefully. "Mike, I want to teach you to use your strength," she said.

"I'm not certain that's something I want."

"After what has happened, you have no choice," Devon insisted. "You have to be able to protect yourself from those who want to harm you."

I ran a hand across the stubble covering my chin. Maybe Devon was right. Maybe I had no choice but to continue my "education" at her hands. Nevertheless, a voice inside told me to be careful. "Why are you doing this?" I asked. "There's something you're not telling me."

"There's a lot I'm not telling you—yet," said Devon. "There hasn't been time, and some things have to be *shown*, remember?"

I smiled. "I remember."

"I can tell you this," Devon continued. "As I said, I was assigned to keep an eye on you. At first it was just a job. Now it's grown to be more than that. If you'll let me, I want to show you what you can become." Then, leaning closer, she pressed her lips to mine.

I felt myself responding to Devon's embrace. Enfolding her in my arms, I pulled her onto the bed. Devon kissed me again, her tongue exploring as our passion began to mount, her breasts warm against my chest. Then abruptly she stopped. "There'll be plenty of time for that," she laughed, rising to her feet. "Your education comes first. I'm going down to the patio to get something to eat. I visited one of the shops downstairs and picked up a few toiletries, some casual wear for me, and a change of clothes for you. Why don't you get dressed and meet me out by the pool for breakfast?"

"Done," I agreed, my curiosity rising. "As long as we cover some questions I still want answered."

"As promised, you'll know everything before the day is over," Devon said, buttoning her blouse. "One caveat, though. As I told you earlier, try to keep an open mind."

After she left, I walked to the bathroom and surveyed myself in the mirror. Though my swollen eye looked better than expected and the gash on my cheek had scabbed over, several days of beard darkened my face, a purplish bruise marked my cheek, and my hair was a tangled mess. All in all, I looked pretty rough. With a rueful shrug I stepped into the shower, deciding that even after I cleaned up, I wasn't going to look much better.

Twenty minutes later—showered, shaven, and wearing a fresh pair of slacks and a short-sleeved golf shirt that Devon had bought for me—I walked onto the hotel patio. To my left the Meliá's seaside pool sparkled in the sunlight, a lone swimmer cutting laps across its width. Ahead, a flight of steps descended through a concrete seawall to the beach; to the right a palm-thatched ramada shaded a pleasant outdoor dining area. On the far side of the ramada I spotted Devon sitting at a table in a deserted area near the pool. She waved when she saw me.

"Here's the program, Mike," she began without preamble as soon as I joined her. "Let me do the talking. If you have questions afterward, then it will be your turn. Now, before we start, do you want something to eat?"

I watched as Devon took a bite of papaya from a plate of sliced fruit. With the exception of a few bags of peanuts I'd had on the plane, I hadn't eaten since dinner in Westwood two nights before. "Definitely," I answered.

"Good." Devon signaled the waiter. "The food here is great." Then, holding a fork in her left hand European style, she squeezed a wedge of lime over her fruit plate and took another bite of papaya. "See those people over there?" she went on, using her fork to point toward a group of young tourists who were clustered around the poolside bar. Already half inebriated, they were drinking Coronas and talking a bit too loudly.

"What about them?"

"And the others by the lobby? And the ones on the beach?"

I nodded, wondering where our discussion was leading.

"You're not like them," Devon said bluntly. "*We're* not like them. The difference between us and them is far greater than you can imagine."

"What do you—"

Devon held up her hand. "I talk, you listen."

"So talk."

Just then a portly Mexican waiter ambled over to our table, order pad in hand. "Would you like breakfast, Señor?" he inquired, stopping beside me.

I picked up a menu. Deftly, Devon plucked it from my fingers. "May I order for you?"

"Sure. But forget breakfast. I'm ready for lunch."

"No problem." Without referring to the menu, Devon spoke rapidly to the waiter in Spanish.

"You speak Spanish extremely well, Devon," I observed as our waiter turned to leave.

"Fluently. Like all the rest."

"The rest? How many languages do you speak?"

"All of them," Devon replied casually. "It's a trick I'll teach you sometime. At the moment I have something else to show you." She raised her hand and called after the waiter. "Señor."

The waiter returned to our table. "Yes, Señora?"

Don't move.

The waiter froze, his face a mindless blank.

Sliding her chair closer to mine, Devon covered the back of my hand with her palm, interweaving her fingers in mine. "It's time you grew up, Mike," she said. I sensed her engaging me in the same mental embrace we had shared in the shower. But this time she guided our conjoined consciousness outward . . .

Without warning, I found myself plunged into the swirling confusion of the waiter's mind!

"See? It's easy when you know how," Devon said aloud. "And once you're in, you can do anything you want."

Hesitantly, I opened myself to a chaos of murky sensation inside the waiter's skull—memories of a childhood in Guadalajara, an unresolved dispute with Maria (his wife?), a nagging pain in his back, the desire for a cigarette . . .

"More to the point, you can make *them* do anything *you* want," Devon added. "Pay close attention. This is where you push."

Take off your shirt.

The waiter raised his hands and began unbuttoning his shirt.

Stop. Leave it on.

The waiter dropped his hands to his sides.

"See how willing they are when you push the right spots?" Devon laughed gaily, continuing her demonstration. "This makes them forget, and this causes pain, and this makes them stop moving, and this . . ."

As one would lead a child, Devon took me on a tour of the hapless waiter's mind. When it was over, she released my hand. I sat dumbfounded, drenched with sweat. I felt sick. Though the experience had shaken me deeply, I realized that our rapelike foray into the waiter's mind wasn't the most appalling thing that had just happened. It was the ease with which we had done it.

The waiter still stood woodenly, his eyes registering nothing. "How . . . how does it work?" I stammered.

"What difference does that make?" Devon replied, her tone telling me she had no idea, either. "You don't *really* understand how any of your other senses work, do you? That doesn't keep you from using them."

I shook my head. "That may be, but there is something fundamentally wrong about this, Devon. Just because you have the ability to force someone to do what you want doesn't give you the right."

"I didn't harm this man," Devon pointed out, waving a hand at the portly Mexican. "He's not even going to remember. Watch."

Forget everything that just happened and bring us our order.

Seeming oblivious to what had just transpired, the waiter turned and hurried toward the kitchen.

"What's wrong, Mike?" Devon chided. "I thought you were going to keep an open mind."

I frowned. "I'm trying to. It's just that what we did to that man makes him, and all the other people around us, seem . . ."

". . . inferior?" Devon finished with a patient smile. "Like sheep, perhaps? Or cattle?"

Instead of answering, I asked, "Why do you and I have this ability? Where did it come from?"

Devon shrugged. "A genetic mutation, possibly? It does seem to run in families," she added, her tone again telling me she didn't really know, nor did she care.

I changed the subject. "Is this what happened at the fundraiser?"

Devon's smile faded. "That was different. And the ones who did it . . . Mike, you don't realize how lucky you are to be alive."

"You said that earlier. Different how?"

"What we just did was strictly one-on-one manipulation. For that the subject has to be *pushed* from close range. A *Deus* engineered the long-range events at Century City."

"*Deus*. Is that Latin?"

"It's based on a language far more ancient than Latin," Devon replied cryptically.

Realizing she wasn't going to elaborate, I decided to try another approach. "I assume you were talking about this *Deus* person when we were at my house in Venice. Are you ready to tell me what you're talking about?"

Devon regarded me somberly. "One thing first. Revealing what I'm about to tell you to anyone outside our circle is punishable by death. Do you understand?"

I shrugged.

"Do you understand?"

I sensed that Devon wasn't going to continue until I said the words she wanted to hear. "Talking about this to anyone outside our circle, whatever the hell that is, is punishable by death," I repeated. "I understand."

Devon regarded me for another long moment. Finally she nodded. "From the very beginning, our kind has always existed, sharing the world with others," she said, lowering her voice. "Those with our abilities are divided into three tiers. There are gradations within each tier, but certain aptitudes within each cannot be exceeded. For example, one born with first-tier abilities can hone their powers, but they can never attain the abilities of the second tier—although one's strengths often ascend a predictable ladder as they become manifest.

"Early in life, those born with first-tier abilities typically exhibit a range of powers that sets them apart from others," Devon continued. "Eidetic memory, precognition, an ability to sense people nearby, heightened intuition, and so forth. If their abilities are extraordinary, occasionally a few first-tier members are invited into our fold. Most are not. Sadly, throughout the ages many with first-tier abilities have ended their lives imprisoned, hanged, or burned at the stake as witches and warlocks. Those with second-tier powers are more fortunate. When fully brought to fruition, their powers make them virtually invulnerable to intervention. I'm second tier, and although you've seen a bit of what I can do, you haven't seen *all* I can do."

"And a *Deus*?"

Devon glanced around nervously. "A *Deus* is extremely rare," she said, lowering her voice even more. "At most, a member of the third tier surfaces every hundred years or so. A *Deus* can control from a distance, and can do so without using verbal commands. It's said they can enter someone at will, taking on a new body like putting on a suit of clothes. Some believe their powers go far beyond that. I'm certain many of the great men throughout history have had it—Alexander, Caesar, Ivan, Napoleon."

I shook my head. "To say the least, I'm having trouble accepting this," I said, struggling to get my mind around the idea that other . . . *beings* inhabited our world, godlike creatures who throughout the ages have lived among us in secrecy.

"Is it any harder to accept than some of the other mysterious truths that have existed since the beginning of time?" Devon demanded. She paused, lost in thought. "You know, Mike," she finally continued, "the difference between a great leader and a monster is often a matter of circumstance. In addition to the Caesars and Alexanders and Napoleons of history, there have been many with the power whom the world now reviles: Vlad Tepes, Gilles de Rais, Countess Elisabeth Báthory, and Fritz Haarman, to name a few. There's a fine line between good and evil, but for better or worse, members of our kind have changed the course of history many times in the past, and we will continue to do so in the future."

"So when Bellamy was killed, a *Deus*—possibly the woman I saw—was pulling the strings," I said, trying to steer the conversation back to the present. "Why?"

"I told you, I don't know."

My mind flashed back to the conference room. "Then maybe you can tell me this. How did I fit into things that night?"

"At this point, I'd rather not speculate," Devon answered. "Let's just say that your abilities appear promising."

Before I could reply, our waiter returned. Cheerfully, he placed several steaming plates of food and a Dos Equis in front of me, acting completely unaware of the treatment he'd received from Devon earlier. Devon glanced at the waiter, then looked at me as if to say, "I told you so."

"Gracias," I mumbled to the waiter as he departed. Then, regarding my food, "What is this?" I asked Devon, grateful for the diversion.

"The fish is grilled Dorado. It's smothered in fresh salsa and garnished with mild chilies and sliced avocado," Devon replied, apparently willing to let our previous conversation lie, at least for the moment. "One of my favorites."

I tried the fish and found it delicious. After several ambrosial bites I tasted the other dish I'd been served—a shrimp-and-rice creation seasoned with a deliciously spicy red sauce. "And this?"

"Shrimp Diablo. The sauce is a blend of olive oil, garlic, Tabasco, lemon, tomato, sugar, and tequila. I thought you'd like it."

"You thought right," I said, concentrating on my food. Each bite of the piquant dishes seemed to beg another, and another. Devon sat in silence watching me eat, absently fingering the gold chain around her neck, the one I had noticed earlier in the shower.

When I finished my meal, I tipped back the rest of my beer, relaxing for the first time since joining Devon at the table. "Devon, you have permission to order for me anytime," I said.

"Glad to be of service," she replied, still toying with her chain.

I looked at it curiously. "What's that around your neck? A key?"

"This?" From beneath her blouse Devon withdrew a gold key with peculiar holes dimpling both sides. "It opens a very special door," she said, smiling. "Perhaps one day I'll show you what's behind it." Then, her smile fading, "Tell me about the hunger, Mike."

From Devon's manner, I realized she wasn't talking about food. Against my will, I recalled the craving that had invariably gripped me during the heat of battle. Again, I wondered how she had known.

"Sooner or later you're going to have to face it," Devon went on. "I'm amazed that you have been able to suppress your natural urges for so long. But why? What do you fear? Are you afraid of what you'll become if you start using your strength?"

"I . . . I don't know what you mean."

"Mike, you have an ability that sets you apart," Devon said. "How you use it will determine what you become, but after what has happened, you *must* use it to survive. Forget morality and all the other outdated concepts that have tainted your thinking until now. There are powerful individuals using this very same ability for their own ends, and you've interfered with them. They now view you as a danger, someone to be eliminated. You were lucky the first time around. You won't survive their second attempt."

"Thanks for the reassurance."

"Wake up!" Devon insisted crossly. "I'm attempting to help you. I'm also putting myself in danger, just being here with you. You could at least try to understand."

"I'm trying, believe me. I'm trying."

Devon paused, then continued more patiently. "Mike, I realize you don't approve of using your powers to get what you want, but isn't that exactly what the strong have always done, one way or another? Besides, what's so admirable about the human race to merit it special treatment? Our leaders have turned our world into a sewer. Overpopulation, pollution, global warming, and nuclear waste comprise just a few of the problems for which humans are responsible. Many of my kind believe it's time for steadier hands to take control."

"Your kind? You're referring to the ones who killed Bellamy?"

"No. They're a breakaway faction, with an agenda of their own. My organization has another, and in time we'll deal with the ones who killed Bellamy. We can use you, Mike. And we can protect you until you're strong enough to stand on your own. I'm asking you to join us."

"And if I don't?"

Devon looked away without answering.

83

Shortly afterward, with nothing resolved between us, Devon announced that she intended to visit the hotel shops, pick out a bikini, and get some sun by the pool. Profoundly disturbed by what she had "shown" me on the patio, I declined to join her, saying I had some thinking to do. I accompanied her as far as the lobby, where we parted company—she to a boutique around the corner, I to our room.

After riding the elevator to our fourth-floor accommodations, I walked out onto the balcony, my thoughts churning. Across the bay, dark banks of clouds were lowering over the mountains, promising rain for the inland jungle. Below, hotel guests were strolling the beach, some stopping to purchase trinkets and souvenirs from passing vendors. Life seemed to be going on as always, but I realized for me it would never again be the same. Though I tried, I was unable to shake the feeling of dread that had gradually enveloped me during my meal with Devon. According to her, she and others like her had the power, and therefore the right, to do or take anything they wanted . . . as did I. I suspected that my newfound ability, a gift whose seductive power could corrupt even the most righteous, might well turn out to be a curse. Nevertheless, the temptation to use it was undeniable. And I *could* use it wisely, couldn't I?

Of course I could, I told myself. I could even use it to fight the group that had murdered Bellamy and tried to harm me, as Devon suggested. But the more I thought about it, the more a nagging suspicion began to crystallize in my mind. Despite her apparent openness, Devon was still holding something back.

What?

Unable to come to a conclusion, I stepped back into the room and tried my cell phone. No service. Deciding to ignore the expense, I picked up the hotel telephone. After a bit of wrangling, I managed to reach the West L.A. Police Station switchboard. The duty officer there transferred me to the detectives' squad room upstairs. Moments later Nelson came on the line.

"Mike, where the hell are you?" my friend demanded, his gruff tones ushering in a welcome touch of reality. "I've been trying to call you since yesterday."

"Sorry, Nelson," I apologized. "I had to leave unexpectedly. It's a long story, but I'm in Mexico. Puerto Vallarta."

"Mexico? Great time for a vacation, pal," Nelson observed angrily. "In case you haven't heard, the media is blitzing Bellamy's murder. Which, of course, means things on my end are going ballistic. There are people here who want to talk to you, including me. For one thing, the pictures you *said* you took of the shooting have vanished."

"What?"

"In fact, according to everyone I talked with at the *Times*, there never *were* any pictures. What's going on?"

"I don't know," I said, puzzled. "I'll have to get back to you on that. In the meantime, have you uncovered anything new on the killings?"

"Off the record?"

"Yeah. Like before."

"Actually, nothing much has turned up," Nelson admitted. "Apparently Arthur Bellamy had no real enemies, at least none who wanted him dead. The only people who seem to be benefiting from his death are his political rivals. To say the least, his murder has put a whole new wrinkle on the governor's race."

"I can imagine. What about the patrol officer who did the shooting?"

"Hidalgo? Nothing there either. For lack of a better explanation, the task force is attributing his actions to a nervous breakdown. I did come up with something on the revolver you gave me at the restaurant, though. We got a hit on a print we lifted from one of the shell casings. The print belonged to a guy named Gregory Tyler, with a list of aliases as long as your arm. Among other things he's wanted for murder, jailbreak, and crossing state lines to avoid prosecution. We matched another print we found on the gun barrel to a second fugitive with a want-list even longer than Tyler's. Roscoe Reese. Seems he strolled out of a maximum-security prison in Florida twenty years ago, disappearing without a trace."

"Well, you can tell whoever's hunting for Roscoe that they can quit," I advised. "Look, I have another call to make, but I'll be in touch. And when I find out what happened to those pictures, you'll be the first to know."

After hanging up, I phoned Hank McCaffery at the *Times*. A secretary answered, then transferred my call to McCaffery. "Mike? Where have you been?" McCaffery demanded when he came on the line. "Never mind. Just get your ass down here. Now."

"Chief, I—"

"No excuses! In my office in thirty minutes."

McCaffery severed the connection. "Damn," I grumbled, starting to reenter Hank's number. I hesitated, then decided to call Taryn instead. When no one answered at her desk, I had her paged. Thirty seconds later she picked up. "Mike? Where—"

"—have I been?" I finished. "Seems to be the question of the day. Listen, McCaffery wants to see me in his office, but there's no way I can make it there in time. I'm in Mexico, but don't tell him that. Try to square things for me, will you?"

"But—"

I cut her off. "I don't have time to explain," I said, realizing that there was no way I *could* explain. "I just talked with Nelson. He says the *Times* doesn't have the pictures I took at Bellamy's fundraiser."

I know," said Taryn quietly. "Something weird happened that night, Mike. Not long after you telephoned, some guy waltzed into McCaffery's office, acting like he owned the place. He left a few minutes later with your pictures."

"What did the guy look like?"

"Dark hair, tall and wiry."

"Tyler."

"Who?"

"One of the mutts who jumped me in the garage. Then what happened?"

"I was curious, so I went down to the photo lab," Taryn went on, sounding increasingly perplexed. "The tech there swore he didn't remember my bringing in the memory card. Said he never printed any pictures for me, either. There's more, Mike, but I . . . I don't want to talk over the phone."

All right," I agreed, my mind racing. "We'll compare notes when I get back. Until then, I want you to do something for me. Got a pen?"

"Hold on a sec." A pause, then, "Okay, shoot."

"Dig up anything you can on Vlad Tepes, Gilles de Rais, Countess Elisabeth Báthory, and Fritz Haarman. I'm not sure of the spellings, but I think they're all historical figures."

"How do they fit in?"

"That's what I'm hoping you'll find out."

"Okay, I'm on it. Hurry back, Mike."

"I'll be there as soon as I can. One more thing. When you speak with McCaffery, tell him I'm onto something big—a story that will knock his socks off."

As I replaced the receiver, an icy shiver ran up my spine. Turning, I saw Devon watching me from the doorway. Her eyes were hooded, her face unreadable.

"How long were you listening?" I asked guiltily.

"Long enough." Devon entered the room and tossed a shopping bag onto the bed. "You can't go public with this, Mike. Not any of it. Even if you did, no one would believe you."

"No?" I tapped my temple. "I have the proof right here. I don't expect you to understand, Devon, but I'm a reporter, and this may be the biggest story of my life. I can't just sit on it."

Devon's expression hardened. "If you try to disclose what you know, you'll be stopped. I told you, the penalty for what you're thinking of doing is death. I couldn't protect you."

"I'll have to take that chance."

"Think for a minute, Mike," Devon snapped. "What you're proposing would be catastrophic for us all, yourself included. Knowledge of our kind would trigger a witch hunt the likes of which the world hasn't been seen for centuries. That's one reason latents like you are so carefully monitored—both by my group and by the others," she added angrily.

"The others?" I said. "What do I have to lose with them? According to you, I'm already on their hit list."

"Please, Mike," Devon begged. "Don't throw your life away. I have one last thing to show you. By the end of today you'll know everything. Please don't do anything foolish until then."

Again I sensed Devon was holding something back. "Fine. I'll keep quiet until I have the full picture. As long as it's soon," I added. "One condition, though. You told me you were assigned to keep an eye on me. I want to know your exact instructions."

Devon shrugged. "I was told to protect you, to find out what you knew, and to keep you from falling into anyone else's hands."

"And?"

"And if possible, to recruit you."

"And what were your orders if I decided not to join your exclusive little club?" I demanded. "You wouldn't answer when I asked earlier today. Now I want to know."

Devon hesitated, then looked away. "In the event you refused, you were to be eliminated," she said.

"And who was supposed to carry out my . . . elimination?" I asked, already certain of the answer.

Though Devon remained silent, her face told me all I needed to know.

Chapter Eleven

After saying goodbye to Mike, Taryn hung up the phone, wondering what to tell McCaffery. Mike seemed to think she could simply smooth things over, as though his absence were no big deal. "Hi, Hank. Callahan is in Mexico, getting some sun. He says he's sorry he's not here to cover the hottest story of the year, but something came up." No way *that* would fly.

Briefly, Taryn considered not saying anything to McCaffery. Mike had made his bed; let him sleep in it. His disappearance had placed everyone at the *Times* in an untenable position, and she didn't blame McCaffery for being angry.

On the other hand, Mike's absence was unlike him. Maybe he had a good reason. Although he'd been secretive on the phone, his hint about being onto something big stuck in her mind. Taryn glanced at the list of names he had given her. Whoever they were, Mike seemed to think that they might be tied to the murders. Shrugging, she stuffed the list into her purse. She could check the names later; first she had to do something about saving Callahan's job.

She had been in the cafeteria when she'd received Mike's page. Now, as she rode the elevator up to her desk in the newsroom, Taryn mentally reviewed the puzzling events of the past days, trying to piece together a plausible explanation for Mike's absence. His recent behavior, especially at the fundraiser, had been puzzling, to say the least. She considered suggesting that Mike was having a nervous breakdown, then rejected it.

Why not just tell Hank the truth? she wondered.

The truth. But what was that?

Taryn knew for certain that Mike's pictures had been printed at the lab; she'd delivered the memory card herself and had waited while the pictures were printed. She also knew that McCaffery had received a set of prints. She had delivered them herself. Now Hank claimed he never saw them. Plus the memory card was missing, and the lab tech swore he had no recollection of receiving Mike's shots, either.

Why were they lying?

Taryn suspected that the answer was linked to the man Mike had called Tyler. Who has the ability to stroll into one of the nation's leading newspapers and walk off with photographic evidence of the murder of a gubernatorial candidate? she wondered. One answer came to mind. *The government.* Taryn's pulse quickened. If someone in Washington, say someone in the CIA, were trying to cover up Bellamy's murder . . .

Upon reaching her workstation, Taryn glanced around the newsroom. Satisfied no one was watching, she leaned down and opened the bottom drawer of her desk. Again she peered around the newsroom. Nothing. Nervously, she reached into the drawer. On the bottom, under a pile of folders, lay a manila envelope marked "Photographs—Do Not Bend."

Mike's pictures.

Actually, most were Jamie's—photos of her dog, her mom working in the garden, Mike and Jamie at the beach. But the last four shots chronicled events at the fundraiser in grisly detail. The first showed the pistol in the police officer's hand as he fired a bullet into Bellamy's temple; the other three were of people in the room, most of them scrambling for the exits.

When Taryn had delivered Mike's pictures to the lab, as an afterthought she had asked the tech to run a second set of prints for Jamie. She had picked up the second set along with McCaffery's. When the memory card and Hank's prints disappeared, Taryn had nearly come forward with Jamie's set. Something held her back.

Without removing the manila envelope from the drawer, Taryn slipped out the bottom four photos, the ones taken at the fundraiser. Studying them, she tried to find something—*anything*—that would explain their importance. The shot taken at the instant of Bellamy's death might be Pulitzer material, but the others simply showed a crowd in panic. All the shots were fascinating in a macabre way, but she saw nothing in them to warrant special importance. Nevertheless, their disappearance now involved more than a missing picture on page one. Yesterday, acting on behalf of the LAPD, the district attorney had served the *Times* with a court order demanding the prints.

Why the cover-up?

Perhaps she should have immediately turned over the extra prints to McCaffery. With a sinking feeling, Taryn realized she could now conceivably be charged with withholding evidence in a murder investigation. Well, she could still turn them in. But to whom?

If she gave them to McCaffery, what would keep them from vanishing like the first set?

The police, then.

But even though the *Times* was denying the photos' existence, the newspaper still technically owned them. If she gave the prints to the police, it could mean her job.

Taryn shoved the photos back into the envelope and closed the drawer, deciding to postpone a decision until after talking with McCaffery about Mike's absence. Maybe she could sound out Hank about the pictures at the same time.

Taryn crossed the newsroom. She hesitated upon reaching McCaffery's glass-enclosed office, noticing that the shades were drawn. McCaffery never drew his blinds. Puzzled, she rapped on the door. Receiving no answer, she poked her head inside. "Got a sec, Hank? I . . ." Taryn's words died on her lips.

McCaffery was sitting at his desk, his face as blank as slate. Behind him stood a tall man with dark hair and granite-grey eyes.

Tyler.

Tyler stared at Taryn. McCaffery still hadn't moved, as if unaware of her presence. Taryn tried to swallow. Her mouth had suddenly gone dry. With an effort, she pulled her eyes away from Tyler. "Sorry, Hank," she mumbled. "I didn't know you were busy. I'll . . . I'll come back later."

Heart pounding, Taryn shut the door and walked quickly back to her desk, at any moment expecting to hear McCaffery's door bang open behind her. To her relief, it didn't. When she arrived at her workstation, she reopened the bottom drawer of her desk. With shaking fingers she withdrew the manila envelope and stuffed it into her purse, all thought of surrendering Mike's photos forgotten.

As she headed out of the newsroom, Taryn realized that whatever was going on, it had to be more than a government cover-up. During those brief seconds in McCaffery's office when Tyler had stared at her, she had seen something evil in his eyes, something that had flooded her with unnamable terror.

Please come back soon, Mike, Taryn thought grimly, clutching her purse to her chest as she hurried toward the elevators. If I've ever needed a friend, it's now.

Chapter Twelve

I still don't understand why you've brought us here," I said, helping Devon from a cab in front of Puerto Vallarta's *Plaza de Toros*.

Briefly taking my hand, Devon swung her long legs from the cab and stepped out. Then releasing my hand, she gazed up at the sizable stadium housing the city's bullring. "You will," she replied.

Devon had declined to talk on the ride over from the hotel, and I had decided not to press. Over the past hours I had gained a new respect for her—a respect based not on the kinship I'd felt earlier, but a respect based on something more basic—something I hadn't felt since my time in the service. As I glanced at the slim, mysterious woman beside me, I realized how easy it would be for her to kill me, were the necessity to arise. She could do it in a hundred different ways—a whisper to a passerby, a haphazard flick of her mind . . .

But would she?

I regarded her warily, realizing I had no choice but to see whatever it was she had left to teach me. After that, well . . . I would worry about that later.

Although not a bullfight aficionado, over the years I had attended several fights in Tijuana and one in Mexico City, and I knew something of the sport—if you could call it that. Each time I'd witnessed a bullfight, the mystique associated with the killing of bulls had eluded me, seeming at best a barbaric and bloody entertainment.

As we approached a line at the ticket booth, I noticed a colorful *cartel* prominently displayed by the entrance. In order of seniority, the poster listed the three *matadores* who would fight that day: Francisco Romeros, a Spanish bullfighter from Madrid who (according to the poster) was completing an immensely successful tour of Mexico; Anton Quintana, a young fighter from Guadalajara; and a local boy named Pepé Montos. Each would face two bulls. Reading from the list, I hoped that the presence of the Spanish matador would raise the afternoon's performances above the clumsy, artless contests I had previously witnessed.

I purchased tickets when we reached the head of the line, and moments later we entered the stadium, making our way through a throng of youngsters selling food, programs, and posters. "I'll see you in a few minutes," Devon said once we were inside. "It's open seating, so try to find seats in the shade, just within the fence." Wondering what she was up to, I watched as she melted into the crowd.

Though smaller than the ring I had visited in Mexico City, Puerto Vallarta's *Plaza de Toros* appeared well maintained. The *barrera*, a stout wooden fence surrounding the sand-covered arena, gleamed with a fresh coat of paint. Occasional advertisements were plastered around the inside of the barrier wall, mostly for Mexican beers—Corona, Dos Equis, Carta Blanca—along with ads for Coke, Pemex, and Pepsi. As I worked my way around to the shady side of the arena, I spotted Devon in a cobbled courtyard where the matadors and their respective *caudrillas*—men including the *banderilleros* and the *picadores* who would assist them—were assembling. The youngest of the matadors there was making practice passes with his cape, but most present were smoking and talking quietly among themselves. Devon stood on the far side, conversing with one of the older bullfighters.

I briefly considered joining her, but something made me think better of it. Instead I continued around the ring, eventually locating front row seats in the shade, separated from the arena by the wooden *barrera* and a narrow passageway running behind it. From my limited experience, I knew that spectators sitting this close were routinely cautioned to remain absolutely still whenever the bull faced them. Any movement, even the slightest, could distract the animal and disrupt the tenuous control the matador held over him. As I sat, it occurred to me that my proximity to the killing ground might lend a new perspective to the fight. In past visits to a bullring I had sat well up in the stands, removed from the action. From this close the contest might take on a different meaning.

Minutes later the first ritualistic phase of the bullfight, the *tercio de varas*, began with a bugle announcing the commencement of the *paseíllo*—the formal entrance of the matadors with their *caudrillas* strung out behind. At that point Devon finally reappeared, settling in beside me. I noted that she had rented cushions to soften the hard arena benches. She handed me one of the pads without comment as the procession of *toreros* moved somberly into the ring, accompanied by brassy music from a band high in the stands.

An official astride a handsomely adorned horse led the *paseíllo*, followed by the three matadors who would fight that day, sparkling in heavily sequined suits of silk and brocade. Being most senior, Francisco Romeros, the bullfighter from Madrid, walked on the left. Second in seniority, Anton Quintana walked to the right, with young Pepé Montos taking the central position. As they approached, I noted that the matador with whom Devon had been speaking was Francisco Romeros. Curious about their conversation, I glanced at Devon. Ignoring me, she studied the ring in silence.

After the matadors, the *banderilleros* entered the ring next, followed by the *picadores* atop their heavily padded horses. As the entire procession began its first tour of the ring, Devon finally looked at me. "Do you believe there can be artistry in death?" she asked.

Puzzled, I shrugged. "If you're referring to the art of bullfighting, you're talking to the wrong guy. The few fights I've attended were pathetic affairs in which the matador barely managed to kill the bull. Actually, I wound up feeling sorry for the bull."

Devon frowned. "Why? Those animals are bred to be sacrificed in the ring, just as cattle are bred to be butchered for meat. You don't get maudlin when you eat a steak, do you?"

"No, but—"

"All life must perish," Devon interrupted. "At least the bull fulfills his destiny when he's killed. For the strong to survive, the weak must die. That's the way of the world."

"Sort of a harsh view of things," I noted.

"Not really," Devon continued. "We're all killers, Mike. We kill to eat; we kill for sport; we kill to survive. Granted, in modern society most people don't bloody their hands. They hire someone to do it for them. They hire slaughterers to kill their meat, exterminators to kill their pests, executioners to kill their criminals. Nevertheless, killing and death are essential parts of life, as common as the dirt under your feet. But when death comes with style and grace, as it does in a truly great contest pitting man against beast, it's possible to appreciate the difference between slaughter and art."

"Sounds like you've been to a couple of bullfights," I interjected dryly, watching as the parade in the arena completed its first circuit.

"I've seen the best matadors in the world," Devon went on, ignoring my sarcasm. "Belmonte, Joselito, Manolete, Arruza. I witnessed the *mano a mano* contest between Ordóñez and Domínguín in which ten ears, four tails, and two hooves were cut in a single afternoon."

"I'm no expert, but even I have heard of Belmonte," I observed. "He fought decades ago. You're not old enough to have seen him."

Devon smiled mysteriously. "Don't change the subject. We're discussing the art of killing. Do you know what makes the best matadors and their accomplishments in the bullring so extraordinary?"

"I have a feeling you're going to tell me," I sighed, beginning to tire of Devon's lecture.

"It's their ability to kill, as the name matador, or 'bringer of death,' suggests," Devon continued, answering her own question. "And to kill not as common butchers—anyone can do that—but as artists. It's a singular gift, given to a very few." She paused to look at me, impervious to my lack of interest. "We all have our fate," she went on. "It's the bull's fate to die. And it's not as if he doesn't have a chance. Occasionally an extremely heroic beast is *indultado*—pardoned and allowed to live. It's rare, but it happens."

Something in Devon's approximate translation of the word "matador" struck me as ominous. "So you brought me here to round out my knowledge of bullfighting?"

"I brought you here to learn of more than bullfighting," Devon answered. "I brought you here to learn of death."

I remained silent, having no idea how to respond to that. Ever since arriving at the bullring, something in Devon had changed. Her generally playful demeanor of the past few days had been replaced by an almost mordant sense of gravity. For some reason she was placing tremendous importance on our being there at the bullring, and though I didn't know why, I decided to keep quiet and see how things played out.

The caravan of men and horses finally retired from the ring. Then, at a signal from one of the officials, the *toril* gates opened. Seconds later the first bull of the afternoon charged into the ring. Black as night, tremendously powerful, angry beyond reason, the huge animal took fierce possession of the arena. A murmur of approval rose from the crowd as he circled the fence, sending showers of dust spraying from his hooves.

As Romeros was the most senior matador of the day, the first bull belonged to him. He stepped into the ring carrying a heavy, brocaded cape lined with yellow silk. To the cheers of the crowd, he began what Devon quietly informed me was the *capeando*—work with the cape alone—engaging the bull in the first stage of a fight that would eventually lead to the animal's death. Holding the cape in both hands, arms held low and facing the bull with one foot slightly advanced, Romeros executed a precise series of *veronicas*, a classic pass that brought the bull's horns and body directly past the matador's waist. Romeros completed the passes slowly and smoothly, and to my eye his performance was flawless. But as the *capeando* progressed, I noticed Devon's mouth tightening in disapproval.

"Something bothering you?" I asked.

"Years ago I saw Romeros in Spain. That was before he lost his nerve," she said. "Now he resorts to tricks. Watch how he takes a sidestep to avoid the horns when the bull charges, then leans in again once danger has passed. There. See?"

97

I saw what she meant, though I wouldn't have noticed on my own. "It makes the horn seem to pass closer than it did. Can't say as I blame him, though."

"Maybe you don't," Devon said. "But I do."

Despite Devon's disapproval, as the fight progressed I found myself enjoying Romeros's gracefully linked passes, as did most of those in the stands. Moments later the matador ended his work with the cape and directed his *picadores* to take the bull. Frustrated by his inability to reach the man wielding the cloth, the bull readily attacked the armored horses, paying no heed to the punishment the men astride them delivered with their lances. As the bull struggled to rip through the horses' protective padding, nearly lifting the animals from the ground with every charge, each picador plunged the triangular steel point of his *vara* into the thick muscle at the back of the bull's neck. In addition to tiring the bull, injury to this muscle gradually forced the animal to lower his head, preparing him for the next stage of the fight.

After the bull had received several lancings at Romeros's direction, Romeros reengaged the bull for the second phase of the fight, the *tercio de banderillas*. With an air of impatience, Devon studied the two *banderilleros* accompanying Romeros, watching as he directed them in the placement of their colorful, steel-tipped dowels. The first man approached the angry animal, running in at an oblique angle with speed and grace. As the bull whirled and lunged, the man leaned over the horns and placed the barbs of his *banderillas* high and close together in the bull's withers, then quickly withdrew. The second man duplicated this near-perfect performance, to the enormous approval of the crowd.

At this point everyone except Romeros exited the ring, leaving the Spanish matador alone with his bull. Devon sat erect, now watching intently. Holding the *muleta*—a small piece of cloth draped over a stick—and a wooden sword, Romeros approached the president's box and dedicated the bull to an older woman sitting with a large entourage. Following custom, he then turned and tossed his hat over his shoulder to the pleased recipient of his salute.

The bull stood in the center of the ring, his shoulders and flanks covered with blood. Impatient for the contest to proceed, he pawed the ground and shook his head, whipping the *banderillas* against his body. Once more Romeros walked out to face the enraged beast, continuing the second stage of the ritualistic fight with the *faena*—work with the light cape to prepare the bull for death. From past experience I knew this was the heart of the battle, and I noticed that Devon was still watching intently.

I also knew from previous visits to a bullring that in order to kill a bull with a sword, the matador must first dominate the animal with the cape. By tradition, the matador has to perform a classic series of passes before he kills, all of which are extremely dangerous, bringing the horns within hooking range of the man's body. The closer the horns, the more thrilling the pass.

With the wooden sword spreading the cloth in his right hand, Romeros challenged the bull, leading him past and then turning him with a flick of the *muleta*. Romeros barely managed to link two passes before losing control of the animal. Conscious of the crowd's dissatisfaction, he shifted the cape to his left hand and executed a number of passes in which the bull charged past the matador's entire exposed body before reaching the cape. Although a false move on any of these passes could mean a horn in the gut, as the fight unfolded Devon seemed to become increasingly disgusted. Nonetheless, by the time the bull stood tired and confused, head lowered and prepared for death, most in the bleachers were cheering the Spanish matador.

Leaving the bull standing fixed after his last succession of passes, Romeros went to the *barrera* to prepare for the third phase of the fight, the *tercio de muerte*. There he exchanged his wooden sword for the *estoque*, a slim, bent-downward-at-the-tip killing sword made of steel. To the sound of a final bugle blast, he cautiously approached the bull, sighting down his slim weapon. He held the cape low in his left hand to keep the animal's head down, exposing the death-notch behind the skull. Then in a sudden rush he reached over the horns and placed the tip of the sword high in the cleft at the base of the bull's neck.

The thin shaft seemed to slip in effortlessly. Romeros shoved down with his palm, sending the sword deep into the beast, ending with his hand almost touching the hump. The bull shuddered. Romeros stepped back, his right hand held high above his head, never taking his eyes from his adversary. An instant later the bull staggered and crashed to the ground, his aorta severed by the thrust.

By petition from the crowd, Romeros was awarded an ear. Trophy held proudly aloft, he took a triumphal circuit of the arena as workers hitched the bull behind two horses and unceremoniously dragged the carcass from the ring.

"I suppose that shows a good kill can save a poor fight," Devon noted with an irritated sigh. She rose from her seat. "I'll be back shortly."

But despite her promise, Devon still hadn't returned by the next fight or by the one that followed, and I wound up watching them alone. The second bull of the afternoon was Quintana's. Occasionally clowning for the crowd and displeasing many of those present, he nevertheless managed to give an acceptable performance in the final phase of the fight.

The local boy, Pepé Montos, nervously took his turn with the third bull. Though his mastery of the classic passes with the heavy cape seemed adequate, he had difficulty controlling his feet, which rapidly moved out of range whenever the bull came too close. Even though Pepé was a local, many spectators whistled their disapproval at this. Clearly embarrassed, Pepé attempted to quiet his feet by executing a number of passes with the *muleta* from a kneeling position. This won the admiration of some who realized what he was doing, especially those from his hometown. He spoiled his fight with a sloppy kill, repeatedly hitting bone before mortally wounding the bull, but the music played and the crowd cheered as Pepé Montos left the arena.

Though still puzzled by Devon's insistence on bringing me to the bullfight, I unexpectedly found myself enjoying the experience, with the exception of the killing. To my surprise, watching the young matador of the last contest overcome his fears had struck a sympathetic chord inside me.

As arena workers completed raking the sand to smooth the bloody patch that marked the previous bull's death, Devon finally returned. Appearing preoccupied, she sat without explanation, nervously scanning the stands behind us.

"Something wrong?" I asked.

"I'm not sure," Devon answered, her eyes darting across the benches above us. "I sense a presence. Don't you feel it?"

"No."

"Well, I do. Be alert."

Disturbed by Devon's words, I shifted uncomfortably, wondering whether we were being watched. Was it possible we had been found already?

A moment later, before I could come to a conclusion, the fourth bull of the afternoon thundered into the ring. This was to be Romeros's final bull. Easily the largest beast to enter the arena that day, the enormous black animal charged across the sand, his hooves tearing the ground. Impressed by his size and fury, the crowd shouted its approval.

Romeros reentered the ring. This time I sensed something different about him. I turned to see whether Devon had noticed it, too. As if in a trance, she ignored me and leaned forward, watching with fierce concentration as Romeros approached the bull.

An uncharacteristic hush fell over the stands as Romeros began a series of poetic, magical passes. Bringing the bull in so close that the horns barely cleared his body, Romeros linked seven beautiful, masterful passes—his feet together and solidly planted during each charge. He ended the seventh pass with a flamboyant swirl of his cape, leaving the bull confused and motionless. Like the stunned animal in the ring, the crowd remained suspended in shock for several seconds, unprepared for the daring display they had just witnessed. Then, as Romeros turned his back on the animal and walked away, the spectators rose as one and filled the arena with a roar.

Seconds later an electric surge passed through the stands as Romeros reengaged the bull, again working with exquisite skill and bravery. Now the crowd shouted with every pass as

Romeros completed a score of intricate moves, ending with a daring pass in which he danced backward from the bull while enticing him to charge with butterflylike flicks of the cape to either side. Then, after directing his *picadores* in the placement of a single *pic* each, Romeros drew the bull away from the horses with his cape. He signaled to the president's box. Again, a hush fell over the arena.

"What's he doing?" I asked.

Devon answered without taking her eyes from the ring. "He's requesting that the *picadores* be led away so he can continue without any further weakening of the bull. Apparently Romeros wants to keep the bull a strong as possible, even though it means running a risk that the animal won't be adequately tired for the kill."

Though puzzled by Romeros's request, the president signaled his assent. After the *picadores* retired from the ring, Romeros called for his *banderilleros*. The agile *toreros* completed their task swiftly, placing their pairs of barbed dowels high on the bull's shoulders. As before, prior to beginning his *faena*, Romeros moved to a position below the president's box and asked to dedicate the bull. Upon receiving permission, he crossed the ring, stopping directly in front of Devon. He stared into her eyes. I felt something pass between them as Romeros raised his hat in salute. Then turning, he tossed his hat to Devon.

As the matador strode back into the ring, I looked at Devon.

"He just dedicated the bull to me," Devon explained before I could speak.

"I got that. But why? And what's happened to him? He doesn't seem like the same man I watched an hour ago."

"I told you that I'd seen him fight years back," Devon answered, still not taking her eyes from the ring. "Today you will see him as he used to be. You will see him fight as he used to fight. Watch, Mike. This is why we're here."

A tremendous cheer rose from the spectators as Romeros again faced the bull, this time with the *muleta* and wooden sword. He began his *faena* slowly, bringing the bull smoothly past his body, then flicking the light cloth to bring him back. For a bullfighter to execute the classic passes of the *faena*, the bull must charge straight and true—passing the matador full-length before turning.

Devon pointed out that Romeros's animal had a tendency to brake with his front hooves partway through his charge, instead of passing the matador without stopping. The Spanish fighter held the bull in the cape and progressively extended his charges with a sweeping movement of his arm, gradually lengthening the beast's runs until he was rushing the cape correctly. Most spectators were unaware of Romeros's training of the bull. They saw only that a previously unpredictable animal was now charging straight and true. Again, it was something I wouldn't have noticed either had Devon not brought it to my attention. What everyone present did know, even those like me who were not aficionados, was that we were witness that afternoon to a consummate display of grace, skill, and courage in the face of danger.

At last, with a swirl of the cape, Romeros again left the bull standing confused and immobile, ending the breathtaking display he had created on the hot sands of the arena. There remained but one thing left to do: to kill, and to kill perfectly.

After exchanging the wooden sword for its steel counterpart, Romeros returned to the bull. But instead of rushing forward and reaching over the horns to place the sword in the death-notch as he had previously, he remained stationary. Then he swung the *muleta*, enticing the bull to charge.

A gasp echoed throughout the stands. Confused, I turned to Devon. "What's he doing?"

"Romeros is going to attempt the kill *recibiendo*," Devon explained, still staring into the ring. "He's been preparing for it all through the fight."

"*Recibiendo?*"

"It's the most beautiful way to kill," Devon murmured. "You could attend hundreds of bullfights and never see it, because it's also the most dangerous. Instead of approaching the bull on foot as is ordinarily done, the matador lets the bull come to him— using the animal's forward momentum to drive home the sword.

A miscalculation can prove fatal." With that, Devon placed a hand over mine, her grip becoming almost painful as she once more interlaced our fingers in her strange, interlocking grasp. At the same time something uncoiled from her mind, snaring me in a viselike grip. "This is why I brought you," she said aloud. "This will be a moment of truth for the matador . . . and for you as well."

An instant later I saw the bull standing before me. In a distant part of my consciousness I still sensed myself in the stands. But now I gazed upon the world through the eyes of Francisco Romeros!

Without words, Devon's thoughts sounded in my mind. *He doesn't know we're here.*

How . . . ?

It doesn't matter. Don't interfere.

A trickle of sweat ran down my . . . down Romeros's back, coursing beneath the heavy embroidered silk suit. I felt the sand shift under my feet, my hand tremble slightly as it raised the sword. *Not my hand*, I thought. *I'm in the stands. This can't be real . . .*

"*It is*, Devon whispered in my mind. *And now you will learn who you truly are.*

I felt the matador's left knee—*my* left knee—bend forward. Without willing it, my hand swung the *muleta* toward the bull. The bull gathered himself, his powerful mass launching into motion. A thrill of panic clutched my throat as the bull thundered toward me.

I held the *muleta* low in my left hand, guiding in the bull and keeping his head low to expose the depression behind his shoulder blades. Time seemed to slow, stretching out before me like a dream.

And then suddenly the animal was upon me. I braced myself and leaned in, aiming for the death-slot. In a moment the sword would slip in until my hand touched the bull's hump and we were joined as one. But at the last instant something went wrong. Against all reason, the bull raised his head. Leaving the *muleta*, he went for me.

I felt the horn rip through my suit, tearing into my chest . . . then a terrible stab of pain and a warm gush of blood spurting from the wound. A roar of horror from the crowd deafened me as I crumpled to the ground. Sand filled my mouth. And again the bull gored me. And again, trampling me under bloody hooves. Vaguely I sensed the other *toreros* rushing into the ring.

Now, Mike. Take his life.

What . . . ?

This is why we're here. His life is spilling. Take it.

I don't understand.

Yes, you do. You feel the hunger. Give in to it.

I started to draw away, sensing that Devon did not have the strength to hold me. But I hesitated, feeling something unspeakable welling up inside. And in that moment, as the unbearable yearning I had fought since the war—the hideous, unfulfilled craving I had long resisted drew me inexorably, irresistibly forward—I realized Devon had spoken the truth.

You want to, Devon repeated. *Join me, Mike. Join me and drink.*

Through a blood-red haze of confusion and horror, I heard my own thoughts, like those of a stranger, echoing in my mind. *Yes. I want to. Show me.*

Unable to abide my shame but powerless to resist, I surrendered at last to the darkness within me. With Devon as my guide, I sucked life's essence from the fallen matador—at first just a trickle, then gushing hot and wet and strong—permeating me with the nectar of death. The pleasures I had shared with Devon in the shower had been the most intense I'd ever experienced, but in comparison, the erotic rapture now suffusing me was far, far greater, leaving me nearly drunk with ecstasy.

It seemed to go on forever, but at last we finished. It was over.

Returned once more to my body in the stands, I watched numbly as the *toreros* carried Romeros's lifeless form from the ring. Immersed in a maelstrom of confusion and self-loathing, I realized I had taken a fatal step . . . a final, unforgivable step from which there would be no turning back. My blood sang with the intoxication of the kill, but shame for what I was—for what I had *become*—burned in my conscience like a fiery brand.

"Now you know," Devon said aloud, releasing my hand.

Yes. Now I know, I thought, realizing that the consuming horrors of my nightmares, the terrors and fears that had plagued me throughout the years, were born of my own true nature, a nature no prayers would ever change.

Sensing my thoughts, Devon regarded me closely, anger flowing like molten iron in her eyes. "Don't be a fool," she spat. "It's your birthright to take what you require."

Realization dawned on me. "This was a test, wasn't it? That man died in the ring so I could—"

"That man was nothing. I created his finest moment; I raised him to the apex of his existence."

"And then you killed him."

"Killed him? The bull killed him," Devon corrected. "At any rate, harvest is a better word. Besides, like the bull, he had a chance. He lost. But in doing so, he fulfilled his destiny by showing you who you are, what you can become," she continued. "Don't be a hypocrite, Mike. Don't lie to yourself anymore. Anyone with the power must eventually accept it and act accordingly. It's the only way."

"I don't think I can do that."

"Then you'll become a pariah," Devon said, her voice softening. "You won't be allowed to live. Mike, I can't carry out my instructions now, you know that. I won't be the one to kill you. But there will be others, and not only from my group. As a rogue, you would represent a threat to us all."

Abruptly, I felt an overwhelming surge of approaching danger. I whirled, spotting one of the *picadores* galloping toward us. The horseman reigned to a skidding stop just outside the *barrera.* His eyes searched the crowd, quickly finding me. Raising his steel-tipped lance like a spear, the man drew back his arm, his eyes boring into mine.

I suddenly realized that Devon had been right when she'd said she sensed a presence in the stands. We *were* being watched. Somehow they had found us.

106

As though it were second nature, I lashed out at the rider with my mind. To my shock, I encountered an armored wall. In desperation, I switched my attack to the rider's mount. Just as the man started to hurl his weapon, I seized the horse's primitive mind and *squeezed.*

Squealing in fright, the animal collapsed. Rage darkened the rider's face as he released his spear, his eyes slits of hate. An instant later he screamed in agony as the weight of his horse crushed him to the sand.

The horseman's lance missed me by inches, striking a spectator sitting behind us. Only a metal guard circling the spear's shaft prevented the blade from passing completely through the man's neck. Eyes bulging, the unlucky spectator clutched his throat and collapsed, a bubble of blood ballooning from his mouth.

As people drew back in horror, I sensed Devon taking advantage of the situation to plunder the essence flowing from the dying spectator. This time she fed quickly. Upon finishing, she looked at me appraisingly. "Nice work," she said.

Then, with an unmistakable glint of hunger, she glanced toward the screaming *picador*, who was still trapped beneath his fallen mount. Reluctantly, she turned away. Taking my hand, she began pulling me toward the exit, merging with a crush of horrified spectators rushing for the gate.

"We have to go," she said. "As I suspected, they know we're here. I don't know how, but they do. They want you dead. At this point they undoubtedly want me dead me as well," she added, panic rising in her voice. "Our only chance is to run."

All at once I noticed something odd. Still moving with the crowd, I turned Devon to face me. "Your eyes . . ."

Releasing my hand, Devon reached into her purse and withdrew a pair of dark glasses. "What about them?"

"They're glowing!"

Donning her sunglasses, Devon increased her pace even more, hurrying toward the exit. She glanced back once, looking at me over her shoulder. "So are yours, Mike," she said. "So are yours."

Chapter Thirteen

Hours later I stood on the balcony of our hotel room at the Meliá, staring across the bay at the lights of central Puerto Vallarta. The storm threatening earlier had finally arrived, soaking the city in a torrential downpour. Most of the storm had now passed, but dark clouds still hid the sky, overlying the town like a shroud.

Upon leaving the bullring, Devon had insisted we separate, reasoning we stood a better chance of evading our pursuers if she were free to act on her own. "I'll meet you back at the room," she told me when we reached the street. "Don't worry, I won't be far. If they make another attempt on your life, I'll be there."

I glanced at the crowd surrounding us, realizing the next attack could come from anywhere. "But if we split up—"

"There's no time to argue," Devon insisted. "Trust me, I can protect both of us better on my own, without having to worry about you. If you have another idea, let's hear it. Otherwise, get moving." Then, drawing closer, she kissed me one last time, her embrace a mix of both passion and regret. "We'll see each other again, Mike," she said. "I promise."

Dusk had come and gone, but Devon still hadn't returned. Although reluctant to admit it, I realized the possibility she had been captured or killed was becoming more likely with each passing minute. As I stood on the balcony, almost invisible in the darkness, two thoughts kept rising in my mind. The first had occurred to me on the cab ride back to the hotel. Somehow our pursuers had tracked us to Puerto Vallarta, so they probably knew where we were staying as well. Remaining at the Meliá could prove fatal. I had to leave. Nothing held me here, except my agreement to meet Devon. But how long could I wait?

The other thought had taken shape over the intervening hours, evolving from a chilling doubt into a burgeoning suspicion. Devon had told me she possessed only second-tier powers. Nevertheless, with me in tow she had entered the matador from across the arena, *putting on his body like a suit of clothes.* True, she hadn't controlled him—at least I didn't think she had—but still . . .

Was Devon a Deus?

And if so, why had she lied?

I realized my fate was tied to a woman I hardly knew, a woman who held the key to forces of unimaginable power, and a woman whose knowledge encompassed far more than she had shared with me. I passed a hand across my face, not knowing what to believe. One thing was certain: I had questions for Devon when she arrived.

If she arrived.

Suddenly a key-card clicked in the door, followed by a metallic snick as the bolt snapped open.

Devon.

Finally, I thought. Stepping back into the darkened room from the balcony, I reached for a light switch. But as the door swung inward, a deadly premonition shivered through me.

The silhouette in the doorway looked wrong—too wide and powerful for that of a woman. Another figure joined the first. Together they slipped into the room and closed the door behind them.

Creeping toward the bed, the first man withdrew what appeared to be a club from beneath his coat. Several pillows lay clumped beneath the sheets. In the dim light mistaking the lump for a man, the intruder brought down his bludgeon in a killing, two-handed stroke.

"Huh?" he grunted as his weapon thumped ineffectually into the bed.

The second man moved forward. He too carried a weapon, something thin and flat. My vision had adjusted to the darkness on the balcony, and I recognized the classic shape of a machete.

Heart hammering in my chest, I gauged my chances of slipping past the men and out the door. No way. They had me trapped. I had to fight. But against two armed men? Then I remembered. What were mere men against me? Feeling something oddly akin to hunger, I flipped on the light.

The men whirled, staring at me with dead, lifeless eyes. The intruder with the club stepped forward. As the other man moved to block the door, I noted that the first man's weapon was a baseball bat—not hollow aluminum, but solid hickory.

I focused my mind.

Drop your weapons.

Nothing.

I tried a second time and failed—both times, as I had with the picador, coming up against an impermeable wall around each intruder's mind.

What else had Devon neglected to tell me? I wondered, trying not to panic. Grabbing a wooden chair as a shield, I backed toward the balcony.

The man with the club moved forward.

Our fourth-floor balcony offered no hope of escape. I made a feint toward the man with the bat and then bolted for the entry door, holding the chair in front of me like a shield.

The man with the machete stood his ground. An instant later he swung his blade toward my face. He changed direction midstroke as I raised the chair, slashing with blinding speed from the other direction. With a sickening thunk, the blade cut deep into a leg of the chair, severing the fourth and fifth fingers of my left hand.

Cursing, the man struggled to retrieve his weapon, which was now solidly embedded in the chair. Blood welled from the stumps of my injured fingers. Ignoring the pain in my hand, I grabbed a fistful of the intruder's shirt and yanked. Off balance, the man stumbled forward. I threw my right fist. A satisfying shock ran up my arm as something in the man's face crunched like dry wood under my knuckles.

He went down. Hard.

Without warning, my ribs exploded in agony!

Clutching my side, I turned to face the other intruder, barely avoiding a second blow from his bat. Again I was forced toward the balcony. The man with the bat stepped over his fallen comrade, sweeping his club in double-handed arcs aimed at my arms, legs, and torso. Several times I tried to rush him, only to be driven back by lightning quick, expertly timed blows.

The man was inhumanly fast, his movements with the bat a blur, almost too quick to follow. Gradually he forced me outside. I gave ground slowly. Knowing that a blow from his club to my head would be fatal, I attempted to take the worst of the beating on my arms and shoulders, hoping for a chance to make it inside the deadly arc of his weapon.

My chance never came.

My retreat ended on the far side of the balcony. Death seemed inevitable, but from the methodical way the man swung his club and the pleasure shining in his eyes, I knew the end wouldn't come quickly. My assailant was toying with me. He intended to break me, bit by bit.

No! It can't end like this.

Without knowing how, I sent my consciousness into the bedroom, finding the other intruder. He was awake. Groggy, but awake. With a shifting, mental twist, I took attempted to mesh my mind with his, as Devon and I had done with the matador in the bullring. But unlike the matador, this man knew I was there.

Get out! his thoughts shrieked in my mind.

For an instant I sensed a second presence inside the man's skull. Then it was gone, slipping away like a phantom. Ignoring the man's silent screams, I fought to make his body submit to my will. It felt like trying to drive an unfamiliar vehicle with someone beside me grabbing at the wheel.

Time was slipping away. I needed to act, and act quickly. Forcing the man into submission with a brutal thrust of pain, I finally took possession. After retrieving the machete, I clumsily marched my commandeered body out to the balcony. I could see my body on the deck outside, crumpled in the far corner. In a remote portion of my mind I could still feel the blows raining down.

As I stepped onto the deck, my assailant with the bat momentarily glanced back. Apparently recognizing his friend, he returned his attention to the unconscious form sprawled on the deck.

Me.

With a grin, he used the tip of his bat to lift the chin of my battered body, setting up my head for a final killing blow. As he did, an eerie thought occurred: What would happen if I didn't survive? Could I continue to live in the body I had just taken?

I had no intention of finding out. As my assailant wound up for a final blow, I grasped the machete in both hands and swung with all my strength.

In the seconds that followed, I discovered that although a machete may be a perfect tool for hacking through dense jungle undergrowth, it is a difficult weapon with which to kill a man—especially a machete with a dull blade like the one I was using. It took several bloody, hideous swings to finish the job.

Shaken, I took the life spilling from the man at my feet, letting the rapture fill me as it had in the bullring, this time experiencing neither shame nor remorse. And when it was over, still hungry but reeling with exhilaration, I turned my thoughts inward, trying to decide what to do with my commandeered body's owner.

As I did, I felt another presence enter the man's mind, the same phantom I had sensed earlier. Against all reason, an unbearable current began flowing through my brain. Stunned by the pain, I staggered. Suddenly the phantom seized control. Before I could react, our conjoined body took two quick steps and vaulted over the balcony railing.

Falling . . . endless seconds of darkness . . .

A wet thump and a sudden burst of light ended our downward rush.

An eternity passed. By degrees, I slowly returned to my own flesh. Gasping for breath, I did a silent inventory of my injuries. My ribs were on fire. I suspected that several were cracked or broken. Otherwise none of my injuries seemed crippling, with the exception of my hand. I lay for several minutes without moving. Then, barely able to stand, I rose to my feet and stumbled into the bedroom, my body racked with pain, my maimed hand throbbing like a rotten tooth. Yet despite my anguish, I felt strangely *alive*. And as I ripped a bed sheet into

112

strips and began binding my injured hand, I realized my feeling of well-being stemmed from more than the mere joy of survival. The life I'd taken from my assailants had made me stronger.

A lot stronger.

When I had finished dressing my wounds, I stood before a mirror in the bathroom wondering what was happening to me, staring into eyes that glowed like an animal's in the dark.

Fifteen minutes later I limped to the downstairs lobby, scrutinizing the room as I entered. Everything looked normal. As yet no one had discovered the broken body in the shrubbery below my room, not to mention the bloodbath on my balcony. But it was only a matter of time.

On the far side of the room several people were having drinks at the bar. Through the lobby doors I could see an older couple exiting a cab. A young Mexican woman, trying hard to stay awake, was stationed at the reception desk. Reaching out with my mind, I examined the people in the bar, checking for danger.

Nothing.

Next I scanned the pair leaving the cab. Then the woman at the reception counter.

Still nothing.

I crossed to the desk.

"Yes, Señor?" the woman behind the counter said when I arrived, regarding my battered face with obvious alarm.

I ignored the question in her eyes. "I'm leaving. I need my bill," I said, giving my name and room number.

"Certainly, Señor Callahan. Do you . . . do you require medical help?"

"No. Just the bill."

Stealing nervous glances at my face, the woman pulled up my name on the hotel computer, printed a copy of my bill, and presented it with a credit card form and various charge slips that Devon had signed for hotel purchases.

I glanced at the itemized bill and shoved it into my pocket. I examined the credit card form next, noting my card number imprinted on it from when I had registered. "Did someone call for credit verification when I arrived?" I asked.

The woman nodded. "Sí, Señor. We always call for credit verification and card limits when a guest checks in."

So that's how they found me, I thought. Stupid. In the future, no more plastic. Devon was right. It's best to fly under the radar and simply take what you need.

"Are you all right, Señor?"

I ignored her query. "What record do you have of my stay here at the hotel?"

"I'm not sure what you mean, Señor."

"In addition to a computer record of my stay, I assume you have a backup system, along with purchase slips for room charges and the like. Anything else?"

"No, Señor."

Give me all paperwork that shows I was here.

The woman complied.

Now delete all computer records of my stay, including any backups.

"I . . . I can't," the woman replied, as if in a daze. "Only the manager has the code for that."

Call him.

Like an automaton, the woman raised the phone. The mental *pushes* I'd directed at her had left her oddly confused, but she did as ordered. She spoke in rapid Spanish, then replaced the receiver. "He's coming."

Shortly afterward I walked into the cool Mexican night, astonished at how easy it had been. Nothing now existed to tie me to the deaths in my room, and neither the night clerk nor the hotel manager would remember me. Ever. Devon had been right once more. It was merely a matter of knowing the right places to push.

Outside, the first in a short line of taxis pulled forward. I slid into the backseat. "¿Adónde, Señor?" asked the driver.

Good question, I thought. They'll be watching the airport. I have no passport, no money . . . what would Devon do?

Devon. After the attack in our room, I had avoided thinking of her. In addition to undoubtedly saving me on that first night at my house, she had been my guide in the nightmare that had unexpectedly become my life. Could I survive without her? She had promised to meet me, but the men who attacked me had used a key-card to enter our room.

Had they taken it from Devon?

With growing desolation, I realized that over the past days Devon had become more than simply my mentor. She was driven by the same compulsions as I, drawn by the same hunger. For all her faults, she was like me, and I like her. And though we were cut from the same cloth, she had somehow learned to accept her nature, even celebrate it.

A mentor? Yes, she had been that. A lover? She had been that, too. But more than that, Devon had become the embodiment of something for which I had been searching since my time in Afghanistan. Despite her chilling views on mankind, in Devon I had seen a chance to find my place in a world turned alien, to find answers to questions I had been unwilling to ask.

"Where to, Señor?" the driver asked again.

"Get me out of here," I answered. "Drive."

As the cabby pulled from the curb, I glanced back, taking one final look at the hotel. Devon would never return. I knew that now. And with that knowledge came a decision that would change everything.

No longer would I play the role of the hunted.

Part Two

Tercio de Banderillas

Chapter Fourteen

". . . give you the next governor of the great State of California, Lyle Exner!"

Lyle Exner, a tall, handsome man with broad shoulders, a bit of a potbelly, and an ingenuous smile, was not given to quick motion. As was his habit, he let the applause swell to a roar before stepping to the podium. Then, raising both arms in his trademark greeting, a gesture purposefully reminiscent of a benediction, he gazed out upon the crowd.

Shoulder to shoulder, row upon row, they had packed the Anaheim Convention Center to hear him speak, to feel the power of his words, to experience the force of his presence. And they will, Exner thought with satisfaction. As usual, a number of second-tier operatives were present in the auditorium to ensure it. Once his team started pumping the crowd, Exner knew he could say or do almost anything, and the audience would react with the same rapturous, bovine adoration as always. Nonetheless, he didn't dare stray from his prepared text . . . not anymore. *She* had put a stop to that.

After earlier rallies he had sometimes joked with insiders about his performance. In the privacy of his hotel suite he had occasionally even given burlesques of his speeches. His voice rising and falling in the deliberate, hypnotic cadence he'd striven to perfect, he would deliver his address replete with practiced gestures and calculated pauses. But replacing the political jargon and pedestrian homilies, he instead spewed forth insults, pornographic allusions, condescension, and scorn. And with only a slight *push*, those in the room sat enthralled.

Well, no more of that. And begrudgingly, Exner had to admit that perhaps she was right. Too much hung in the balance. Bellamy's death had been a masterly stroke, removing a significant obstacle to Exner's election and at the same time tainting any Republican candidate who might resume the campaign of the late Arthur Bellamy.

Nevertheless, a difficult road lay ahead. Even with Bellamy out of the way, the conundrum of public inertia remained. Lacking the *pushes* they'd been using in the auditoriums, Exner's TV and radio spots had proved largely ineffective, and it was nearly impossible to reach the numbers he needed solely with rallies and debates. The race promised to be close.

One hour, Exner thought to himself as he began his speech. An hour, hell. Ten minutes with everyone herded together within range of a few judicious mind-pushes would do it . . .

Well, larger groups would come later.

Three minutes into Exner's presentation, the second-tier operatives in the audience began hitting the crowd. Exner relaxed as he sensed the waves of conviction washing over the stands. This was the part he liked—thousands hanging on his every word, submission shining in their eyes. As he spoke, he let his gaze range the room, spotting Chrissy Adams sitting with several other campaign workers in the front row. Ms. Adams was tall, slim, and had curves in all the right places. Her résumé stated that she had graduated from Stanford with a degree in political science, and that she planned to return to college after the campaign to pursue postgraduate work. She had signed on several weeks ago, but as yet Exner hadn't found the time to greet her personally. That was an omission he planned to rectify.

Perhaps tonight.

Like the others around her, she sat in rapt attention—her expression nearly vacant. Her short plaid skirt had accidentally ridden up well past her knees. As Exner ran his eyes over her shapely legs, he came to a decision. Definitely tonight. And just for fun, maybe he would let her remember.

At least for a while.

Hours later when someone knocked on the door of his hotel suite, Exner was lounging on a couch wearing a blue terrycloth robe, his slippered feet propped on the coffee table. He took a sip of bourbon. "Come in."

"Hello, Mr. Exner," Chrissy Adams said uncertainly as she entered. "When you sent for me, I wondered . . . I mean, I hope nothing's wrong," she stammered.

Exner noted that she was still wearing the plaid skirt and white blouse she'd had on at the rally, but apparently she had taken time to freshen her makeup and brush her hair. "Nothing's wrong, Chrissy. May I call you Chrissy?"

"Of course, Mr. Exner. I'd like to say what an honor it is to be working on your campaign." Chrissy glanced at Exner's robe, which had parted at the top to reveal a patch of coarse, dark chest hair. "Uh—what did you want to see me about, sir?"

Exner finished his drink, setting the empty glass on the table. "You've been with us about a month now, haven't you?"

"A bit over three weeks, sir."

Exner patted the couch. "I think it's time we got acquainted," he said with an unctuous smile, nearly laughing out loud as he saw the uncertainty in her eyes change to realization. That's right, sweetheart, he thought. Did you think I asked you here to discuss campaign strategy?

"It's late, sir," Chrissy mumbled. "If it's okay with you, I'll—"

Exner flicked at her with his mind.

Come here.

He saw her eyes widen in pain. He hadn't pushed that hard. It appeared she was sensitive . . . very sensitive. "What a beautiful creature you are," he murmured as she crossed the room and sat on the couch beside him. Beneath her stunned exterior he could feel her mind writhing liked a trapped animal.

Take off your clothes.

Chrissy tried to resist. Exner *pushed* again, harder this time. She groaned under the blow. Tears streaming down her cheeks, she began unfastening the buttons of her blouse.

Exner watched, his excitement growing. Instead of prodding the girl with pain, he just as easily could have used his power to make her a willing partner. He didn't. He liked it like this.

Now your bra. Hurry up.

Her breasts were larger than he had expected, her skin smooth and flawless. He cupped a breast in each hand and squeezed, feeling her pink nipples puckering under his palms.

"No, please . . ." Chrissy moaned.

Shut up. Don't open your mouth till you're told.

Exner smiled at the tantalizing image that suddenly popped into his mind. No, not yet. Make it last, he told himself, shoving the girl down on the couch. Her legs dangled over the side, drawing her skirt tight against her thighs and raising the enticing mound of her groin under the soft woolen material. Exner lifted her knees and spread her legs, running his hands up her flawless skin.

By then Chrissy's dress had climbed almost to her waist, exposing a flash of silky underwear and the tempting shadow of her sex. Forcing a hand under the girl's hips, Exner shoved her skirt the rest of the way up. Then with a brutal jerk he pulled down her underwear, leaving the lacy garment dangling from one ankle.

Grinning, he knelt between her knees, his swollen organ now poking through his robe like a misshapen slug, peeking out from beneath the flab of his belly. He stared at the helpless girl beneath him. Her tawny hair lay in a swirl around her face, her breasts still showing the livid imprints of his fingers. She tried to cover herself with her hands. Exner slapped them away, punishing her with another whiplike slash of his mind. Though she made no sound, her chest rose and fell in a series of shuddering sobs.

Exner's need had grown unbearable. Though he had promised himself to make it last, the girl's torment had driven him too quickly to the edge. He had to have her now.

*   *   *

Wearily, Taryn rubbed her eyes, shaking her head at the stack of reference books piled on the table before her. Both puzzled and intrigued after completing an internet search of the names Mike had given her, she had decided to flesh out her research with a trip to the library. The clock on the wall behind the librarian's desk read a few minutes to ten. Closing time.

"The things I do for you, Callahan," Taryn muttered, collecting her papers. Rising, she flipped through a handful of yellow sheets covered with her tight scrawl. Not for the first time that evening, she wondered what it all meant. Mike had given her the names on those sheets in the apparent belief they somehow related to Bellamy's murder, but for the life of her Taryn couldn't see how they fit. For one thing, all the people on Mike's list were long dead, most of them executed.

The first name he had given her—Vlad Tepes, otherwise known as Vlad the Impaler—was the most familiar. Like his father before him, Vlad Tepes was an accomplished warrior. Nonetheless, although the military genius he displayed in battle against the Islamic Turks convinced some to overlook his sadistic excesses, his barbaric executions shocked many of his contemporaries, even the most hardened. In the early years of his reign of Wallachia, now a part of modern Romania, he would typically impale prisoners on a wooden stake, deriving perverse pleasure from watching them die an excruciating death.

Vlad's cruelty wasn't limited to his enemies. As on the battlefield, his anger as a ruler often proved quick and unpredictable. On April 2, 1459, as a result of a disagreement with local merchants, Vlad drove from their city the entire population of Brasov—20,000 men, women, and children. The stink of their burning village filling their nostrils, they trembled on a knoll at the edge of town, watching as he sacked their homes. Then, astride a black charger and dressed in full battle attire, Vlad rode to the top of the hill, his eyes blazing with unearthly fire. The townspeople of the luckless city stood strangely silent, even the children, as he pronounced their sentence: death by impalement.

Curiously, on that day outside Brasov, thousands lined up without resistance to meet their fate. Though historians are not in agreement, witnesses reported that many victims appeared to have cooperated in their own torture, some even thrusting themselves upon the sharpened stakes, as if embracing death.

123

The next name Mike had given her—Gilles de Rais, also known as Baron de Rais—had been a respected Marshal of France during the fifteenth century. To all appearances a pious man, in 1440 he stood trial for the torture and murder of over 140 young boys and girls. In the proceedings that followed, the grisly details of his killings were revealed. In his final confession Gilles de Rais admitted his monstrous deeds, revealing that lost in the throes of sexual transport, he murdered his victims with a stab to the throat, allowing blood from their severed arteries to spurt over him—washing himself in it, even drinking it.

More recent was the case of Fritz Haarman, brought to trial in 1924 in Hanover and later executed for the murder of twenty-four young boys, although the actual number of his kills is thought to have totaled far more. Haarman owned a small butcher shop, selling roasts, chops, and sausage to a post-World War I Germany hungry for meat. During his seventeen-year murder spree he prowled Hanover's railway stations, enticing young boys to the rooms behind his shop with promises of shelter and a hot meal. Once there he overpowered the unwary youths, nailing them to the floor and then killing them with a savage bite to the throat. One particular detail of Haarman's later confession sickened the citizens of Hanover more than his bloody murders. Over the years Fritz Haarman had ground many of his victims into sausage meat. Some he ate, but most he sold to his customers.

Countess Elisabeth Báthory, the final name on Callahan's list, proved the most puzzling . . . and the most bizarre. For generations a thread of madness had run through the blood of her ancestors, with sadists, masochists, and murderers more the rule than the exception. Elisabeth ran true to form. At fifteen she married Ferencz Nàdasdy, becoming Countess Elisabeth Báthory of Hungary. While Ferencz campaigned in lengthy wars abroad, Elisabeth amused herself at home with the torture of servant girls, deriving ecstatic sexual pleasure from her victims' pain.

After the death of her husband, Countess Báthory graduated to murder. By then she had grown to be a vain, beautiful woman. As she aged, she increasingly came to believe it possible to preserve her youth by drinking and bathing in the blood of others. To that end, in the recesses of her dungeon, the countess and her helpers—a nurse, a valet, and a nanny—carried out a multitude of sordid acts. One of the countess's favorite methods of torture involved the use of a cylindrical metal cage fitted with inward pointing spikes. After locking a victim inside, the countess would then hoist the cage and command her helpers to prod the screaming girl with red-hot pokers, causing her victim to flail against the spikes. All the while the countess sat below, showering in and drinking the rain of blood splattering down.

In the end Elisabeth's inability to dispose of the bodies proved her undoing. Shocked by the multitude of corpses appearing in the fields surrounding her castle, villagers brought complaints to Count György Thurzo. Over the course of a five-day trial that followed, it came out that no fewer than 650 girls and young women had met their deaths at the hands of the countess. The court sentenced her helpers to public torture and execution, but Countess Báthory herself managed to escape any such indignity. Instead, workmen walled up the doors and windows of her bedroom in Csjethe Castle, leaving only a small hatch for food as they sealed her inside. It was there that Elisabeth spent her final years, confined to the utter blackness of that room. Strangely, it was rumored that near the time of her death, guards peeking through the food slot reported seeing Countess Báthory sitting in the center of her chamber, her eyes burning with a strange, satanic glow . . .

Vlad Tepes, Gilles de Rais, Fritz Haarman, Elisabeth Báthory. All monsters, all guilty of horrific crimes, all dead. How did they tie in with Bellamy's murder? Taryn wondered. Had Mike sent her on a wild-goose chase, or was there a piece of the puzzle she couldn't see?

Stuffing the notes into her purse, Taryn headed for the library door. *If I don't hear from Callahan soon, I'll have to do something,* she thought uneasily, remembering the photos she had taken from her desk.

But what?

*   *   *

Exner tried to shut out the sound, but the phone kept ringing. Now, of all times. Red-faced and grunting, he struggled to maintain his rhythm, slamming his engorged member into the limp body on the couch.

The phone kept ringing.

There's gonna be one sorry sonofabitch at the front desk when I get through with him, Exner thought angrily. I made it clear I wanted all calls routed to my aides. That is, all except . . .

"Shit," Exner groaned, shoving away the girl.

Don't go anywhere. I'm not done with you yet.

With a sinking feeling, Exner grabbed the phone. Why was she calling him here? Had he done something wrong? He raised the receiver. "Exner," he said, hating himself for the tremor he heard in his voice.

"Good evening, Lyle. What took you so long to pick up?"

It *was* her, and from the sound of her voice, something was wrong. "Sorry, Ms. Varkoff," he mumbled. "I was busy."

"Is someone there with you?"

"Just someone I was having a little fun with. Nothing wrong with that, is there?"

"As long as you're discreet," she answered. "Erase or eliminate your indulgences, Lyle. You know the rules."

"I'll take care of it," Exner promised, glancing at the girl on the couch. But not till I've finished what I started, he thought, realizing that Ms. Varkoff hadn't called to criticize him for a minor dalliance. If he had committed some error, she would have already broached the subject. "So how's your problem in Los Angeles going?" he ventured, relaxing a little.

"What problem?"

"The latent who showed up at Bellamy's goodbye party."

"Lyle, this isn't a secure line."

"Sorry. I just thought—"

"It isn't your job to think. It's to do as you're told. Understand?"

"Yes."

"Thank you. Now, to business. I'm moving up the time of our meeting. I have some loose ends to tend to in L.A., as you mentioned, but I'll see you in New York on Thursday. Please call the others and inform them."

"But I'm scheduled to speak in Sacramento. I can't—"

"Do you have a problem with this, Lyle?"

"No. No problem," Exner backpedaled. "I'll call Dr. Menninger and Blaumpier tonight."

"Fine. I'll see you at the meeting."

The line went dead. Exner slammed down the receiver. God damn her! he fumed. One of these days . . .

Suddenly he remembered the girl. Trying to cover her nakedness, she was still cowering on the couch, staring at him like a fawn caught in the headlights.

Exner watched her squirm. Slowly, he felt the tension drain out of him. Pursing his lips, he placed his fingertips together, attempting to decide which would give him more pleasure— eliminating Chrissy when he'd finished, or simply erasing her memory of the evening. Her work as a volunteer had been useful, and he might enjoy having her revisit his room again in the future. On the other hand, he hadn't fed for several weeks. In either case, thinking about it was making him hard again. Smiling, he opened his robe.

He could make his choice later.

Chapter Fifteen

M iss Callahan? Care to join us?"
"Huh? Oh, sorry," Jamie mumbled. Flushing with embarrassment, she forced her mind back to the classroom. "I was . . ."

". . . daydreaming?" Mr. Gray completed her thought. "Yes, that's obvious. Would you like to share with the rest of the class whatever it was you found so interesting?"

Snickers sounded from the back of the room.

Mr. Gray, Jamie's fourth-period biology teacher, stood near his desk awaiting her reply. Mr. Gray had the reputation of running his classes with a no-nonsense attitude, but unlike many of the teachers at George Washington Junior High, he did so with humor and wit. He also had the rare ability of being able to present his subject in a way that often made it fascinating. As a result, despite his strict demeanor, most of his students liked him, including Jamie.

Jamie shifted in her seat. "It was nothing."

Not true, a voice inside her corrected. You wish it were nothing, but it isn't.

She still hadn't heard from her father, not a word since he had dropped her at home on Sunday. As promised, her mother had checked at the *Times* following her meeting on Tuesday. No one there had seen her dad. Later her mother had even visited his house in Venice. Her father's motorcycle and car had been in the garage, but no sign of her dad. At Jamie's insistence they had telephoned hospitals, friends, even the police. No one had seen him.

But now the sense of impending danger that had hounded Jamie these past days was worse—*different* somehow from the concern she had previously felt. Jeez, what's wrong with me? she wondered. Is this what an anxiety attack feels like?

"So, Miss Callahan," Mr. Gray continued, "as you're apparently unwilling to share whatever it was that previously had your attention, and as we *are* supposed to be discussing biology, perhaps you'd like to answer the question that the rest of us were considering."

"Yes, sir. Uh—what was it?"

More titters from the back.

"I asked for a definition of the DNA structure called the telomere, and an explanation of its function."

"Oh," said Jamie, relieved to be back on familiar ground. "The telomere is the noncoding structure capping each end of every chromosome."

"And its form and function?"

Jamie searched her memory, easily bringing the information into the focus of her mind's eye. "It's a terminal segment of nucleotides containing the bases thymine, adenine, and guanine. TTAGGG is the basic unit, repeated hundreds of times. Although the segment carries no genes, it's vital to chromosomal integrity. Because the same identical sequence occurs at the ends of chromosomes of all bony fish, amphibians, reptiles, birds, and mammals—animals that haven't shared a common ancestor for more than four hundred million years—it's clearly an important component of the DNA strand."

Mr. Gray looked pleased. "Anything else?"

Jamie hesitated, noting several classmates beginning to glower at her. Nuts, she thought. Only a few weeks into the new school year, and already I'm developing a reputation as a brain. Well, who cares, anyway?

Doggedly, she continued. "Most nonreproductive cells lose telomeric subunits as they divide. And when the telomere is finally depleted, the chromosome decays, resulting in the death of the cell."

"And in the end, the entire organism?"

Jamie felt another premonition of danger. "I guess so," she agreed, glancing at a clock over the door. Still twenty minutes to go. I have to get out of here, she thought, fighting a feeling of panic. I have to . . . what?

The room had settled into an uneasy silence. Mr. Gray regarded Jamie curiously. "Any idea why the telomere is shortened during replication?"

Jamie shrugged. "That wasn't in our assigned reading."

"I asked what *you* thought, not what you read in a book," said Mr. Gray. "For someone who considers paying attention in class optional, you're doing extremely well. Please go on."

"Well, I suppose the answer could be tied in some way to the mechanisms involved in replication," Jamie ventured. "Possibly the reason that the new DNA strand is shortened during transcription is that the duplication enzymes take up room on the DNA template, and the covered part isn't reproduced."

Mr. Gray scratched his chin pensively. "The reason your text doesn't cover this," he said, "is because it isn't in there. It will be interesting to see whether future research supports your conjecture."

"Mr. Gray?"

"Yes, Jamie?"

"I'm really sorry," Jamie said. Leaving her books on the desk, she rose from her seat. "I have to go home."

"Is everything all right?"

Jamie started for the door. "I don't know," she answered truthfully. Over the past few minutes her sense of dread had grown to full-blown panic. "I just know that I have to go home." And without looking back, she left the classroom and raced down the hall toward the exit.

Partway up Sunset Boulevard Jamie caught a ride with two secretaries returning to work after lunch in Brentwood. They dropped her at Chautauqua, admonishing her to be careful in the future hitching rides. Jamie thanked them, numbly acknowledging that Los Angeles was a dangerous place. Heart in her throat, she ran the rest of the way home.

As Jamie mounted the walkway to her front door, she knew for certain something was wrong. She could sense danger flowing from her house, radiating outward in sickening, ever-widening waves.

Her mother's Jaguar sat out front. A second car Jamie had never seen before—a white Mercedes SL convertible—was parked close behind. Her mother never came home from work during the day, and rarely did she bring clients to the house.

Cautiously, Jamie opened the front door. Winded from her sprint, she paused in the entry to catch her breath. Other than the sound of her own ragged breathing, she heard nothing. Yet something in the silence made every fiber of her being tremble with fear.

"Mom? Are you home?"

No response. Nervously, Jamie crept deeper into the house. As she rounded the staircase, her foot encountered something. She looked down.

Georgie.

Her dog lay crumpled on the hardwood floor, tongue lolling from his mouth, his eyes open and unseeing. Kneeling, Jamie cupped his head in her hands, blinking back a rush of tears. "Aw, Georgie," she whispered, realizing with a shock that he was dead.

"Mom?" she called again, a fist of panic now slamming in her chest. "Mom, where are you?"

Jamie found her mother in the living room.

Susan Callahan was sitting erect in a wooden chair, hands folded in her lap, her eyes registering nothing. A beautiful, dark-haired woman stood beside her, scrutinizing Jamie with a vitreous stare. A hawk-faced man stepped from behind the door, joining the woman. "Party time, Ms. Varkoff," the man said with a grin.

"Who are you?" Jamie demanded, her voice quavering. She glanced at the man, then back at the woman. "What happened to Georgie? And what's wrong with my mom?"

"Ah, you must be Jamie," the woman said. She smiled, displaying perfect, even teeth, but not a trace of warmth touched her piercing green eyes.

A renewed wave of terror coursed through Jamie. "Who are you?" she repeated.

"You may call me Devon," the woman replied, never looking away.

Suddenly Jamie was unable to move, unable to breathe.

"You and I are going to be very close," the woman said softly, her eyes beginning to glow.

Chapter Sixteen

Taryn had nearly passed her exit on the 405 Freeway when she finally spotted an opening in the right lane. Ignoring a horn blast from a delivery van, she tucked her Volvo in behind an eighteen-wheeler just in time to make the Westwood off-ramp. Screw you, she thought, resisting an impulse to flip off the delivery van's driver, who'd ridden her bumper all the way to the exit.

Reaching the bottom of the off-ramp, Taryn breathed a sigh of relief. She was returning from another late night at work, but even at nine in the evening, well after the supposed end of rush hour, the concrete arteries serving Los Angeles were still as clogged as those of a quadruple-bypass candidate. It seemed traffic couldn't get much worse, but from experience Taryn knew that it would.

I have to get out of this town, she thought with a sigh, swinging west on Wilshire Boulevard.

Leave town, and then do what? she asked herself as she passed the Veterans Administration grounds and turned right on San Vicente Boulevard. Your job is here; your friends are here; your life is here. You're not going anywhere, so quit complaining and make the most of it.

An accident had snarled traffic on San Vicente. Impatiently, Taryn sat at the light on Barrington, watching as it changed from red to green and back again. As she waited, she idly watched a number of late-night joggers passing the majestic coral and magnolia trees lining San Vicente's grassy median, each runner's arms and legs pumping, lungs straining to suck in a double ration of car exhaust. Eventually succumbing to boredom, Taryn set her parking brake and turned on a CD: Etta James's *Seven Year Itch.* Cranking up the volume, she settled back, letting Etta's soulful tones wash over her.

Ahead, a tow truck eventually finished removing the smashed remnants of a Toyota. Shortly afterward traffic began to move again, and a few blocks farther on Taryn turned left on Bundy

Drive. Years back, following the death of her father, she had used a small inheritance for a down payment on a condo in Brentwood. The cross-town location meant a long drive to work at the *Times*, but the relatively clean air near the ocean made it worthwhile.

Minutes later, with a feeling of contentment, Taryn passed a wrought-iron security gate and pulled into a parking space beneath her building. She was home.

Taryn twisted off the ignition and stepped from her car. As she did, she sensed movement in the shadows behind her.

"Who's there?" she called nervously into the darkness.

*　　*　　*

"Is your daughter sick, ma'am?"

"She's just frightened," Jamie heard the woman named Devon reply. "It's her first flight," the dark-haired woman added, turning in her seat to face Jamie. "You'll be fine, won't you, darling?" she asked, taking Jamie's hand.

As if in a horrible dream, Jamie felt her head swivel like a ventriloquist's dummy, turning toward the aircraft cabin attendant. "I'll be fine," she heard herself say. But deep inside, Jamie knew she wasn't going to be fine.

Not now; not ever.

As the giant turbines powering the aircraft began spooling up for takeoff, the dark-haired woman reached across to tighten the seat belt across Jamie's lap. Inwardly, Jamie cringed at her touch. Outwardly she showed nothing, concentrating instead on silencing the scream that had been building inside her ever since—

No! Don't think about that!

To Jamie, it seemed as if the woman were radiating an almost palpable force, its tendrils extending throughout the first-class cabin. Why couldn't anyone else sense it? Jamie felt it smothering her, penetrating to the very core of her being. Unable to move, she closed her eyes and held her breath in a fruitless effort to shut it out.

Minutes later her stomach lurched as the plane rose into the air. Shortly afterward she felt the invisible coils that had held her loosen. They weren't gone entirely, but they had withdrawn enough for her to regain some control of her body.

Enough to attempt an escape?

The woman had placed her in a window seat. Jamie would have to climb past her captor to get out. And then where would she go?

"Don't even try," the woman whispered, as though she had heard Jamie's thoughts. "Please remember what I told you."

When they had first entered the airport, Jamie had noticed her captor's hold easing as the woman dealt with others in the terminal. When Jamie had felt the woman's control slip to its weakest, she had tried to flee. Punishment had been swift and ruthless.

In less than a heartbeat Jamie's world had turned into a crucible of pain. There in the terminal, surrounded by hundreds of travelers, she had silently suffered a degree of agony few will ever be unfortunate enough to experience. And when it had ended, when the woman called Devon had taken Jamie's face in her hands and gazed into her eyes, anyone watching would have only seen a concerned mother comforting her child. "If you try that again," she had said, "I promise you will regret it."

Hours passed. Jamie sat motionless as the jetliner hurtled eastward, her eyes fixed, her hands folded quietly in her lap. Inside, however, her mind was racing. Though the woman had fallen asleep, Jamie knew that a bond still existed between them, tethering her to her captor. But were Jamie ever to escape, she knew that now was the time to form a plan.

You'll never escape, a small voice flickered in Jamie's consciousness.

Jamie shivered, wondering whether her mind was playing tricks on her.

Barely turning her head, Jamie glanced at the woman beside her, listening to the rhythmic sound of her breathing. She appeared to be asleep. Strangely, the voice Jamie heard had seemed to have come from inside the woman, yet it hadn't been Devon, of that she was certain. *What's happening to me? Jamie* wondered. *Am I going insane?*

You're not insane, the lonely, childlike voice returned, floating like a phantom in Jamie's consciousness. *Not yet, anyway.*

Who are you? Jamie asked silently, turning her thoughts inward.

Mine. What you see is mine. Devon took my body . . . stole it from me.

She took your body? But how . . . ?

Silence.

Please, Jamie thought, struggling to direct her question at whomever had spoken. Although she didn't understand what was happening, she knew this might be the only chance she would ever have. *Tell me what to do. Please, please talk to me.*

She's afraid of you. But you'll never get away. Never, never, never. Oh, God, she's coming!

Jamie felt the other's presence skitter away. Turning, she found her captor's eyes boring into hers, pinning her in their glacial depths. "I see you've been visiting with my companion," said Devon.

Hatred for the woman surged up in Jamie. Yet at the same time, Jamie knew her hatred was not for the woman alone. Part was for herself, for her weakness and her fear and for what she had—*No! Don't think about that . . .*

All at once, though she tried to banish the loathsome images from her mind, they came flooding back, all of them, filling her with their horror. The knife . . . and the blood . . . and . . .

Oh Mommy, I'm sorry. I'm so sorry.

Alone as never before, Jamie Callahan sat aboard Delta Airlines flight 2262 to New York, staring out the darkened aircraft window as the jetliner arrowed through the night. Folding her arms across her chest, she rocked back and forth, her body racked with silent sobs, her eyes squeezed tight against tears she could no longer contain.

*   *   *

I stood watching from the shadows as Taryn parked her car, unwilling to reveal myself yet. There was something I had to do first.

Who's there?" Taryn called, peering into the darkened garage.

"Don't turn around," I said quietly. "You're being watched."

"Mike?"

"Yeah. It's me. Go up to your condo. I'll be up after . . . I'll be up soon."

"But what—"

"Please. Just do it."

Twenty minutes later I rapped softly on Taryn's door. "It's me," I said.

Taryn fumbled with the deadbolt for what seemed forever before finally getting the door unlatched. "Thank God you're back," she cried, throwing her arms around my neck. "I don't know whether to kiss you or slug you. What took you so long?"

"I ran into some trouble."

Taking a step back, Taryn looked at me, clearly unprepared for what she saw. Adding to my previous injuries, a huge purplish bruise now covered the entire side of my face— extending from beneath my collar, past my swollen lips and the dark glasses I had on, fading into my scalp. The rest of my body had similar bruising, a result of the beating I'd taken in the hotel room. Scabs crusted the knuckles of my right hand; a filthy bandage concealed most of my left.

"Not much to write home about, huh?" I said ruefully. "It's a long story. I'll tell you later."

"At least give me the short version."

I shook my head. "The less you know, the better. I shouldn't have involved you by coming here, but some guys are staked out at my house, and I—"

"Shouldn't have involved me?" Taryn interrupted. "Callahan, I'm already involved. I was there when Bellamy was

136

murdered, remember? I was the one who took your pictures to the *Times*. And now, according to you, I'm being watched."

"I took care of that."

"How?" Taryn asked, glancing at my bandaged hand. "Never mind. First things first. We need to get you cleaned up." Taking my arm, she began leading me into the kitchen. "Let's check that hand. If the bandage is any indication, it's probably already infected."

"My hand's fine, Ms. Nightingale. Forget it."

"I'm going to get that dressing off and clean you up," Taryn said firmly. "Meanwhile, start at the beginning and fill me in."

Reluctantly, I accompanied Taryn to the kitchen sink, watching in silence as she worked with a damp sponge and a small pair of scissors to remove the crusted bandage from my hand. Amazingly, the stumps of my missing fingers had ceased throbbing earlier that day, as had all my injuries—my pains gradually being replaced by an almost pleasurable sensation of well-being and rejuvenation. Though I didn't understand why, I had never felt stronger in my life.

"Come on, Callahan," Taryn prodded without looking up from her task. "Give."

How much could I tell her? I wondered. More to the point, how much would she believe? I hesitated, then forged ahead. "Okay, the short version for now. I told you that two men attacked me at Century City. I managed to get away, but afterward one of them drove to the *Times* and retrieved the pictures."

"Tyler."

"Correct. Then when I got home later that night, I found a woman named Devon Summers waiting there for me. She said she knew who was responsible for Bellamy's death, and that I posed a threat to whomever it was. If I wanted to live, I had to make myself scarce."

"So you hopped on a plane and zipped off to Mexico. With Devon, I assume."

"Well . . . yeah."

"Great timing, Mike. Speaking of which, I wasn't able to cover for you at the paper. I tried, but . . ."

"I'm fired?" I asked, expecting the worst.

"I'm afraid so," Taryn answered. "McCaffery asked me to tell you. I'm sorry, Mike. But considering the circumstances, you can't really blame him. I can't believe you did this to yourself."

"You had to be there," I mumbled. "At any rate, when we arrived in Mexico, things went bad. Really bad. They found us. I think they killed Devon."

Taryn, who had nearly finished removing my bandage, looked up in shock. "They killed her?"

"I think so . . . although I'm not certain. At any rate, I never saw her again. At that point I knew I had to get away. I figured they would be watching the airports in Puerto Vallarta and Los Angeles, so I took a cab to Guadalajara, flew to San Diego, and rented a car. And here I am."

"That's it? Callahan, you're either leaving out one hell of a lot, or—Oh, dear God!"

Taryn had the dressing off. I stared at my mutilated hand, feeling as if I'd been kicked in the stomach. A growth of pink skin already covered the stumps of my severed fingers. And from the center of each, translucent but clearly visible, grew the bud of a new finger.

I pulled my hand from Taryn's grasp. With a mix of both wonder and horror, I stared at my newly sprouting digits.

Taryn's face went white. She inhaled sharply. "What . . . *happened* to you?"

"I lost them in a fight."

"Lost them? People don't grow new fingers."

"That's right," I said, struck by how truly alien I had become. "*People* don't."

"What other surprises do you have in store?" Taryn asked shakily. "How'd you get that bruise on your face? Is that why you're wearing shades?" Her hand darted out to remove my sunglasses.

"No!"

Too late. Taryn snatched away my glasses. As she did, her face filled with shock. "Mike! Your eyes . . . they're glowing!"

"Don't look if it bothers you," I said harshly. "It'll go away."

"Don't look if it bothers me? Callahan, I'll tell you what bothers me. I'm tired of being kept in the dark. I'm your friend and I want to help, but you have to tell me what's going on. All of it."

"I can't."

"Yeah, sure. The less I know, the better. Well, I'm not buying that. I'm up to my neck in this. I didn't want to tell you on the phone, but I have another set of those pictures you took at the fundraiser. If I'm in danger because of them, I want to know."

"You have the photos? But I thought—"

"The lab guy ran a second set for Jamie. When the memory card and the first set disappeared, I decided to hang on to them until you returned. You want to see them? Talk."

"Taryn—"

"Talk."

"All right," I sighed, realizing that whether I liked it or not, Taryn was caught up in my nightmare, and nothing I could do would change things. "I'll tell you everything. But I'm warning you, you're not going to believe it."

"Try me."

Remembering Nelson had said the same thing, I hoped I'd have better success with her. "I will," I agreed. "On one condition. Actually, several conditions."

"And they are?"

"One: You do whatever I say if things get out of control. And I mean *whatever* I say."

"I'm a big girl, Callahan. I can take care of myself."

"Promise, or no deal."

"Okay, okay," Taryn grumbled. "I promise."

"Two: First thing tomorrow, you're moving out of your condo. They were watching your place when I arrived. I fixed that for now, but they'll eventually send someone else. When they do, I want you to be where they can't find you."

"Whatever," Taryn mumbled, clearly trying to sidestep the issue. "Anything else?"

"Yeah. One more thing. Lend me the use of your shower," I replied with an attempt at a smile. "I'm so ripe I can barely stand myself."

Taryn smiled back. "Gladly. I think I can scare up a change of clothes for you, too. Last time my brother Robbie visited, he left a few things in the dryer. He's a big guy like you, so they should fit."

"Thanks, Taryn. I . . . I'm just sorry I got you involved."

"We already settled that," said Taryn. "I asked *you* to the fundraiser, remember? Now, go clean up while I make some coffee. Then it's time for the truth."

". . . so that's about it. You know everything else." I took a sip of coffee and glanced across the table, awaiting Taryn's reaction.

Taryn had listened quietly as I related details of the past days that I had previously omitted, telling her everything except the shower experience I'd shared with Devon, and our time in the bedroom afterward—for some reason deciding to leave that part out. In any case, I wouldn't have known how to describe what happened. Not the shower part, anyway.

Taryn's lips had tightened when I described my experience in the bullring, but otherwise she had shown no reaction. Now she sat with her elbows on the table, chin resting on her hands, regarding me dubiously.

"Well? What do you think?" I asked. "I know it's a lot to swallow . . ."

"No argument there," she replied dryly. "But it *would* explain a lot. The way you acted at the fundraiser, the missing photos, and so forth. When I surprised Tyler in McCaffery's office, I swear that man stared right through me. Those eyes of his were . . . creepy."

At the mention of eyes, I glanced away, wondering whether the strange fire still burned in mine.

"It's gone," said Taryn, as though reading my mind. "Which reminds me. I researched those names you asked me to look up."

"What did you find?"

"I'm not sure." Taryn crossed to an alcove off her living room, returning with a manila envelope and a yellow sheaf of handwritten notes. "Here," she said, sliding the yellow pages across the table. "I think you'd better read this for yourself."

Quickly, I scanned Taryn's notes. By the time I finished, things were beginning to fall into place, in an insane sort of way. I felt sick. I pressed my temples, unable to rid myself of the image of Elisabeth Báthory waiting for death in her sealed chamber, her eyes glowing in the darkness . . .

"This has been going on for a long time, hasn't it?" Taryn said softly.

"Yeah. I'm afraid so."

"I'm scared, Mike."

"So am I."

"What does it all mean? Is *blood* the common denominator? The people on your list bathed in it; some even drank it. I know it sounds crazy, but are we talking about vampires?"

"Something along those lines," I said grimly. "Only worse. A lot worse. I don't know how else to explain it. One thing I do know: Bram Stoker's vampires were a work of fiction, but long before he wrote his novel, they existed in folklore and myth. Like many legends, this one apparently has a basis in fact. Believe me, these people, if you can call them people, are real, and unfortunately I don't think holy water, garlic, and crucifixes are going to be much help against them.

"And the blood?"

I considered a moment. Vampires of legend drank the blood of their victims, at least according to Stoker, as did several of the historical figures in Taryn's research. Recalling my experience in the bullring, it seemed to me that *drinking* was the essential part of the equation, not blood. When I had taken the lives of others, initially with Devon's help and then later on my own, the experience had been strangely akin to drinking—possibly even drinking and eating at the same time. It also appeared from the rapid way my injuries were healing, not to mention sprouting a new pair of fingers, that Countess Báthory might have been at least partially correct in her belief that taking . . . or *drinking* the lives of others was the key to preserving her beauty.

At last I replied. "I think the blood connection is incidental," I said. "An insane perversion of the *hunger.* More important, from what I just read in your notes, it seems the longer it takes their victims to die and the more profound their agony, the more pleasure these . . . creatures derive from the kill. And it's not just the masochistic thrill of domination, either," I added softly. "The ecstasy of death is . . ."

I hesitated, staring at my injured hand. "I can't describe it, but blood is only a part. What these creatures ultimately take from their victims is far more precious than that."

"And you have this power?"

"Yes."

"Show me."

"No."

"You're asking me to accept an awful lot on faith, Mike. If you could just—"

"No," I repeated, my thoughts traveling back to the night I had stood helpless in the parking garage. What had happened to me at the hands of Roscoe and Tyler had been rape, pure and simple. "You wouldn't like it," I added. "Take my word for it."

"All right . . . for now," said Taryn. "I'm simply trying to understand. The others—you're not like them. Was it the hunger you mentioned that drove them to commit such horrible acts?"

I avoided Taryn's gaze. "I think so. That, and the belief they are superior beings and as such they have the right to do anything they please. In some respects, I'm no different from them, Taryn. I feel that same hunger, that same pull drawing me with an irresistible, addictive . . ."

"Stop." Taryn took my uninjured hand, forcing me to look at her. "You're not like them, Mike. You're not."

I glanced away. "I wish I could believe that."

"Trust me, you're not," said Taryn firmly. Then, changing the subject, she passed me the manila envelope she had also brought from the alcove. "Here, look at these."

I opened the envelope. It contained several dozen of Jamie's photos, shots that had been on her memory card. Rapidly, I shuffled through them. Toward the bottom I found the self-portrait Jamie had taken of us at Neptune's Net. I stared at the print, thinking that although it had been only a few days, it seemed like a lifetime.

I flipped to the next shot. In gruesome detail, it depicted the moment of Arthur Bellamy's death. I studied the picture, trying to find something in it that might shed some light on the murder.

In the photo, the patrol officer was kneeling beside Bellamy, his pistol jammed to the candidate's head, explosive gases and flame exiting the barrel against Bellamy's temple. In the background several of Bellamy's aides were rising from their seats. As I examined the photo, I sensed that something was not quite right, but I couldn't pin it down. Giving up, I flipped to the final three shots, the ones I had taken of the crowd. "Do you have a magnifying glass?" I asked.

"I have an eight-power loupe around here somewhere," Taryn answered. "For checking proof sheets. Want me to get it?

"Yeah. Bring a light, too."

Taryn went back to the alcove, returning with a small, conical-shaped magnifier and a brass lamp. I set the lamp on the table beside the photos, then placed the loupe on the first shot of the crowd. After a minute I moved on to the next.

"What are you looking for?" asked Taryn, leaning over my shoulder.

"I'm not sure," I replied, scanning faces in the room. Nothing jumped out at me. I proceeded to the final shot. "But whatever it is, I think I'll know it when I see it," I added, suddenly spotting Roscoe and Tyler near the back.

I froze, staring through the loupe in horror. I had found the woman I'd seen by the door after the killings. She was standing with Roscoe and Tyler. She had a hand on Tyler's arm. The brim of a hat partly covered her face. Nevertheless, as surely as I was alive, I recognized the piercing green eyes that were just beginning to light with a strange, unearthly fire. Although a malignant mask of rage twisted her lovely features, I felt for the first time that I was truly seeing her.

Devon!

A hollow realization settled like a stone in the pit of my stomach. Devon had deceived me from the very beginning. But why? And more to the point, how could I have been so blind?

"Find something, Mike?"

I nodded, unable to speak.

Clasping her hair in one hand, Taryn leaned over and peered through the loupe. "The tall guy in the back," she said after a moment. "Tyler."

"And the ape to his left is Roscoe. Those are the two who mugged me in the garage," I said, barely finding my voice.

Still clasping her hair, Taryn continued looking through the loupe. "Is there . . . Oh, my God! The woman standing with them. Her eyes are glowing. Who is she?"

"Devon Summers," I said quietly.

"The woman who took you to Mexico?"

I nodded again. "She lied to me about knowing Roscoe and Tyler. Actually, she probably lied about everything," I said, realizing there had never been a need for anyone to trace me to Mexico. Thanks to Devon, they had known exactly where I was all along. And to think I had been worried about Devon's safety. What a fool I had been.

"What's with her eyes? Is it like that Countess Báthory woman? You know, where her eyes were glowing when she was sealed up in her room?"

"Their eyes get like that when they . . . feed."

Taryn regarded me strangely, undoubtedly recalling that my eyes had looked like that when I first arrived. I watched as her expression turned from puzzlement to shock.

"I . . . I'm in a lot more trouble than I thought," I mumbled, absently thinking that I had probably just uttered the understatement of the century.

"Damn, Callahan."

"Of one thing I'm certain," I continued. "Those three are responsible for Bellamy's murder, and the police officer's death as well."

Taryn considered a moment, her brow furrowed in concentration. "So where do we go from here?" she asked.

"*We* don't go anywhere. I'm handling this alone."

"Wrong," said Taryn. "No way you're cutting me out of the biggest story of my life."

"Taryn, this has nothing to do with a news story. Whoever killed Bellamy—"

"I'm in, and that's all there is to it."

I glared. Taryn glared back. Finally, realizing I had no choice, I shrugged. "All right," I reluctantly agreed. "As long as you realize that the only way I'm coming out of this alive is by getting to them before they get to me. You can't be a part of that."

"Are you nuts? Let the police handle this."

"The police are powerless against them."

"And you're not."

"I don't know, Taryn. I just know I don't have a choice. You can help, but if things get ugly, remember your promise."

Innocently, Taryn raised an eyebrow. "What promise?"

"Damn it, Taryn . . ."

"Take it easy, Mike. Where's your sense of humor?"

"I lost it. Along with a few other things."

"Well, it wouldn't hurt to lighten up a bit. Anyway, the problem still remains—where do we go from here?"

I considered carefully. "First, we need to learn more about Devon Summers, if that is actually her name. For that we need the police."

"I thought you said they couldn't help."

"They can help with something like this. Nelson's task force has the resources to investigate every person at that fundraiser, if necessary. These photos should narrow the field."

"What makes you think the task force will share information with you?"

"Oh, they will," I said. "One way or another."

Taryn shifted uncomfortably, hearing something in my tone. "So we call Nelson?"

"Right. Not on your phone, though. Whoever put a tail on you could be listening to your conversations." Though I still had my own cell phone, I had removed the battery and stopped using it before leaving Mexico. At the time I had mistakenly thought that whoever had located Devon and me in Mexico had probably run a trace on my credit card. I didn't know what other resources they had, but I knew from watching too many TV cop shows that my cell phone could be traced. Now, although things had changed, I intended to continue playing it safe.

Frowning, Taryn thought for a moment. "I'm friends with the woman next door. She waters my plants when I'm gone. I'll call her . . . I'll *walk* over and ask to use her phone."

"Good idea. I'll go with you."

Taryn's neighbor turned out to be an attractive, garrulous young African American woman named Wilhelmina Dobbs— Willi for short. After several knocks Willi opened the door, her eyes swollen and red, a box of Kleenex in her hand.

"You okay, Willi?" asked Taryn.

"I'm fine," Willi sniffed. "I've just got rotten taste in men, that's all. Come on in. I could use some company. Who's your friend?"

I extended my hand. "Callahan. Mike Callahan. Listen, Willi, may I use your phone? Taryn's is out of order, and I need to make a call."

"So *you're* Mike Callahan," said Willi. Brightening slightly, she took my hand. "Taryn's always talking about you. I've read your stuff in the *Times*. I'm a big fan."

"Back off, Willi," laughed Taryn.

"Already spoken for?" Willi glanced at Taryn, then back at me. "Well, can't blame a girl for trying. Of course you can use my phone," she added, crossing to a table in the entry where she pulled a cell phone from her purse. "And if there's anything else you need . . ."

"Nope, this will do it," I said with a grin, taking the phone. "Thanks. I appreciate it."

146

"Anytime," Willi replied, flashing me a brief, flirtatious smile. With a patient shake of her head, Taryn took her friend's arm and steered her into the living room.

I stepped around the corner into Willi's kitchen and tuned out the sound of the two women chatting in the adjoining room, Willi doing most of the talking. Aware that Nelson's task-force duty had probably taken precedence over his usual work schedule, I decided to try him at home. On impulse, however, I punched in my own number first. My answering machine picked up on the second ring, meaning I had messages. I entered my access code. Moments later I heard Jamie's recorded voice.

"Hi, Dad. Just checking to see whether you got my call last night. Don't worry about the camera. I can get it anytime. Give me a ring when you get a chance. I love you. 'Bye."

One by one, my other messages began to play.

"Mike, this is Taryn. Call me as soon as you get in. I don't care what time. We need to talk."

"Callahan, Hank McCaffery here. Get your ass down here on the double. We need you, for chrissake."

"Hi, Dad. Me again. Sorry to keep bugging you, but I've been getting this creepy feeling . . . Are you all right? Gimme a call, okay?"

"Callahan, if I don't hear from you by five o'clock, you're fired!"

"Mike, this is Nelson. I've been trying to reach you all day. I need a set of those pictures, and the *Times* is giving me the runaround. Those photos are evidence in a murder investigation, pal. Don't make me play hardball. I'll be expecting your call."

"Mike? Taryn. Where are you? Please, please, call."

The next message sent a chill up my spine.

"Keep your mouth shut if you want to live, asshole."

Three hang-ups followed, then nothing. I listened to the final message once more. I couldn't be certain, but it reminded me of a deep, guttural voice I had first heard in the Century City Hotel parking garage. Tyler.

Next I called Nelson at home. He answered almost immediately. "Nelson Long here."

"Nelson, this is Mike."

A pause. Then, "It's about time you got back to me, amigo."

"Sorry, Nelson. It's a long story. We need to talk."

"You've got that right. When?"

"Now.   And Nelson?   I have the pictures from the fundraiser."

"Where are you?"

"Brentwood." Covering the receiver, I called into the living room. "Taryn, what's the name of that pizza place with all the stuff on the walls? Honest Abe's?"

"That dump on San Vicente? Regular John's," Taryn replied.

I removed my hand from the mouthpiece. "I'll meet you at Regular John's Pizza Parlor. San Vicente near Wilshire."

"I know the place," said Nelson curtly. "I'll be there in twenty minutes."

Chapter Seventeen

Arriving at Regular John's before Nelson, Taryn and I took a booth in the back. "Place hasn't changed much," I said fondly, glancing around as I slipped into the booth beside Taryn.

At the far end of the dining area two teenagers were manning the order counter; behind them an older man in a white apron was working at a bank of stainless-steel pizza ovens. Tables with red-checkered tablecloths jammed the center of the room. Booths similar to ours lined three walls, and a cluster of video games took up the fourth. The remainder of the interior—doors, windows, ceiling—displayed an eclectic assortment of dust-covered memorabilia.

"Nope, it's still the same," Taryn agreed, rolling her eyes. "Nothing here I couldn't fix with a match and a gallon of gasoline."

"You may not appreciate the décor, but the food's great. Want anything?"

"Just a beer."

"Suit yourself." I got up and placed an order at the counter, returning minutes later with pitcher of beer and three glasses. As I reached our booth, I spotted Nelson coming through the door. "Nelson! Over here," I called.

Nelson made his way back. He wedged his blocky frame into the booth, settling in across the table from Taryn and me. "Hi, Taryn," he said, reaching for the pitcher and pouring himself a glass. "How're things?"

"Actually, Nelson . . . things have been better."

"No argument there," Nelson replied. After taking a pull on his beer, he shot me a sulfurous stare. "Callahan, you put me in one hell of a spot these past few days. First you—" He stopped, abruptly noticing my face. "Damn. You look worse than the last time I saw you. Have you looked in the mirror lately? Take my advice and don't."

"I've been hanging with a rough crowd," I mumbled. "Look, I'm sorry about running out on you. It couldn't be helped."

Nelson withdrew a pack of Camels from his coat pocket, shook out an unfiltered cigarette, and placed the pack on the table. "So you say." Noticing Taryn's glance at the cigarette, he added, "Don't worry, I'm not going to light it."

"Mike told me you were quitting," Taryn said, raising a questioning eyebrow.

"One thing at a time," said Nelson peevishly, rolling the unlit cigarette between his fingers. "Rochelle wants me to cut down on the groceries until I lose some weight. She's got me on a diet, and it's killing me."

Ignoring this interchange, I reached into my coat and withdrew Taryn's manila envelope.

"Ah, the missing photos," said Nelson, reaching for the pictures. "Unfortunately, at this point they're not going to make much difference. Like I said, the powers-that-be want to put the investigation behind them ASAP. In the absence of evidence to the contrary, the brass has ordered the case closed. Officer Hidalgo had a nervous breakdown, shot Bellamy, and killed himself. Period."

"Look at the pictures."

Nelson opened the envelope and began shuffling through. "What are these—shots of you and Jamie at the beach?"

"Some of Jamie's photos are in there." I grabbed the stack and found the shots I had taken at the fundraiser, then shoved the rest of the prints into my pocket. "Here."

Nelson studied the photo on top—Officer Hidalgo discharging his pistol into Bellamy's temple. "Well, if there were ever any uncertainty about who did the shooting, which there isn't, this certainly clears things up," Nelson muttered, shuffling to the next photo. "What have we here—people in the room?"

I nodded. "Check the final picture. Taryn, did you bring the magnifier?"

"I did." Taryn rummaged through her purse and passed Nelson the loupe.

"The guys by the door," I prompted as Nelson placed the magnifier on the photo.

"Well, well. Gregory Tyler," said Nelson, squinting through the loupe. "He's older, but I recognize him from his mug shot. I assume the gorilla beside him is Roscoe Reese."

"Right. Now look at the woman with them."

Nelson peered through the magnifier. "What is this, some kind of trick photography?"

"No trick, Nelson. Her name is Devon Summers—at least that's what she told me. She's your murderer. Their eyes get like that when they kill."

"Who'd she kill?" Nelson demanded, flipping back to a picture of Bellamy and Hidalgo. "The patrol officer shot Bellamy," he said, tapping the photo with a thick finger. "The evidence is right here."

I was about to answer when something about the photo of Hildago caught my eye. "Let me see that," I said, abruptly realizing what had troubled me earlier. I pointed to Hidalgo's holster. "Here."

Taryn and Nelson leaned closer. "It's empty," said Nelson. "So?"

"He's wearing it on his right side."

"I see now," interjected Taryn. "His holster is on the right side, meaning he's right-handed. But he's holding the pistol in his left."

"Correct," I said. "Bellamy held the gun in his left hand, too."

"Hold on, pal," said Nelson. "We're not back on that story you tried to feed me at Chuck's, are we?"

"I know it's hard to believe, but—"

"Hard to believe? It's *impossible* to believe." Nelson tapped his unlit cigarette on the table, packing the tobacco. "Lemme pose a couple of dumb questions here. Your photos prove that the guys who *allegedly* attacked you in the garage also attended Bellamy's dinner. What else do the pictures prove? Nothing," he said, answering his own question.

"But they wanted the shots I took of—"

"There could be any number of reasons for that," Nelson interrupted. "Roscoe Reese and Gregory Tyler are known fugitives. It stands to reason they might not appreciate having their picture taken. Let's move on. Officer Hidalgo was right-handed, but he shot Bellamy with his left. So what? That's not proof someone forced him to do it."

"No, but—"

"Next you have a picture of some broad whose eyes appear to be glowing. There could be a rational explanation for that, too. Maybe your camera flash bounced off her contacts. Taryn, excuse my language, but you're not buying this horseshit story of Mike's, are you?"

"I didn't at first," Taryn said. "But . . . things kept adding up. The way the photos vanished at the *Times*, for instance. I know my editor got the prints. I delivered them myself. But after Tyler showed up—"

"Tyler was at the *Times*?"

Taryn nodded. "And he walked out with Mike's photos. I saw him take them. Here's the weird part, Nelson. Either McCaffery and the lab tech are lying, which I doubt, or neither of them recollects anything. It's as if Tyler somehow erased their memories."

"And you're claiming that's possible?" Nelson scoffed.

"It's not only possible, it's what happened," I said.

"Bull."

"Nelson, why don't you try listening for a change?"

"I'm too old to listen to this kind of crap, amigo."

I started to respond, pausing as a teenager from the order counter approached. "One of you order a beef sub?" the youngster inquired.

"If it's got extra cheese, jalapeños, and French dressing, it's mine," I replied.

"This be the one," said the boy, plopping down a plastic basket overflowing with chips, pickles, and a huge chunk of French bread stuffed with meats and cheese. "Anything else?"

"Nope."

Nelson glanced hungrily at my sandwich. Absently, he started to light his cigarette, stopping as he realized what he was doing.

"Let's all calm down," suggested Taryn. "Nelson, you're correct in pointing out that the photos don't actually *prove* anything, but you have to admit that a lot of things have been happening that are hard to explain. For instance, what do you make of this?" Grabbing my sleeve, she pulled my wounded hand from beneath the table.

Nelson's mouth dropped open in astonishment when he saw the nascent digits growing from of the stumps of my severed fingers. "How do I explain *that*?" he said slowly, staring at my hand in disbelief. "I don't. I'm a cop, not a doctor. But whatever it is, it has nothing to do with Bellamy's murder."

"But it does," said Taryn quietly.

Wearily, Nelson replaced his cigarette back in the pack. Shoving the pack into his shirt pocket, he gathered the fundraiser photos and rose from the table. "Look, it's late," he said. "I've had a long day. Why don't we all get some sleep and—"

"I'm sorry for what I'm about to do," I interrupted. "But I need you to believe me."

"That ain't gonna happen, pal," Nelson grumbled. "I'm keeping these photos, and I'll see you at the station tomorrow for your state—"

Sit down.

A puzzled expression crossed Nelson's face. Then his eyes went wide with shock. Stunned, he resumed his seat.

"Wha—"

Don't talk.

"What . . . what are you doing?" Taryn stammered, staring first at Nelson, then at me.

"He wanted proof," I explained. "I'm giving it to him."

Nelson sat immobile, a tic pulling at the corner of one eye.

"It's terrible, isn't it?" I said, leaning closer. "In this state you'll do anything I want. If I say: *Raise your arms* . . . you'll do it."

As though jerked by invisible wires, Nelson's arms shot up over his head.

"And if I say: ***Quit smoking*** . . . you've puffed your last Camel," I continued. "And if I told you to kill—believe me, Nelson, you would."

Nearby diners were staring openly at Nelson, who still had his arms raised in the air. Lowering my voice, I continued. "The people who murdered Bellamy will eliminate anyone who gets in their way, Nelson. And I'm in their way. This is more than a news story for me. It's my life."

A moment later I released my friend.

"You son of a bitch!" Nelson shouted. He lunged across the table, his face mottled with rage. Grabbing my shirt, he dragged me from my seat. I offered no resistance as his right hand formed a fist.

"Nelson, don't!" yelled Taryn.

Ignoring her, Nelson drew back his arm. Still I didn't resist, waiting for a blow I knew I deserved.

For a long moment nothing happened. Then, slowly, fury drained from Nelson's face. He lowered his fist. Both of us slumped back into the booth. By then an uneasy silence had fallen over the entire restaurant. Wisely, no one chose to approach our table.

"I'm really sorry, Nelson," I said. "It was the only way I could get you to believe."

Nelson looked away.

"Will you help me?" I asked.

Instead if answering, Nelson absently started to pull out his pack of cigarettes. He froze in the act, staring at the pack as if he were holding a snake. Groaning, he tossed the cigarettes onto the table, realizing he was done with them for good.

A long silence followed. "Yeah, I'll help," he said finally. "Another demonstration like that for the brass will definitely get the case reopened."

I shook my head. "No one else can know. If I were to go public with this, I wouldn't last a day. If the opposition didn't take me out, I'd probably get hustled off to a locked room in some top-secret government facility, strapped to a dissection table."

"So what do you want me to do?"

"You said the investigation is officially closed. Leave it that way. Just help me find who's out behind this. I'll take it from there."

"You'll take it from there? That's not the way things work, pal."

"We'll talk about that later. Will you do it?"

Another silence. "Yeah, I'll do it." Nelson cracked his knuckles. "It could mean my job if the wrong people get wind of this, but I'll do it." He pulled out his cell phone and rose from the table. "I've gotta make a couple calls."

Taryn and I watched as Nelson walked outside. Then Taryn turned to me. "I thought he was going to clobber you. Why didn't you stop him?"

"Because I deserved it."

"Don't be so hard on yourself, Callahan. I don't understand what you just did, but as you said, you had to make him believe."

I nodded. "I still deserved it."

Minutes later Nelson returned. "I called in some markers and got two of my best guys to work with me on this," he said. "Detectives Kane and Deluca. They'll do it on their own time and keep their mouths shut. I'm meeting them after I leave here. We'll try to get a start on it tonight."

"What did you tell them?"

"Nothing. They were on the Bellamy Task Force, too. Like me, they think something stinks about the way the brass squashed the investigation. Nobody likes being told how to do his job."

Nelson thought for a moment, then continued. "First we need to finish checking names on the dinner list. Now that we have your pictures, maybe we can get something on your mysterious woman. Too bad we don't have more to go on."

"Actually, I do have something else that might help," I said. I pulled out my wallet and extracted a thick wad of bills. Taryn stared at the money. "What'd you do, rob a bank?"

Ignoring her question, I repaid Nelson for my dinner at Chuck's, shoved the rest of the cash into my pocket, and passed the empty wallet to Nelson. "Devon Summers, the woman in the photo, visited me at home after Bellamy's murder," I explained. "She claimed to represent an organization fighting the people who murdered Bellamy. Turns out she was lying. She was up to her neck in Bellamy's murder. She briefly had my wallet in her possession. Maybe her prints are still on it."

"Maybe." Nelson lifted the wallet with the handle of his fork and deposited it into Taryn's manila envelope. "I'm gonna get moving on this," he said, shoving the envelope into his pocket as he rose from the table.

I extended my hand. "Thanks, Nelson. I appreciate your help."

Nelson stared at my outstretched hand, then turned for the door without taking it. "I'll be in touch," he said over his shoulder.

Realizing I had probably just lost a friend, I toyed with my sandwich, then shoved it away, suddenly not hungry.

Taryn placed a hand on my arm. "When did you last sleep, Mike?"

I rubbed my eyes. "I don't remember."

"Come on, let's go home. You can sleep on the couch in my living room. Things are bound to look better in the morning. We can figure out what to do then."

Chapter Eighteen

How long had he waited there in the darkness?
A bone-thin sliver of moon had long since disappeared behind the western ridge; a wintry chill had seeped into his limbs hours before. But somehow, against all reason, it seemed he had kept his vigil far longer than the mere hours spent that night on the castle battlement. Though he tried, he was unable to recall what compulsion had brought him, or what need now forced him to stay. His mind whirled in confusion, reason confounded by contradiction and half-remembered truth. Nevertheless he waited, hands gripping the cold granite wall, eyes searching the night.

As he watched, an icy mist crept through the lowlands, clinging to the valleys and hollows of the rugged countryside surrounding the castle foundations. No sound reached him from the forest to the west—no creaking of wind in the trees, no rustling in the thickets. Yet something called to him from the stillness, growing stronger with each passing hour, filling him with unnamable terror. Without knowing how, he realized he had been there before and would be there again . . . and again . . .

Still, he waited.

There. A light.

He stood spellbound, watching as it drew closer. Flickering, it moved ghostlike through the forest—now suspended in darkness, now gone, now returning. And from somewhere, dancing on the threshold of perception, came the sound of a stringed instrument, its tones deep and disturbing, playing a cloying, almost remembered nocturne.

The light stopped at the edge of a clearing. He could now see that it was a torch held high above some invisible bearer, the flame beckoning him with a power he could neither fathom nor resist. He knew it was for this that he had waited.

Without willing it, he stumbled down a long, darkened passageway to the outer gates of the fortress, pausing near the castle's southern rampart. Although the cold night cut through his vestments like a dagger, rivulets of sweat soaked his tunic, trickling down his sides. His heart thundered in his chest, deafening him to all but the rush of his own blood. Clutching his cloak tightly to his body, he turned to retrace his steps. He found himself unable.

The glimmering light again began to move, beckoning him onward. Powerless to resist, he followed, staggering through the night. Gradually the swell of music grew louder, its unsettling melody unfolding, the torch always just ahead, leading him deeper into the forest. He clawed through a tangle of twisted trunks and clinging branches, thorns ripping his clothes and skin. At last a rock amphitheater came into view, illuminated by an encircling ring of torches.

A mantle of evil seemed to charge the scene before him. Crouching, he peered through the underbrush. In the light of the torches he saw men gathered around a pit of blazing coals, tongs and irons thrust into its center. Two of the men wore suits of leather armor and appeared to be doing the bidding of a third, a dark figure presiding over them from a great throne hewn into the living rock. A hood concealed the third man's face, but his imperious eyes glowed like beacons as he directed his minions with an occasional wave of his hand and a sporadic, muttered command. The others present, a man and two boys who'd been stripped of their clothes and bound with strips of hide, knelt helpless before him.

As the figure on the stone seat listened impassively, the bound man begged for the lives of his sons. When the man had finished, the hooded monarch laughed cruelly. Then he signaled to his men. The soldiers dragged the younger of the boys into the circle and threw him facedown on the ground. Refusing to acknowledge the heartrending pleas of the father, they fastened the boy's wrists to a post. As one held his legs, the other went to the edge of the clearing, returning with a six-foot stake the thickness of a man's wrist, one end blunted so as not to result in too quick a death.

The boy died twenty minutes later. Twenty minutes . . . but for him an eternity.

As had the first, the second boy suffered greatly. And finally, impaled on a stake between the bodies of his sons, the father met his own savage fate. His tormentors had saved their most imaginative torments for him, and as is true of all men in the face of torture, he did not meet death well.

He watched from the darkness, unable to look away. And when it was over, when the last bloodcurdling wail had echoed into eternity, the hooded figure turned to where he lay hidden. "Come out!" the dark monarch bellowed.

He tried to run. To his horror, he found he could not.

Rough hands dragged him into the circle—past the pit of live coals, past the broken bodies, past the stench of death. He cowered at the feet of the hooded master, afraid to meet his glowing eyes.

"Look at me."

The thrum of ghastly nocturne rose in the night, ascending to an insane, monstrous crescendo . . .

Look at me.

Against his will, he raised his head.

Something familiar . . . The dark figure's cowl was suddenly pulled back, revealing teeth bared in a mocking smile and a face he knew too well.

It was his own face! His face! Laughing, laughing . . .

With a wave of utter, bottomless despair, he covered his eyes, attempting to banish the horror he had discovered within himself, knowing in his heart he could not.

And then he began to scream.

"Mike! Mike . . . wake up."

"Wha—?"

"Wake up, Mike. You were having a nightmare."

I sat up in panic, my eyes searching the darkness. Taryn stood beside the couch, light from the hallway seeping past her into the room. "I . . . I thought I was over those," I stammered.

"Over what?"

"This isn't the first time I've had that particular dream," I mumbled. "If it is a dream. It's always the same, everything so real, as if I were actually there. It started after I got back from Afghanistan. I . . . I eventually got rid of it. Until now."

Taryn sat beside me on the couch. "It might help to talk about it," she suggested. As she sat, her robe parted slightly, exposing a hint of satin nightgown beneath.

"I don't think so," I said, looking away.

"Come on, Mike. Nightmares are never as bad if you talk about them."

I shook my head.

"Please?"

I didn't reply. Though ashamed of my hideous dream, a part of me realized it was something beyond my control. Even after all these years, maybe it would help to share it with someone. Someone like Taryn.

"Tell me, Mike."

Finally, with a reluctant shrug, I agreed. "Okay," I said. "But don't say I didn't warn you." And then I told her, holding nothing back.

When I had finished, Taryn took my hand. "You've been keeping that inside for a long time, haven't you?"

"Wouldn't you?"

"I don't know," Taryn replied softly. "I'm just glad you shared it with me." She hesitated, then continued. "Listen, Mike, I need to tell you something. This may come as a big shock, but you're not half as bad a guy as you think you are." And to my surprise, she kissed me.

At first Taryn's lips lingered tenderly on mine. Gradually they grew more insistent, her embrace igniting a long-suppressed desire between us. I felt her heart quickening under her thin negligee as she moved into my arms.

A wave of conflicting emotion swept through me, warring desires I was unable to resolve. For years Taryn had been my associate, my confidante, my friend. By tacit agreement we had avoided a romantic entanglement that might jeopardize our friendship. Now I realized I wanted more. Yet at the same time, I knew that could never be. I had placed Taryn in danger by seeking her help, and I couldn't make things worse. With a surge of guilt, I recalled the spectator at the bullring who had died simply because he'd been sitting too close. Gripping Taryn's shoulders, I gently pushed her away. "Taryn, I can't do this."

"Why not?" she asked. "After all these years, are you still in love with Susan?"

I hesitated, caught off guard by a question I hadn't considered for quite some time. "I don't know," I answered truthfully. "Maybe. But that's not the reason. I'm caught up in something that isn't going to end well. I don't know whether I can come out of this alive, but I'm going to try. In the meantime, I can't put you in any more danger than I already have."

"I told you, I can take care of myself."

"Not against these people, you can't."

"I don't want to hear that," Taryn said stubbornly.

"Taryn, people are going to die. When that time comes, I don't want you to be one of them. When that time comes, I don't want you anywhere near me. Maybe when this is over—"

"Please don't say anything more, Mike," Taryn interrupted. "I'm frightened enough as it is. Just shut up and hold me. Please . . . just hold me."

Hours later the telephone rang. When it became obvious that whoever it was had no intention of giving up, Taryn pulled her robe around her and rose from the couch, where we had both fallen asleep. "Don't go anywhere," she murmured. "I'll be right back."

Taryn made her way to her phone in the bedroom. Seconds later I could hear her end of the conversation drifting into the living room. "Hello," she mumbled, her voice still thick with sleep.

A pause. "Oh, hi, Nelson."

I sat up, straining to hear.

Another pause, a long one this time. Then Taryn's voice came again, sounding oddly subdued. "Okay. We'll be right over."

"What is it?" I asked.

161

Taryn reappeared in the doorway, her face ashen. "That was Nelson. One of his detectives answered a call in Pacific Palisades . . ."

"Taryn, what is it?"

"Jamie is missing," Taryn said. "Nelson is on his way over there now. He wants us to meet him. And Mike . . . he was evasive on the phone, but I think something has happened to Susan."

Chapter Nineteen

Twenty minutes later Taryn and I arrived in Pacific Palisades. Police cruisers had sealed off Susan's street, blocking both ends of the block. Unable to proceed, we parked Taryn's Volvo one street over and covered the rest of the distance on foot.

As we approached Susan's house, I noticed more squad cars parked out front, their flashing lights illuminating the overhanging sycamores and jacarandas in sickly hues of red and blue. A radio squawked, sending garbled phrases into the night. In the driveway several police officers were lounging against a squad car. Across from the police barricade, a gaggle of wide-eyed neighbors stood gawking at the house.

I spotted Nelson talking with a heavyset detective on the walkway. Both men had their LAPD shields hung from their coat pockets. A dozen feet beyond them Susan's front door stood ajar, a young patrol officer stationed just inside. A stutter of strobe flashes lit the interior hallway.

Taking Taryn's hand, I ducked under a strip of yellow POLICE LINE DO NOT CROSS tape strung around the perimeter of the property. As I did, a scowling police officer moved to block our way. "Stay on the other side of the tape, sir," the officer directed.

Go away, I ordered quietly.

The policeman looked momentarily confused. Then he turned and walked off as if we didn't exist.

Still holding Taryn's hand, I strode across the lawn. "Hey, Nelson!"

Nelson turned, glancing in our direction. "Mike, Taryn," he said somberly when we arrived. Although he still seemed distant, his animus toward me from Regular John's seemed to have lessened. "This is Detective John Banowski," Nelson continued, indicating the thick-necked man beside him. He'll be handling the investigation—"

"What investigation?" I interrupted. "Is Jamie all right? You said she's missing? Where's Susan?"

"I take it you're the husband," said Banowski.

"Ex. What's going on?" I demanded.

Banowski stared at me. His eyes had the look of a man who has seen too much, his body showed signs of muscle going to fat, and the creases in his face put him on the wrong side of forty. Nonetheless, he stood a solid six feet tall, and he clearly didn't like looking up at someone when he spoke. Instead of answering my question, he pulled out a pack of Marlboros, lit one, and inhaled deeply, all the while scrutinizing me skeptically. "The crime-scene unit is almost done," he said at last. "Wait here. I'll talk to you shortly."

"I don't think so," I said. Bulling my way past, I started for the front door, determined to find out what was happening.

"Hold it right there," Banowski ordered. At his signal, several burly officers moved to block my way.

My eyes narrowed. Before I could act, Taryn took my arm. "Don't do anything foolish, Mike," she pleaded, drawing me aside. "Please, just let these guys do their job. I'm sure they'll tell us what's going on as soon as possible," she added, pointedly eyeing Banowski.

"That's right, lady," Banowski retorted. Turning to one of the officers he had summoned, he said, "Go get the neighbor." Then, staring again at me, he flipped his half-finished cigarette into the bushes. "We'll be getting to your friend Mike here real soon. Count on it."

Frowning, Nelson shook his head. "What's with you, Banowski?" he asked. "When you told me to get Callahan down here, I thought it was because—"

"With all due respect, Lieutenant," Banowski broke in. "I know this guy is your longtime buddy, but this is *my* investigation. Lemme do it my own way. Believe me, I have my reasons."

At that moment a three-man forensics team, along with an individual whom I recognized as an investigator from the coroner's office, exited the front door. Trailing behind were two uniformed policemen, one of them the young officer I had seen posted inside in the entry. The young officer was walking slowly, apparently upset. As the crime-scene technicians stopped to confer with Banowski, the rookie's partner put an arm around the youngster's shoulders, leading him across the lawn. I could hear the two men talking as they passed.

"It's nothing to be ashamed of," the older cop was saying. "A lot of guys lose their lunch the first time they work a case like this."

"You've seen something like *that* before?" the young officer asked weakly.

"Well . . . no. Not that bad, anyway," the older cop admitted.

"You know what got me?" the young officer mumbled. "I heard the coroner's investigator say that when that was done to her . . . she was still *alive*."

Heart in my throat, I slammed past several startled policemen, heading for the front door. Behind me I heard Banowski snarl for assistance. As I entered Susan's house, I glanced back to see a knot of police officers charging toward me, Banowski leading the way.

I took the stairs to the upper floor two at a time. At the top, the door to Susan's bedroom stood open. I froze in the doorway.

Susan's body lay on the bed, eyes staring sightlessly into the void. Her head was twisted to one side, her auburn hair sticky with blood, clinging to her face in a tangled mass. A fresco of red spattered the wall. Blood had soaked through the bedding, collecting in a dark puddle on the floor.

I stared at the savaged body that had once been my wife. In life, despite our divorce, she had remained my touchstone— former lover, steadfast friend, mother of my child. Now, in death, she seemed small and sad and alone. A blinding rage rose inside me, bolts of white-hot hate coursing through my veins. Someone would pay.

Breathing hard, Banowski appeared at the top of the stairs, several uniformed officers close behind. "Don't touch anything," he ordered angrily. Noting that I wasn't moving, he signaled for the other officers to stop. "That your ex-wife?" he asked.

I nodded, fighting back tears as the shock of Susan's death became real, and with it the realization there was nothing I could do to change things. Nothing. "Jamie . . . where is she?" I asked, feeling a surge of panic welling up inside.

"Maybe you can tell me." Banowski stepped past me into the room, avoiding the dark puddle at the base of the bed. He withdrew a pen from his pocket and used it to press the play button on an answering machine on the nightstand. A moment later I heard Jamie's voice.

She was crying. "Oh Daddy I'm sorry I'm sorry I couldn't stop her . . ." Abruptly her voice shifted. It was still Jamie, but *different*, somehow. "This is a warning, Mike. Keep your mouth shut and stay out of our way." Then Jamie's voice again shifted to normal. The sound of her sobbing ended the message.

"Why would your daughter leave a message for you on your ex-wife's phone?" asked Banowski. "Did she think you would be stopping by? Or maybe you'd already been here and planned to come back?"

Whoever did this had meant to send me a warning. They had succeeded. "I don't know," I said, a sense of abject, utter hopelessness enveloping me.

Banowski smiled cynically. "I figured you'd say that. Let's go downstairs. Maybe you'll feel more like talking there."

Taryn and Nelson stood waiting at the bottom of the staircase. Taryn watched as I descended, her eyes brimming with concern. Nelson looked confused.

"Keep an eye on Mr. Callahan here," Banowski said to several officers waiting there. "Don't let him out of your sight till I get back."

Nelson spoke. "Banowski, what the hell are you—"

Banowski cut him off. "With all due respect, Lieutenant, I have my reasons, like I told you," he said, stepping outside.

"Damn," Nelson muttered once Banowski had left. Shifting from foot to foot, he turned to me. "I'm so sorry, Mike," he said softly. "When I called you at Taryn's, I didn't know the full story. I didn't know about Susan. If I had, maybe I could have, I don't know . . ."

"It wouldn't have made any difference," I said, barely able to speak, unable to drive the image of Susan's mutilated body from my mind. "I'm the only one who could have prevented what happened here tonight. And I didn't."

"You can't blame yourself for this," said Taryn.

"No?" I said, stricken with guilt. "I've been underestimating these people from the very beginning—starting with Devon. I should have made certain they couldn't get to me through my family, or my friends, either. It won't happen again." Coming to a decision, I looked at Taryn. "As of now, you're out of this."

Taryn shook her head. "But—"

"I can't risk having you hurt. You made a promise, and you're going to keep it. Even if I have to force you," I added. "I need to move fast, and I can't risk having anything happen to you. As long as you're around, you're a target."

"Be reasonable, Callahan," Taryn objected. "You'll need all the help you can get to find Jamie. You don't even know where to start looking."

"I have a few ideas," I said, turning to Nelson. "I know there hasn't been much time, but have you and your guys made any headway on identifying the woman at the fundraiser?"

"The one with the glowing eyes? Maybe," Nelson replied wearily. "We've been at it since I left you. We lifted several prints from your wallet. I twisted some arms and got them run right away. They turned out to be yours, Tyler's, and a third person's that didn't make sense—some kid who disappeared twenty years ago. Her prints were in the Department of Justice missing child database. We don't know what to make of that."

Nelson thought a moment. Finally he shook his head and continued. "Bottom line, the prints looked like a dead end. But in comparing known aliases for Tyler against the dinner list, we got a hit. Tyler was registered at the fundraiser as Jay Watkins, an assumed name he was using years ago. When we checked the contribution roster, we discovered that the same corporation that paid for Tyler's meal also sprung for two others. One was probably for Roscoe. We think the other was for your lady with the weird eyes. She was listed as a Ms. D. Varkoff."

"What company made the contributions?"

"Some outfit I never heard of. Had a funny name—oh, yeah. The Elysian Foundation."

"Now it makes sense," Taryn jumped in.

Curious, both Nelson and I turned toward her.

"It's simple," Taryn explained. "The question has always been: Who would benefit from Bellamy's murder, right? Well, one name definitely tops the list. Lyle Exner, Bellamy's political opponent."

Nelson looked dubious. "Yeah, but—"

"Exner divested himself of all financial holdings prior to declaring his candidacy," Taryn went on, her excitement growing. "It's a matter of public record. Guess what company he used to own—at least a big part of it."

"The Elysian Foundation?"

"Bingo."

Nelson scratched his chin. "Even if that's true, it's not enough to hang a murder rap on him. Having two of the FBI's most-wanted on their payroll could cause the Elysian Foundation considerable embarrassment, but that doesn't prove the foundation was responsible for Bellamy's death. Not with any explanation that would hold up in court," he added, glancing at me.

"Don't worry about proving anything in court," I said. "I'll take it from here."

"*You'll* take it from here?" said Nelson. "I told you before—things don't work that way."

"They do now."

"Damn it, Mike—" Nelson halted midsentence as Banowski strode up.

Banowski stopped in front of me. "Step outside, Callahan," he ordered.

"Why?" I asked, getting tired of taking orders.

"Because there's a witness I want you to meet," Banowski explained. "A neighbor lady heard screams, right around the time we estimate your wife was murdered. The neighbor didn't call it in right away, thinking it was a domestic spat and none of her business. She got suspicious after seeing your daughter leave with someone. Let's step out to the front yard and see if we can find out who that someone was."

Outside, a woman in her early fifties stood near one of the squad cars. She had on a long coat with her collar turned up, hands shoved deep in her pockets. The moment I saw her, an alarm went off in my head.

The woman removed her right hand from her coat pocket, pointing. "That's him! He's the one who left with the girl."

Strong hands grabbed me from behind, pinning my arms. I struggled to free myself. I couldn't. In the periphery of my vision I saw Nelson moving forward, yelling at Banowski. "John, you idiot, Callahan didn't do it!"

"Is that right?" Banowski replied. "He may be your bosom buddy, Lieutenant, but I have a witness here who says different." All eyes were on the two detectives when the woman pulled her other hand from her coat. This time it wasn't a finger she was pointing. It was a .45 caliber automatic.

"Mike, look out!" Taryn screamed.

I saw the pistol lock on my chest. All at once someone was rushing in from the side, grabbing for the gun . . .

Nelson.

A split second later the .45 jumped in the woman's hand, sending a deadly lick of flame stabbing into the night.

*　　*　　*

Cold.

Jamie hugged her knees, shivering in the darkness. The sweater and jeans she had worn to school the previous day provided little protection against the dank confines of her cell. Her legs ached from sitting on the frigid concrete floor. Groaning, she shifted her position, attempting to relieve the bone-numbing chill that had settled into her limbs. Clenching her chattering teeth, she rose, trying to shake the feeling of helplessness that had enveloped her since they'd fastened a metal shackle around her neck and chained her to the wall.

Is it really this cold, or am I just afraid? she wondered, unable to stop her shivering.

Deciding it was probably both, Jamie extended her arms, groping in the blackness that surrounded her, hoping to find something she'd missed, however small. Something that might help her escape. She had just enough chain to almost reach the front wall. If she stretched, she could touch the heavy wooden door with her foot. *Terrific,* she thought grimly. *If I get hungry, I can bang for room service.*

When they first led her in, Jamie had managed to get a brief glimpse of her windowless concrete prison. It was about ten feet square, featureless except for a naked bulb hanging from the ceiling. That, and a metal drain in the floor. Pulling her chain to full length, Jamie inched to the far wall. As she did, she stumbled on the final object in the room. The bucket. She had forgotten about that. She found it with her hands, smelling the fetid odor of excrement and something else she couldn't quite identify—cloying yet at the same time nauseous, like the reek of rotting meat. Retching, she set the bucket upright, realizing with disgust that she would have to use it before long.

Following the side wall, Jamie ran her fingers along the concrete. At regular intervals of every ten inches or so, raised horizontal lines broke its surface. She recognized them as marks made by forming planks. It was a poured wall. Solid.

Still using her fingers, she examined her chain next, testing each link—praying for a flaw, a gap in the metal, anything.

She found nothing.

Suddenly she heard a low roar starting up outside her cell, like a powerful engine shuddering to life. Smoother, though. More continuous . . . like a furnace.

A sliver of yellow filtered under the door.

Jamie quickly glanced around, seizing the opportunity to reexamine her cell. As she'd thought, the stark concrete walls offered no hope of escape. She turned her attention to her bonds. Tucking her chin, she could just make out part of a padlock securing the iron shackle circling her neck. The lock was heavily constructed, similar to many she had seen at the hardware store.

The chain appeared unremarkable as well: three-eighths-inch galvanized, each link welded. She followed her tether to its termination. The chain ended in an iron ring that had been spread and rewelded after being passed through the terminal link of her chain. A pin and metal eyelet secured the ring to the wall, several feet above the floor.

Jamie placed her lips close to the wall and blew at the base of the pin, revealing a slight gap between the concrete and the shaft of the pin.

A bolt. They had used an expansion bolt to secure the ring to the wall, she thought. If there's a weak point, that has to be it.

Jamie sat on the floor, placed her feet on either side of the ring, and pulled. Failing with a steady tug, she yanked, using all her strength. The bolt didn't budge.

Though she didn't know how, Jamie abruptly sensed the presence of someone outside her cell. More than one. The dark-haired woman and someone else. Someone old, very old.

"Clean up this garbage," Jamie heard the dark-haired woman named Devon order, her tone as cutting as a knife. Then, creaking, the door to Jamie's cell swung open. As light flooded in, the foul stench Jamie had noted earlier worsened. Her dark-haired captor stood silhouetted in the doorway, her face hidden in shadow. Swallowing hard, Jamie squinted into the glare. "Why are you doing this?" she asked, trying to keep her voice steady. "What do you want?"

No answer came from the dark figure. Not even the slightest intimation she had heard.

Jamie peered into the light, attempting to pierce the shadows masking the woman's face. Though she could see little but an eerie glow that seemed to illuminate her captor's eyes from within, she sensed something about her had changed. A chill prickled Jamie's spine as she realized what it was. The woman was smiling.

Jamie tore her eyes from the woman in the doorway, using the opportunity to search the space beyond. She could make out what appeared to be a number of thick metal bars leaning against a distant wall. Closer to her prison cell she saw a massive table with perforated leather straps—each leather restraint as thick as a barber's strop. A spatter of dark stains covered the table's wooden surface. Across the room, hulking in the gloom, sat a huge furnace. Jamie shivered, realizing she had been right about the source of the roaring sound.

Abruptly, someone else came into view. It was an old woman. As Jamie watched, the woman groped under the massive table, reaching for an oblong metal tub. Straining, the woman began dragging the container across the floor toward the furnace. The stench grew worse. Jamie gagged, her stomach heaving.

The dark-haired woman turned in the doorway. An instant later Jamie's cell door banged shut. But as it did, Jamie saw something spill from the tub, slapping like wet meat onto the floor in front of the furnace. Though it was horribly mutilated, and though Jamie quickly looked away, she had no trouble identifying the severed object that had slopped from the tub.

Outside her cell, the roaring of the furnace increased. Jamie huddled in the corner, covering her ears. And at that moment, in the darkness of her solitary prison, Jamie Callahan realized she was going to die.

*   *   *

"No!" I shouted as the blast from the pistol ripped into Nelson's chest. Shrieking with rage, the neighbor again brought up her weapon. This time I was ready. With a flick of my mind I froze her in place, arm extended, finger on the trigger. A heartbeat later several police officers opened fire.

"Stop!" I yelled.

I was too late. A barrage of gunfire slammed the woman into a holly hedge, copper-jacketed slugs plucking at her coat like invisible fingers. Her body caught on the prickly branches, then slumped to the ground, her death negating any hope I'd had of questioning her.

Choking with frustration, I knelt beside Nelson. A bright red flow welled from his chest, as though some vital dam had broken inside. Nelson lay still, his eyes glazing.

Then Banowski was there, kicking the gun from the woman's lifeless hand. Other officers moved in rapidly, weapons drawn. And then Taryn was there, too. "Oh, sweet Jesus," she whispered when she saw the blood soaking Nelson's coat.

Satisfied that the woman was dead, Banowski leaned over to feel Nelson's throat. He shook his head. "He's gone."

"No," I said. "He's not dead."

"I'm sorry, Mike," said Taryn, placing a hand on my shoulder. "I'm so sorry."

"He's not dead," I repeated.

"Unfortunately, he is," Banowski said, his face flushed, still charged with adrenaline from the gunfight. He grabbed the back of my coat. "On your feet, Callahan. You're under arrest for the murder of your ex-wife. You have the right to remain—"

I looked up. Seeing something in my eyes, Banowski stumbled back in surprise. "What the . . . ?"

I rose to my feet.

Don't move.

Banowski froze, as if turned to stone.

I noted that others nearby were watching us uncertainly. I stepped closer to Banowski and spoke in a low voice.

Have someone bring a car.

As directed, Banowski signaled to the rookie I had seen earlier. "Get a cruiser over here!" he yelled.

As the young officer ran to one of the vehicles parked in the driveway, I again glanced at the other police officers in the yard. Several had moved to surround the fallen woman, but most were still watching Banowski and me. Many of the onlookers across the street were staring at us, too.

"What . . . what are you doing?" asked Taryn, who had moved to stand beside me.

"I'll explain later. Right now I have to get Nelson to a hospital."

"Nelson's dead, Mike."

"No. He's not. Not yet, anyway. I don't know how, but I'm connected to him. I'm keeping him alive. But I can't keep it up much longer. Please trust me, Taryn. I need to get him to a hospital."

Trembling, Taryn stared at me, then at Banowski, "What can I do to help?" she asked.

"You can help by going back to your condo—no, forget that. You said your neighbor waters your plants when you're gone. Does she have a key?"

"Yes," Taryn replied. "Why?"

"Until this is over, you're not going home. I want you to call Willi and have her throw together a few things for you— whatever you'll need for a week or two." I thought a moment, then added, "What did you do with my clothes, the ones I had on when I arrived?"

"They're on top of the washing machine."

"Good. Have Willi check for some papers in my pants pocket. Tell her to bring everything to you someplace away from your condo. And tell her to make sure she isn't followed," I added. I was fairly certain that it was still too soon for the man I'd eliminated outside Taryn's condo to have been replaced, but I didn't want to take any chances.

And then?"

"You and I will meet later. I need those papers," I answered. "After which, you're getting out of L.A."

"I told you, I'm not running away."

"Don't you realize what just happened here?" I demanded. "You could be next."

"But—"

"You made a promise, Taryn, and I'm holding you to it. Do you have a place to go, somewhere nobody knows about?"

"My sister lives in Fresno," Taryn said reluctantly. "I suppose I could stay with her."

"No good. They could trace you too easily. Someplace else."

Taryn paused. "Well, my folks owned a getaway cabin in Montana near Kalispell, right on Flathead Lake," she said. "After Dad died, my sister and brothers and I decided to keep it. Nobody's been up there for years."

"Perfect. The drive will take a few days. Stay there until you hear from me."

"Until I hear from you? But—"

"If I'm alive when this is over, I'll find you," I interrupted. "I promise."

By then the young LAPD officer had wheeled his cruiser up Susan's driveway, crossed a bricked terrace, and fishtailed across the lawn. Tires skidding on the damp grass, he pulled to a stop nearby.

I turned back to Banowski, who was still standing frozen. "Do you know who I am?" I asked softly.

"Callahan," he answered, barely moving his lips.

I'm not the man you want.

Something changed in Banowski's eyes. "You're not the man I want," he repeated.

The woman who shot Lieutenant Long knew nothing of Susan's murder.

Banowski nodded. "She knew nothing of your wife's murder."

I'm taking Nelson to UCLA. You won't stop me. And you will remember nothing of what just happened.

Banowski's eyes fluttered for an instant. Then, with a mental tap, I released him.

Dazed, he glanced around the yard, then back at me.

"Where's the nearest trauma-care unit?" I asked.

"This time of night, UCLA is probably best," he answered. "Listen, Callahan. I'm sorry about—"

"Later," I interrupted. "Help me get Nelson into the car. I'm taking him to UCLA."

Finally coming out of his fog, Banowski signaled to several officers nearby. They hurried over. At my direction, they helped Banowski and me place Nelson's body in the back seat. When that was done, I climbed into the front beside the young officer already behind the wheel. "Get on the radio and tell them we're bringing in a gunshot victim," I said to Banowski, rolling down the passenger window.

"Right," he said. "Get moving, Callahan."

"I'll meet you at the hospital, Mike," called Taryn.

Before I could reply, the cruiser's engine roared to life. Lights flashing, we crossed the yard, hopped a curb, and shot down Hartzell. Grimly watching a parade of houses slipping past my open window, I sat in the front seat, feeling my life draining into Nelson.

It felt like I was bleeding. Somehow Nelson was feeding on me, as I had fed upon others. But how long could it go on? "I'm sorry, Nelson," I said aloud, glancing into the rear seat where my friend lay unmoving, as still as death.

"Seems like I'm poison to everyone around me," I added softly. "Susan, and Jamie, and now you. I'm not certain you can hear me, but I know you're in there, and I promise you this: I won't let you die."

Chapter Twenty

I glanced up to see Taryn hurrying toward me across the nearly deserted UCLA Medical Center surgical waiting area. I was sitting alone in a corner, cradling my head in my hands.

"Sorry I couldn't get here sooner," she said as she arrived. "The police wanted to get my statement, and I—" She stopped short when she saw my face. "My God, Mike. Are you all right?"

"I'm okay," I mumbled. I had looked at myself in the bathroom mirror earlier, and I knew what she was seeing. Deep lines creased my face; folds of flesh hung loose under my eyes. Even my hair seemed to have grayed over the past hours. I looked old, as though life itself had been drained from me. Which it had.

"How's . . . how's Nelson?" Taryn stammered, clearly shaken by my appearance.

"Still in surgery," I answered wearily. "When we got here, the emergency room staff didn't believe he was alive. It took some convincing," I added. "I'm not connected to him anymore. Once they got the life-support machines hooked up, there was nothing more I could do."

Taryn sat beside me. "What happened to you?"

"Keeping Nelson alive took a lot out of me," I replied. "A lot more than I expected. I'll be fine, though. I just need to . . . *eat*."

Understanding flared in Taryn's eyes. She looked away, struggling to conceal her revulsion. "Sorry," she said. "I don't mean to judge."

"It doesn't matter," I said with a tired shrug. "In your place, I would probably feel the same."

Color rose to Taryn's face, turning the thin scar on her chin livid white. "Don't tell me how I feel," she shot back. "You have no idea how I feel."

"Maybe. As I said, it doesn't matter anymore."

Taryn started to ask what I meant by that, hesitating as a thin, wiry Asian man wearing green surgical scrubs entered the room and began making his way toward us. We both stood as he arrived. I stuck my injured hand into my pocket to conceal it. "How's Nelson?" I asked. "Is he going to be all right?"

The man looked at me, then at Taryn. "I'm Doctor Watanabe," he said, not offering to shake hands. "And you two are . . . ?"

"Friends of the family," Taryn replied. Glancing at me, she added, "Speaking of which, did anyone call—"

"I asked someone at the desk to telephone Rochelle," I said, anticipating her question. "She should be here soon." Then, to the doctor, "How is Nelson?"

Dr. Watanabe pinched the bridge of his nose, clearly exhausted. "I should wait to talk to the immediate family, but to tell you the truth, I . . . I don't know what to say. I've never seen anything like what happened here tonight," he replied wearily.

"What do you mean?" Taryn asked.

Dr. Watanabe hesitated, then continued. "By all rights, Lieutenant Long should be dead. When he came in he had no pulse, his respiration was zero, and his eyes were fixed and dilated. An emergency room physician had already pronounced him when one of the nurses saw him blink. Everyone thought she'd imagined it, but she kept insisting he was alive. Apparently caused quite a stir. Anyway, when the ER physician reexamined Lieutenant Long, his vital signs were still nonexistent—except that now his eyes were open and alert."

"So he *was* alive," said Taryn.

Dr. Watanabe shrugged. "Depends on what you call alive," he went on, seeming as if he needed to talk to someone, anyone—even if we weren't family. "When the ER staff transferred your friend to surgery, I examined him myself. He *still* had no pulse, no blood pressure, no respiration. Nevertheless, though I don't understand how, when we got him into the operating room his EEG showed normal activity—even though the blood supply to his brain had been cut off for almost forty minutes."

"That happens sometimes, doesn't it?" Taryn asked, again glancing at me. "People are revived as much as an hour after drowning, right?"

"It's rare, but possible," Dr. Watanabe conceded. "Usually though, irreversible damage occurs as early as six minutes after the oxygen supply to the brain is stopped. The only exceptions are cases in which victims have been submerged in very cold water. In all such cases the victim invariably loses consciousness. This was different. Lieutenant Long's body temperature was normal, and somehow, for much of the time we were working on him, he was conscious. For him, that had to be the most terrible . . ."

The surgeon rubbed his chin. "Anyway, there's more. Because your friend initially had no respiration or circulation, it was impossible to sedate him or even to administer pain meds until we got him on heart-lung support. His eyes were alert the whole time we were opening his chest. He was . . . watching us." The doctor hesitated a moment, lost in thought. "Another thing. When we cracked his chest, we found that his blood hadn't begun the postmortem clotting changes normally associated with a cessation of circulation," he continued. "It was as if everything had somehow been put on hold."

Doctor Watanabe ran his fingers through his hair, appearing progressively mystified. "The bullet severed his aorta and right pulmonary artery, along with several lesser vessels," he went on. "Injuries of that type are routinely fatal, with the victim rapidly exsanguinating—bleeding to death. In this case that didn't happen. Again, I have no explanation."

"But he's going to recover?" asked Taryn.

"It's too early to tell," Dr. Watanabe hedged. "But he has a good chance."

"When can we see him?" I asked.

"He's sleeping. Perhaps tomorrow, if there are no complications." The physician checked his watch. "I'm sorry, I have to go. Please tell Mrs. Long to page me when she arrives."

"We will," I said. "And Doc . . . thanks."

After the surgeon departed, Taryn turned to me, wonder filling her eyes. "You saved him, Mike. You really did."

I looked away, thinking that if it hadn't been for me, Nelson wouldn't have needed saving. "Are your bags in the car?"

Reluctantly, Taryn nodded. "Yes, but—"

"Good. Here." I thrust a thick roll of currency into her hand. "Please wait until Rochelle arrives and let her know what's happening. Tell her I'm sorry and . . . tell her I'll call her. Then it's time for you to get out of town. Pay cash for everything on your way to Montana. Don't use your credit card. And don't use your cell phone, either. Most important, don't tell anyone where you're going. And I mean *anyone*."

"You don't have to be alone in this, Mike. Are you sure this is what you want?"

"I'm sure," I said. "If you don't hear from me in a couple of weeks, come back and forget you ever knew me. One more thing. Did Willi find those papers I asked for?"

"The ones in your pants pocket?" Taryn rummaged through her purse, pulled out a wad of invoices, and handed them to me. "What are they? Hotel records?"

"Yeah." I scanned the itemized list I'd taken from the desk clerk at the Meliá. I quickly found what I wanted—Devon's long-distance telephone charges.

"Do you have your cell phone with you?" I asked.

Taryn searched her purse again, found her phone, and handed it to me.

"Until this is over, this will be the last time this phone gets used," I said.

Taryn nodded. "I understand."

With a sickening feeling of certainty, I punched in the phone number Devon had called from the Meliá. A pause. Then a phone at the other end rang once . . . twice . . .

A recorded message came on. "You have reached the Manhattan offices of the Elysian Foundation. Office hours are Monday through Friday between eight A.M. and five P.M. Please call back during that time."

Angrily, I disconnected.

"What is it?" asked Taryn.

"I just got final confirmation that Devon Summers, aka Devon Varkoff, played me for a fool," I answered. "As I said earlier, I'm in more trouble than I thought, if that's even possible. I have to find Jamie—" My voice broke as I recalled my daughter's hysterical sobs.

"I want to help, Mike," said Taryn. "Please let me."

"Thanks, but I can't risk it," I said. I removed the battery from Taryn's phone and handed the phone and battery back to her. "I have to do this alone. Good-bye, Taryn. Take care of yourself. And please tell Rochelle that she and Nelson will be in my thoughts and prayers."

Taryn called after me as I started for the exit. "How are you going to find Jamie?"

"I'm not sure," I replied without looking back. "But I have a good idea where to start."

Chapter Twenty-one

Pulse quickening, Devon Varkoff opened a door that accessed a closet beneath her entry staircase. Smiling, she stepped inside. The large, roomy recess she entered had, at one time or another, served as a storage locker, a coat closet, and a utility room. But regardless of the role the space had played over the years, one thing about it had never changed: A section of paneling at the rear had always remained unobstructed.

Closing the closet door behind her, Devon paused, letting her anticipation grow. Then, almost greedily, she pressed a concealed latch. With a muffled click, a section of wall paneling slid back, revealing a ponderous oak door with thick metal straps running from each of the door's four hinges. Tipping her head, Devon gathered her hair from her neck and slipped off the delicate chain that held her gold key. Excitement growing, she inserted the key into a slot in the door. The key turned easily, sending back a hidden bolt. Placing a hand on the door's rough surface, she shoved. Hinges squealing in protest, the heavy door swung inward, revealing a staircase leading down.

Devon paused on a landing at the top, peering into the darkness. She could have easily turned on a light. Habitually she chose not to, preferring instead to enter her secret realm in darkness. Somehow it heightened the experience for her. Besides, she knew the location of everything in the labyrinthine rooms below as well as she knew the reaches and limits of her own body.

As she stood, sounds came to her through the darkness: the creak of a beam, the whir of a sump pump, the slow drip of water into one of her stainless-steel sinks. Placing her hand on the staircase railing, Devon descended, counting the steps as she went.

Twenty-three, twenty-four, twenty-five.

Sixteen feet below her mansion's main floor, she stopped on the first landing, which accessed an intermediate loft level filled with a warren of rooms and passageways. The loft's heavy planks partially hid the basement's deepest chamber, which lay another twenty feet farther down the stairs.

Years before, prior to the Hamptons becoming a fashionable retreat for New York's rich and famous, Devon had built her rambling estate on a tract of secluded acreage overlooking Georgica Cove. The grounds outside her house were protected by a guarded gate and an electrified fence that ran the entire length of a thirty-foot-tall hedge surrounding her property— privacy measures that often caused passersby to comment on the estate's fortresslike quality. Over the decades, however, more than one unfortunate guest had discovered the true nature of Devon's security precautions. Upon entering her gates, her home became a prison.

Starting out once more, Devon entered the intermediate level and made her way forward in the darkness, moving from chamber to chamber. She explored with her hands as she went, touching each apparatus she encountered in turn—running her fingers over leather restraints, metal buckles, blades, irons, pliers—occasionally lingering on items that for her held some special memory. Many of her devices, like the giant wheel used for slow disarticulation or the iron boot into which one could pour scalding oil, dated back to the Middle Ages. Most were diabolically simple, had few moving parts, and required little maintenance. More important, all were still in excellent repair.

Walking slowly, Devon traversed a narrow passageway and entered what she knew to be a large, open area. Here she proceeded cautiously, knowing that farther back the floor suddenly gave way to the deepest chamber beneath her mansion—a cavernous space hewn from solid bedrock. The unprotected drop was, in Devon's estimation, one of her basement's most utilitarian features, for over the years it had proved ideal for activities requiring suspension of a victim from above. Inching forward, she peered into the chasm. In the faint glimmer of a flickering pilot light, she could make out the outline of an enormous furnace below. More an oven, actually, its construction had been modeled after the giant crematoriums used in Germany during the war. The furnace's features included a large vent and auxiliary blower to supply fresh air from the outside, as well as an exhaust chimney equipped with afterburner scrubbers to remove any noxious smells that might offend neighbors. Over the years the oven had served Devon not only to warm the chambers beneath her house, but also to eliminate certain troublesome materials whose nature precluded conventional disposal.

Devon considered the oven to be one of her finest designs. But there was another nearby in which she took even more pride. And pleasure. She regarded it now in the dim light, studying a monstrous orb hanging over the pit like an oversized Christmas ornament—hinged on one side, split apart and waiting—each hemisphere lined with daggerlike spikes.

The iron cage.

Contemplating the enjoyment that would soon be hers, Devon felt a shiver of anticipation course through her. For a moment she considered immediately taking her pleasure. No, she told herself, irritated by her weakness. The child could wait. In time the girl would bring an even bigger fish into her net.

After leaving Mike Callahan in Mexico, Devon had followed his development with growing interest. She had taught him much without his being aware she was doing so, helping him explore a nature he had long attempted to deny. And the cost had been minimal. Now his education was nearly complete. If he lived, he would prove either a powerful ally or a worthy opponent, neither of which she had experienced in a very long time. Either way, in the end he would come to her, his head lowered and horns shining, charging straight and true. And then she would take him *recibiendo*—upstairs, as consort, or in these chambers beneath her mansion, as sustenance.

Perhaps both.

And afterward, in the fullness of time, she would have the child as well.

Tomorrow . . . or the day after.

Soon.

Part Three

Tercio de Muerte

Chapter Twenty-two

"What's with you, Tyler? Somethin' got your pantyhose in a bunch?"

Tyler took a sip of tepid coffee, struggling to control his anger. Without answering, he turned and stared out the car window, carefully inspecting Mike Callahan's house down the street. No change.

Tyler sighed. Night stakeouts were bad enough, but pulling a double shift with a punk like the assistant sitting beside him was making this one torture. Tyler's head ached, his back hurt, and he hadn't slept for days. He knew it wouldn't take much to send him over the edge.

"Givin' me the silent treatment, huh?"

"Shut up, Carlos."

"It speaks," Carlos crowed. "Well, that's a start. C'mon, man, talk to me. We gotta do somethin' to pass the time."

Tyler set his coffee on the dashboard, turning toward the garbage they had given him as a tool. The punk's hair was greased back from his forehead, and a tattooed tear dribbled from the corner of one eye, proclaiming to anyone who knew what it meant that Carlos had made his bones. Real class. Tyler thought about simply killing his sorry helper right then—just marching him around the back of Callahan's house and drowning him in the canal. Later he could say the kid wandered off, got in a fight, whatever.

No, he thought nervously. If Devon caught him in a lie . . .

But what could go wrong? Either Callahan showed up, or he didn't. If he didn't, no sweat. And if he did—well, Tyler could handle that, too. Payback time for what Callahan did to Roscoe that night in the parking garage. Payback time, just like Devon had said. Either way, Carlos's disappearance would probably never be noticed. Still . . .

Carlos jabbed a grimy finger into a paper sack sitting on the seat between them, exploring the paper-wrapped remainder of a fast-food breakfast sandwich Tyler had bought earlier. "You gonna eat this?"

"Not anymore," Tyler answered, thinking that the punk had no idea how close he was to crossing the line. Standard operating procedure on an assignment like this called for using a disposable pawn to take the fall. Enter Carlos. Tyler knew that if the necessity arose, he wouldn't hesitate to kill his irritating assistant. And if there were any possibility of making things painful, that's the way it would go down.

Carlos devoured the rest of Tyler's sandwich, washed it down with a swig of Coke, and belched. "Mind if I smoke?" he asked, leaning back in his seat.

When Tyler didn't respond, Carlos pulled a crumpled joint from his pocket. After straightening the joint and lighting it, he took a few tokes, carefully blowing smoke out the window. Something about Tyler made him jumpy. Carlos couldn't put his finger on it, but the guy was . . . well, *spooky*. And when Carlos was nervous, he talked. "What's so important about this Callahan guy?" he asked.

"None of your business."

"Clue me in, man. We've been sittin' on this dude's house so long my ass is cracked. He ain't never gonna show, is he? But if he does, I get to pop him, right?" Carlos grinned, stroking the butt of a pistol protruding from his belt.

"Sure," said Tyler. "You can plug him—once I'm finished with him. At that point you'll be doin' him a favor."

Carlos's grin broadened. "Okay by me. Hey, let's move the car closer. We're so far down the block, he coulda slipped in already and we'd never know."

"If he comes anywhere near, I'll know."

"You mean like how you knew when that broad showed up? Callahan's old lady?"

"Yeah. Like that." Tyler recalled the hours he'd spent with the Callahan woman—Sally, Sarah, whatever her name was. He hadn't had as much fun as he would have liked . . . but enough.

"That was radical what you done to her, man. How'd you do that? Can you show me?"

"No," Tyler snapped, weary of their conversation. "Don't you get it, dirtbag? You either have it or you don't. And you don't. So shut up."

"No need to get nasty."

Tyler pressed his thumbs to his temples. His headache was worse. If Callahan didn't arrive soon, he decided to just do Carlos, leave, and worry about the consequences later.

"How come you're so sure Callahan is gonna turn up here, anyway?" Carlos persisted.

"I'm not," said Tyler. Christ, the kid just wouldn't shut up.

"But you told me all the stuff we were gonna do to him when he gets here. Not *if* he gets here, but *when.* I thought—"

"You thought wrong." Tyler finished his coffee and crushed the paper cup. True, *he* hadn't thought Callahan would show up here again, but Devon had. She had known somehow, just like she knew a lot of things. "Sooner or later, Callahan will return to his house," she had told him with absolute conviction. "When he does, I want you there. I think there will be a surprise in it for both of you."

Recalling Devon's words, Tyler shifted uncomfortably, wondering what she had meant by that last bit. For that matter, why had she insisted on his being here at all? Callahan might be a chump, but he wasn't stupid. No way he'd be coming back to his house—especially after what had gone down at his ex-wife's. But Devon had seemed so certain. Why?

Then another thought occurred. Maybe Devon had some dirty little secret, something she wasn't sharing. As Tyler tried to puzzle it out, Carlos pulled out his piece, a nickel-plated .32 automatic. It was a woman's gun in Tyler's opinion, but still deadly at close range. Carlos passed it from hand to hand, then practiced sighting on a mailbox down the street. Tiring of that, he withdrew the magazine from the butt, checked the loads, and slammed it home again.

"Get rid of that till I tell you," Tyler grunted.

"Anything you say. You're the man." But instead of putting away the weapon, Carlos racked the slide and chambered a round.

"Didn't you hear me, asshole? I said put it away."

Strangely, Carlos acted *exactly* as though he hadn't heard. Instead of doing as he'd been told, he stared straight ahead, his eyes vacant. Then he turned. "Who gives you your orders?" he demanded. "For instance, who ordered you to be here tonight?

"Who said anything about orders?"

"It's obvious you're just some sadistic piece of trash who's following orders," said Carlos. "It was a woman, right? What's her name?"

Tyler couldn't believe his ears. "You greasy turd," he snapped, deciding right then that Carlos was dead. "Nobody talks to me that way."

"First time for everything," Carlos replied casually, his voice sounding changed somehow. "Tell you what. Start talking and I'll let you live. Where's Callahan's daughter? Where's Jamie?"

Tyler popped a knuckle, trying to decide how best to kill Carlos—drowning him in the canal as he'd previously contemplated, or simply blowing his brains out.

"I'm waiting, Tyler."

"You'll do your waiting in hell, asshole." Focusing all his power, Tyler *pushed.*

Gimme the gun.

Carlos laughed. "You want the gun? Take it."

Tyler *pushed* again. And a third time. Nothing happened. Something inside Carlos had turned as hard as granite.

"Who . . . who are you?" Tyler stammered, feeling a sudden prickle of fear. No answer came. Instead, Carlos's gun locked on a point just above the bridge of Tyler's nose. "I'll . . . I'll talk," Tyler said quickly.

Carlos smiled. "It's different when you're on the other end, isn't it?"

"Please, I'll tell you anything you wanna know. Just please don't . . ."

"Sorry, Tyler. Now that it's come to this, I wouldn't know whether you were telling the truth. No, there's only one thing to do."

"Please . . ."

"You don't think I'd shoot you?" Carlos said coldly. "That would be too easy. Here, I'll show you what I mean." In one brisk motion he jammed the gun into his own mouth and jerked the trigger.

A deafening explosion rocked the car. A chunk of Carlos's skull lifted from the back of his head, spattering a pudding of blood and brains on the headliner.

Tyler covered his ringing ears, staring at the pulpy mess that had once been Carlos. Suddenly he was aware of a presence outside. He turned. A dark figure stood beside the car, not two feet away. How had he arrived unnoticed? Tyler felt a chill, noting something familiar about the man. But, oh Jesus, his eyes were . . .

"Callahan?" Tyler whispered. He risked a look at Carlos's body, gauging his chances of grabbing the gun.

"Don't even try."

Tyler smiled nervously. "I wasn't—"

Shut up.

Without warning, Tyler found himself unable to move, unable to turn away from eyes that were tunneling like hot pokers into his brain.

No secrets, Tyler. You're going to tell me everything, a voice spoke inside his skull.

A feeling of bottomless despair gripped Tyler as he sensed the tendrils of another consciousness flooding his mind. He tried to resist. He couldn't. The other was far too strong.

As he spiraled down into his own private hell, Tyler heard the other's thoughts once again. *One more thing*, the disembodied voice echoed in his mind. *When I said I'd let you live . . . I lied.*

Chapter Twenty-three

Detective John Banowski sat outside the all-night burger joint, morosely watching a string of cars rumbling past on Lincoln Avenue. Though it was barely light out, a steady stream of traffic had already jammed both freeway-bound lanes, piling up at a traffic signal on Pico. Banowski took a swig of Coke, wondering what all those assholes were doing up so early—going to work, coming back from a night out, sticking up a liquor store?

Giving up on the mystery, Banowski finished his chili-cheeseburger and considered ordering another. In his opinion, *Tommy's* made the best burgers in town—thick, juicy, and smothered in chili, cheese, and onions—exactly the way he liked them. Too bad his stomach didn't feel likewise. Maybe he should have skipped the chili, he thought sadly, fighting a case of heartburn that had been stoking in his gut ever since he'd left the crime scene in the Palisades.

As usual after investigating a case like that, Banowski had been unable to sleep. Last night he hadn't even tried. Later he would feel rotten at work, but anything was better than spending another sleepless night at home.

The first thing he'd done after leaving the murder scene was to head over to UCLA Medical Center and check on Lieutenant Long. He wound up spending most of the night at the hospital. Despite all the contradictions the evening had brought, Banowski was certain of one thing: Lieutenant Long had been dead. If Banowski had learned one thing during his years on the homicide unit, it was how to tell when somebody was dead. And Long had definitely been dead. Now the surgeon was saying he was going to make it. It didn't add up.

Other things about the case didn't add up, either. None of the witnesses' statements jibed. Everyone seemed to have seen something different. Some of their stories even bordered on the bizarre. Granted, he had been wrong about Callahan. This time the killing hadn't been done by the victim's nearest and dearest, but the brutality of the murder and the daughter's hysterical phone message made no sense. And the lady next door, a solid citizen according to neighbors, shooting Lieutenant Long—how did *that* fit in?

Banowski levered himself from the plastic bench and headed back to the counter, deciding that if he had to endure a case of heartburn, he might as well go all the way. He had just finished ordering a second burger and a side of fries when his cell phone rang.

"Banowski," he said, answering his phone.

"Detective Banowski, this is Sergeant Kingsford, West L.A. Sorry to call so early, but we need you down here ASAP."

"What's up?" asked Banowski, motioning for the counterman to cancel his order.

"We have some guy in custody named Gregory Tyler. He just walked in off the street. Said he wanted to talk to you. Ever heard of him?"

"Nope."

"Well, apparently he's heard of you. What's more, he's been on the Feds' want-list for years—armed robbery, murder, unlawful flight, and so forth. Claims he wants to make a statement, but he'll only do it if you're present." Kingsford paused. "Listen, everyone heard what happened to your lieutenant," he added quietly. "Some of the guys are heading over to the hospital when their shift's over."

"Yeah, I was gonna drop by again myself," Banowski mumbled.

"Maybe I'll see you there. In the meantime, get down here fast, okay? The captain wants to get Tyler's statement before the FBI hotshots show up."

"No problem," said Banowski, already heading for his car.

Chapter Twenty-four

Jamie huddled in her cell, listening. Coming from somewhere in the chamber outside she could hear the steady drip of a faucet, along with the hiss of the furnace. Otherwise, nothing. Nevertheless, she sensed a presence outside her door as surely as she felt her own heart pounding in her chest.

She's there. Just beyond the door.

With a plunge of terror, Jamie pressed her back to the concrete wall, wishing she could hide. From the chamber beyond her cell came a feeling of anticipation, and of growing excitement, and of ravenous, unrelenting *hunger*.

At last, after what seemed forever, Jamie felt the woman leave.

How long before she comes back? Jamie wondered. *There has to be a way out of here. Think. There has to be a way, something . . .*

Think!

Once more, though she didn't understand how, Jamie sent her consciousness into the space outside her cell. This time she sensed nothing. The chamber beyond was deserted. But how did she know?

All her life Jamie had experienced queer premonitions, unexplained *feelings* that seemed to rise unbidden in her mind. As a child she had astounded adults with an uncanny ability to guess who was at the door, to divine the contents of a wrapped package, to uncover the most carefully guarded secrets. At first she'd thought everyone had that ability. Later, when she discovered otherwise, Jamie began to hide her strange gift, eventually suppressing it altogether. Now it was back. Why?

The darkness? Jamie moved a hand in front of her face, unable to discern anything at all. *I've never been in total darkness before, not really. There's always been at least some light. Is this what it's like to be blind?*

Jamie knew that blind persons routinely developed a heightened acuity of their other senses—smell, hearing, touch, taste. Is that what was happening to her? Or had the woman's presence simply awakened a power in her that had long lain dormant?

Who cares? Jamie thought. *The important thing is—can I use it?*

Think!

The woman who'd taken her prisoner had wielded her power like a bludgeon—pushing, prodding, bending others to her will. Strangely, no one in the airport or on the plane had been aware of her doing it. It seemed to Jamie that she alone had sensed the hideous force emanating from the woman. Again, why?

Is it because I'm like her?

No! Jamie recoiled at the thought.

Why not? After all, what do you know of her?

One by one, Jamie mentally ticked off the things she knew of her captor. First: The dark-haired woman possessed an ability to force others to do whatever she wanted, and for some reason only Jamie seemed aware of it. Second: The woman's capacity for cruelty seemed boundless. Third: The woman hadn't chosen Susan at random, nor had she taken Jamie without a reason. Something else was involved. Some*one* else.

Dad?

You're missing something. Come on, think!

Suddenly Jamie recalled the ghostly voice she had heard on the plane. The voice had come from *inside* her captor, but it hadn't actually been the woman. How could that be, unless . . .

What had Devon said when she'd awakened?

I see you've been visiting with my companion.

Was someone else, *a separate entity*, living inside Devon?

Jamie tried to bring back the words she had heard in her mind. In a rush they returned. *Mine. What you see is mine. Devon took my body . . . stole it from me.*

Finally understanding, Jamie shuddered, trying to imagine living trapped inside her own body, a body that someone else controlled—sensing the world around her but unable to act, stripped of everything save her own thoughts. Compared with sharing herself with someone as evil as Devon, anything would be preferable. Even death.

Snap out of it! You're not dead yet. The voice said something else. What?

All at once she had it. She replayed it again and again, puzzling over its meaning.

She's afraid of you. But you'll never get away. Never, never, never.

She's afraid of you. But you'll never get away . . .

She's afraid of you . . .

She's afraid of you . . .

Her thoughts turning inward, Jamie weighed myriad options and possibilities—testing, probing, exploring. Someone watching might have thought her asleep. But Jamie did not sleep. And hours later, her internal voyage bore fruit. Though tenuous, she seized upon it and held tightly, clinging to something now as vital to her as life itself.

At last, Jamie had hope.

Chapter Twenty-five

I stood in the airport boarding area, impatiently waiting for my call to go through. Minutes earlier I had "borrowed" a cell phone from an unwary traveler, someone who would never remember meeting me after I returned it.

"Times. Hank McCaffery's office," a female voice finally answered.

"Sonja, this is Callahan. I need to speak to McCaffery."

"He said he doesn't want to talk to you, Mike."

"I'm not surprised. Listen, it's important. Could you get him anyway? Please?"

"Well, for you . . . I'll risk a lecture from the boss," the secretary reluctantly agreed. "I'll have to track him down. He's not in his office."

"Thanks, Sonja." I checked a clock on the LAX departures board: 6:55 A.M. "Make it quick, okay? I don't have much time."

As I waited, I swept my eyes over the crowded room. I could see nearly everyone in the semicircular boarding area—business commuters, families, college students. I quickly touched the mind of each, finding nothing threatening. But upon completing my search, I found myself strangely disappointed. Taking the life of Tyler's accomplice had gone a long way toward restoring what I'd lost keeping Nelson alive. With a surge of shame, I realized I *wanted* trouble to find me.

I was still hungry.

"Callahan? McCaffery's voice came on the line. "Give me one good reason why I shouldn't hang up on you right now."

"To tell you the truth, Hank, I can't," I replied. "At least not one you're going to buy over the phone. I'm asking as a friend. Give me two minutes."

"Two minutes. The clock's running."

"Thanks, Hank. First of all, Taryn is leaving for a few weeks. She'll be back when things cool down."

"What do you mean, when things cool down? Have you got her in some kind of trouble? Damn it, Mike—"

"She's fine, at least for now," I broke in again. "I sent her away. They . . . they killed Susan," I added, my voice breaking at the memory. With the thought of Susan came a sudden, almost paralyzing sense of loss. With an effort of will I focused my mind on the present, promising myself there would be time to mourn Susan later. Right now I had to find Jamie. "They kidnapped my daughter, too. And it was all because of me. Taryn could have been next."

"Mike, I'm . . . I'm sorry," said McCaffery, his tone softening. "I'm so sorry. I didn't know. But who—?"

"I don't have time to explain. Please just listen. Early this morning, an FBI fugitive named Gregory Tyler gave a statement to West L.A. homicide detectives." I paused, remembering the difficulty I'd had refraining from killing Tyler outright, instead marching him into the West L.A. police station and forcing his confession. "Believe me, it's a statement you'll want to hear," I continued. "Ask to speak with Detective John Banowski. By the way, during the past week Tyler visited you at the newspaper more than once."

"I don't remember—"

"It doesn't matter. What's important is that Tyler has confessed to being complicit in the murder of Arthur Bellamy. Tyler showed up in one of the pictures I took at the fundraiser, which could explain why the photos disappeared."

"You mean the nonexistent photos."

"They exist. The police have them now. Contact Detective Banowski or Lieutenant Long."

"Back up a sec," said McCaffery. "An off-duty patrol officer killed Bellamy. How does Tyler fit in?"

"It's complicated, but he and the people for whom he works forced the patrol officer to shoot Bellamy," I explained. "They used some sort of brainwashing, hypnosis, blackmail, whatever," I added, knowing that there was no way McCaffery was ready for the truth. "The important thing is that the police are taking Tyler's confession seriously, and that's definitely news. There's more. Bellamy's election committee kept a list of contributors. Guess who paid for Tyler's meal at the fundraiser."

"Who?"

"The Elysian Foundation. Ring a bell?"

"Yeah. That's Exner's company. At least it was before he divested. How do you know all this?"

"I can't tell you, except to say I've had an inside track on things from the beginning."

"I'll have to accept that—for now," McCaffery said. "I'm going to have someone contact Exner and the Elysian Foundation for statements. You head over to West L.A. and—"

"Hold on, Hank. You fired me."

"So I'm hiring you back. Get your ass—"

"Sorry," I interrupted. "Thanks for the offer, but I have other business."

Other business. With a surge of anger, my thoughts turned to what I had learned during my foray into the sewer of Tyler's mind. I knew what had happened to Susan. I knew where Jamie was being held. And I knew who was responsible. I knew it all.

"Mike—"

"Good-bye, Hank."

Minutes later, wearing dark glasses and a leather jacket, I walked to American Airlines boarding gate sixty-seven. An agent there glanced up from a computer screen as I approached. Disregarding others waiting in line, I leaned across the counter and spoke quietly to the agent. The man's eyes fluttered briefly, as though he were having a minor seizure. Then, with a cheerful smile, he abandoned his station and ushered me through the boarding gate to the plane beyond.

The plane was almost ready for takeoff. I spoke briefly to a cabin attendant upon entering the aircraft. Ignoring other passengers already aboard, I took one of several empty seats in the first-class section, fastened my seat belt, and closed my eyes.

At 7:17 A.M., flight 185 nonstop to New York Kennedy International cleared the runway at LAX, banked over the ocean, and climbed into the rising sun. As the jetliner leveled out at

33,000 feet, for the first time in my life while traveling on an aircraft, I slept.

And as I slept, I dreamed. Racing toward a fate that seemed to have been ordained for me from the very beginning, I dreamed of a stone battlement on a moonless night, and of a torch flickering in the forest, and of an imperious hooded monarch, and of a hideous nocturne that drew me ever onward into the past.

Chapter Twenty-six

Once more Jamie was aware of a presence outside her cell. As before, she focused her mind. She sensed someone descending a flight of stairs. But this time whoever approached was proceeding at a slow, plodding pace, not stealthily as before.

Not her. *The other one, the old woman.*

Jamie closed her eyes and concentrated, probing with a part of her consciousness that seemed to be growing stronger with each use.

Pain. A weary, rheumatic throb . . . bending to ease the ache in her back. Her breath coming hard, and something in her right hand—a wire handle—biting deep into her palm. Turning on the middle landing, then proceeding down, wooden stair treads rough under her bare feet. Standing in front of a door now, bending to set down her load. A bucket. Then gnarled fingers reaching for an iron bolt . . .

Jamie scrambled to her feet. Somehow she had been inside someone else's skin, seeing through someone else's eyes . . .

No! It isn't possible.

Or is it? Isn't it similar to what the dark-haired woman did when she forced me to—

Jamie clamped down on her thoughts. An instant later her cell door creaked open. In a faint glow from the furnace, Jamie recognized the old woman whom she had first seen dragging the metal tub. The woman stood hunched in the doorway, a bucket at her feet. Jamie stared in wonder, struck by the enormity of what she had just done. And she *had* done it. She didn't know how, nor, at the moment, did she care. Because maybe, just maybe . . .

The woman bent to lift the bucket, slopping water as she raised it. Without looking at Jamie, she set the bucket inside the cell so Jamie could reach it, then turned to go.

"Wait!"

The woman stopped. Even in the dim light Jamie could see that she was incredibly old, her wrinkled skin hanging like a loose garment on her bones.

"Will you help me?"

The woman shrank back.

"Please! I have to get out of here. I'll pay you anything. My dad has money, and so does my . . ."

At the thought of her mother, Jamie's voice caught in her throat.

Glancing furtively over her shoulder, the woman retreated another step and began closing the door.

"Don't!" Jamie pleaded. "Please don't shut me in."

The door continued to close. Only a small rectangle of light remained. Then a crack, a slit . . .

"No!" Jamie cried.

The woman fumbled at the bolt.

"No!" Jamie screamed again. Then, with a feeling of profound, almost paradoxical release, she felt something well up inside her. Giving vent to her frustration, she lashed out at the woman in an explosive burst.

Stop.

Jamie had no more understanding of what she had just done than does a fledgling spreading its wings to leave the nest. But it worked. Experimenting with her newfound ability, Jamie struck at the woman once more.

Open the door.

The door to Jamie's cell swung open.

Stooped and pathetic, the woman cowered in the doorway. Seeing her there, Jamie guiltily recalled a similar horror she had experienced at the hands of her own captor. *Worry about that later*, Jamie told herself. *Just get out of here. And do it fast.*

She focused her mind.

Release me.

The woman winced as though she'd been struck, but she made no move to comply.

Taking the chain in her hands, Jamie repeated her command.

Release me.

Tears trickling from her rheumy eyes, the woman glanced away. Though she seemed willing to comply, for some reason she was unable. With a sinking feeling, Jamie demanded, "Who has the key?"

The woman's eyes darted back up the stairs.

"She has them? What about tools, then? A bolt cutter, a hacksaw . . . ?"

The woman shook her head.

Jamie's mind raced. It couldn't end this way. There had to be something. Abruptly she remembered the metal bars she had seen across the room. She peered past the woman. Almost hidden in the gloom, the bars were leaning against a wall near the table she had noticed earlier.

Bring one of those bars.

Heart in her throat, Jamie watched as the woman shuffled across the floor. After passing the table, the woman picked up a short, curved poker shaped like a branding iron.

"Not that. One of the longer ones," Jamie called. "Yes, that one. Quickly. Bring it here."

After what seemed forever, the woman returned dragging a heavy metal shaft. When she arrived, Jamie ripped it from her hands. The bar was nearly six feet long, pointed at both ends, and about an inch and a half in diameter. It was too thick to fit into the links of her chain, but it would pass through the connecting ring that fastened her to the wall.

Hands slippery with sweat, Jamie gripped the bar and shoved the tip of the shaft into the metal ring. Using the bar as a lever, she pulled. The ring didn't budge.

Help me.

As the woman moved forward, Jamie sensed someone at the top of the staircase, opening the door to the cellar.

Her!

"What's taking so long?" Devon's voice floated down through the darkness.

Don't panic, Jamie told herself, her heart pounding so hard she thought surely her captor must hear. *There has to be a way.*

The woman stood immobile, still bound by Jamie's will. "Go," Jamie whispered. Voice still lowered, she added a final command.

Shut the cell door, but leave it unlocked.

The woman stumbled out, raising her eyes to look at Jamie as she closed the cell door. As she did, Jamie thought she detected something in them she hadn't seen before. Resignation, hopelessness . . . pity?

The prison door swung shut, again plunging Jamie into darkness. Holding her breath, she said a silent prayer that she wouldn't hear the bolt sliding home. She didn't. Careful not to make a sound, she withdrew the iron bar from the ring.

Where to hide it? A corner? At the base of the wall? Beside the door?

Jamie sensed Devon descending the staircase, moving toward her like an approaching storm.

Does she know what I did to the old woman? Is that why she's coming?

Willing herself under control, Jamie tried to remember where in her cell the shadow had been deepest when her captor had last visited. She glanced around. All at once she realized she could see!

Jamie turned. From behind her came a faint thread of light. To her horror, she saw that her cell door had swung ajar.

It was only open a crack . . . but enough for Devon to notice?

Soundlessly, Jamie placed the bar at the base of the back wall and shrank into a corner, a panicked litany running like quicksilver through her mind.

Don't let her come down, don't let her come down, oh please, God, don't let her come down . . .

*   *   *

Devon hesitated on the middle landing, her mind probing the chamber below for . . . *what?* Something was out of place. For a fleeting instant she had sensed a presence. But the grounds were secure, every servant lay under her control, and the child still cowered in her cell—bait for a bigger fish to come. What, then?

Devon scowled, hearing the old woman approaching. "What took you so long?" she demanded.

204

The woman refused to meet her gaze.

"What have you been doing?" Devon asked pleasantly. "Nothing to say? Well, silence has always been your finest attribute. It remains the one reason I allow you to live. Now, go. I'll find out what you've been up to later."

Devon waited until her servant had disappeared at the top of the stairs. Then she turned, again searching for the source of her vague apprehension. But though she tried to concentrate, her mind kept returning to other matters. In the end she decided that whatever it was, it could wait until after the meeting.

The meeting. Over the past hours Devon had considered canceling it. After all, she had moved up the date of the council's monthly assembly to discuss the near-thwarted assassination of Arthur Bellamy, and that problem had resolved itself nicely. Nevertheless, she decided she might as well go. For one thing, Exner had been growing progressively irksome. If nothing else, seeing him in person would provide an opportunity to put him in his place.

Devon hesitated a moment more, then remounted the stairs. Upon reaching the light at the top, she glanced at her watch. Her helicopter stood fueled and ready at the airport, but even if she were to leave immediately, she would still be late for the meeting.

So what? she thought as she exited her basement chambers. With a smile, she withdrew her golden key and relocked the heavy oak door behind her.

Let them wait.

Chapter Twenty-seven

The East Hampton Airport lay only a few miles north of Devon's estate. Nevertheless, by the time Devon's limousine nosed past a line of private hangers and pulled to a stop beside an executive transport helicopter bearing Elysian Foundation logos, she was already thirty minutes late for her meeting.

Upon leaving the chambers beneath her mansion, Devon had returned to her second-floor bedroom suite, where she took her time getting ready. Afterward, on the drive to the airport, she listened to a Brahms piano sonata. Refusing to be hurried, she elected to remain in the air-conditioned car until the end of the first movement. Lost in thought, she spent several leisurely minutes more in the back seat of the limo. Finally exiting, she crossed the tarmac to the waiting aircraft. Although three of the world's most powerful men awaited her, she knew they would do so without complaint. They had no choice.

A male attendant assisted Devon as she boarded the aircraft, offering her a drink as soon as she had settled into one of the plush seats lining the cabin. Devon declined. Then, deciding to pass the short flight to the city continuing to listen to music, she began riffling through a selection of classical recordings stored in a cabinet beside her seat. "Notify the pilots that I'm ready to depart," she told the attendant. "And tell them to fly down the coast this time. I'm tired of looking at the expressway."

After the attendant departed, Devon completed her perusal, selecting a CD recording of Schoenberg's *Guerrelieder*. Shortly afterward, a slight vibration of the helicopter's twin 450-horsepower engines signaled the aircraft lifting into the air. Slipping on a pair of headphones, Devon started the CD and settled back in her seat.

Devon had always preferred classical music to the popular efforts of the day, refusing to abide any musical work she didn't consider a serious composition. Ignoring the coastline rushing past beneath the aircraft, she closed her eyes and let

Schoenberg's incandescent melodies spin their drama of doomed love and transcendence. And as the stormy cycle of themes progressed, Devon's thoughts turned to Mike. To her surprise, with those thoughts came an unexpected thrill of desire, the intensity of which surprised her. Irritated, she opened her eyes and stared out the window.

As instructed, the pilots were taking a route that traced the course of Dune Road down the coast. Below, Devon could see the blue waters of Moriches Bay, sailboats threading through the narrow inlet at the top. Moments later the aircraft left them behind, skimming over Smith Point Bridge and arcing down the long sandbar known as Fire Island.

Mike was near. Devon could feel it. And as much as she was loath to admit it, she realized he had become more than an amusement, more than the mere dalliance she had originally intended. He had become dangerous. Why didn't I just kill him that first night at his house, she asked herself, not for the first time. Things would have been a lot simpler.

Simpler, of course. But not nearly as interesting.

Devon knew she had taken a considerable risk by letting Mike live—not that she had been in any real danger from the ludicrous hammer with which he'd threatened her that first night. No, the danger Mike posed involved far more than a hammer. For one, he knew too much about the Bellamy killing. As a latent, even with his undeveloped powers, he could conceivably go to authorities with information about the late candidate's demise—an embarrassing situation for both Exner and the Elysian Foundation—especially with those infernal photographs as corroborating evidence. After recovering the pictures, the natural course would have been to eliminate Mike. But she hadn't. Many times since she had asked herself why. And many times since, the answer had astounded her.

That first night Devon had glimpsed something in Mike Callahan that had intrigued her, something that he himself only dimly suspected. Though still dormant, there was a power in Mike that was virtually equal to her own. And in a rare moment of introspection, Devon finally realized what she had seen in Mike, the mystery that had so drawn her, was herself.

Could it be? she wondered. Another like me? Mike, an equal?

Maybe. If so, the possibilities were staggering . . . and potentially lethal. Mike had become an unknown quantity. An unknown quantity, but *interesting*—a welcome diversion from the deadening boredom of the centuries.

Yes, the risk had been justified, Devon decided, thinking back on the incredible joining they had shared in the shower, followed by their surprisingly satisfying lovemaking in the bedroom afterward. That afternoon alone had made it all worthwhile. That, and what they had experienced together in the bullring. Another first.

In the beginning Devon had felt certain that once Mike had fed, he would abandon his qualms about taking human life. He had disappointed her, proving far more rooted in his quixotic morality than expected. Once again she had considered eliminating him. And once again, rejected it. Instead, she had set Mike free, discreetly arranging for his continued "education," hopeful his awakening hunger would complete the seduction she had first begun.

Now, although she had managed for the most part to negate the damage caused by his interference in the Bellamy affair, Devon knew that Mike's myopic refusal to accept his true nature might still necessitate his death. A multitude of lifetimes had taught her caution. She had hedged the danger of letting Mike live by taking his child as hostage, knowing he would seek her out. He would come to her, and on her terms.

And then she would test him, one final time.

The helicopter banked, taking a more northerly course to avoid the traffic pattern over JFK Airport. Shortly after that the Brooklyn Bridge spanning the East River came into view, and the aircraft began its descent to the heliport. What fate lies in store for Mike? Devon wondered as they turned on final approach. To be my partner?

Never.

To join me as consort and ally?

Possibly.

Or will Mike simply provide the pleasure of feasting on one of my own ilk?

Minutes later as the helicopter touched down, Devon concluded that however things turned out, she was certain of one thing: Mike Callahan had definitely been worth the risk.

*   *   *

Lyle Exner gazed out a window on the forty-ninth floor of the GE Building in Rockefeller Center, also thinking about risk. *His* risk. Current developments had placed him in extreme danger. It was not Devon Varkoff who was in jeopardy. Nor were the other members of the council, nor the foundation itself. Should the Bellamy fiasco blow up in their faces, it was he alone who would roast in the media spotlight.

For years the Elysian Foundation had leased the entire forty-eighth and forty-ninth floors of the GE Building, also known as 30 Rock, the 850 foot-tall flagship building of Rockefeller Center. The conference room in which Exner now stood encompassed the complete northeast corner, affording a view of Central Park to the north, the eastern skyline to Roosevelt Island, and beyond. Below, Exner could see Prometheus Fountain, the skating rink, and a procession of beetlelike vehicles moving on the streets below. Where the hell is Devon? he thought angrily.

"Ms. Varkoff will be along soon enough," said a deep, guttural voice behind him. "Pacing like a caged animal won't speed her arrival, Lyle. Sit down."

With a murderous glare, Exner turned to regard Hans Menninger, an elderly man who was reclining in a leather chair at the head of the conference table. An immensely wealthy German industrialist who had risen from the ashes of his shattered homeland years before, Menninger was old now, his skin as thick and wrinkled as a turtle's. He was also a potent member of the second tier who was functioning at the height of his powers, as were they all. "I don't take orders from you, old man," Exner replied, his eyes narrowing.

Copeland Blaumpier, the third member of the council, sat several seats to the right of Menninger. Rolling folds of blubber encasing his androgynous body, he glanced up from a scrapbook of newspaper articles, his eyes as unreadable as marbles. "In view of present developments, Lyle, I don't think this is the time for you to be making enemies," he advised.

"Enemies?" Exner shot back. "We're all in this together."

Both men stared at him coldly.

Exner hesitated, realizing that if he were going to stand up to Devon, he would need the support of both Menninger and Blaumpier. He walked to the window, fighting to quiet his anger. Then, turning back to Menninger, "I didn't mean any disrespect," he said, attempting to appear contrite. "I'm under a lot of stress. You understand."

From his coat pocket, the German withdrew a cigar. After snipping an end, he rolled the fat brown cylinder between his liver-spotted hands, lit it, and regarded Exner as if examining a specimen under a microscope. "I do understand," he said. "And you're correct. We are all in this together. However, recent developments *do* seem to indicate that of everyone present, you have the most to lose, my friend."

"You've got that right," Exner retorted, his temper flaring anew as he realized Menninger had been scanning his thoughts. "But if I go down, you're coming with me, *friend.*"

"That could be," conceded Menninger. "But as we can do nothing until Ms. Varkoff arrives, I reiterate my earlier suggestion. Sit down and shut up."

With ill concealed anger, Exner slouched into a seat across from Blaumpier, who had resumed working on his scrapbook. Deciding to change the subject, Exner stubbed a finger at a clutter of clippings that Blaumpier had spread across the table. "Anything new?"

Blaumpier glanced up. "I do have a few things you might find interesting," he conceded. Wetting his lips with a lizardlike flick of his tongue, he selected several articles and passed them across the table.

On other occasions Exner had thumbed through some of Blaumpier's newspaper mementos. Many articles in Blaumpier's scrapbook dated back more than thirty years, a span indicating that Blaumpier had begun amassing his trophies before he was ten years of age. In spite of himself, Exner had been impressed by their scope and savagery: fires, assassinations, serial killings, airline crashes, and Blaumpier's specialty—particularly bloody public executions.

Exner picked up the newspaper clippings Blaumpier had passed to him. One article detailed an unexplained hotel fire in Las Vegas—sixty-four dead. Another chronicled a mass murder in a fast-food restaurant in California, with a follow-up piece about a postal worker who had wiped out most of his coworkers the very same day. But it was the final article that caught Exner's eye. "Attempt on Pope's Life!" the headline proclaimed.

"That was *you*?" asked Exner.

Blaumpier nodded. "I don't usually keep a record of my failures," he admitted, retrieving the articles. "But the exploding crucifix lent a novel touch, don't you think?"

Menninger, who had listened to this exchange in silence, drew deeply on his cigar. He inhaled a bit of the smoke, then let it flow in a thin stream from his leathery lips. "Such a trivial waste of your talents, Copeland," he remarked acidly. "Almost puerile, hmmm?"

Color rose to Blaumpier's cheeks. As he started to reply, Devon Varkoff strode into the room. "Good afternoon, gentlemen. You're in my seat, Dr. Menninger," she said. "Please move, and dispose of your cigar."

The German rose. "Of course, Ms. Varkoff," he said deferentially, his lips drawing back from tobacco-stained teeth in the semblance of a smile.

Devon continued, addressing Blaumpier, "This is no time for your souvenirs. Please put them away."

"Yes, Ms. Varkoff," replied Blaumpier, gathering his papers.

"What, no kind words of greeting for me?" grumbled Exner. "After all, I'm the reason you called this meeting."

"I said good afternoon, Lyle. And of course we all know why we're here. Nevertheless, the matters we need to cover encompass more than you."

"Speaking of which," Menninger noted, "I think we would all like to proceed with the meeting you felt so necessary to convene on short notice. You want to discuss our ongoing problems in Los Angeles, correct? That, and how you plan to deal with them?"

"Correct," said Devon. "Although I wouldn't call our problems in Los Angeles 'ongoing.' Everything is well in hand. We simply need to—"

"Well in hand?" Exner interrupted.

"Wait your turn to speak, Lyle," said Menninger. Then, to Devon, "This problem you say is 'well in hand' seems to be causing Mr. Exner a great deal of concern. In many respects, I quite agree."

Devon shrugged. "Granted, our plan to remove Bellamy was compromised, but no one could have predicted that a latent would be present, or that he would be able to interfere with our actions. Nevertheless, in the end we achieved our goal. Bellamy is dead. In addition, we retrieved the latent's photographs and controlled the news coverage. Now all we have to do is—"

"Christ!" Exner broke in again. "Haven't you heard? Didn't you see that throng of reporters downstairs? The story is all over the networks."

"What story?"

Instead of answering, Exner strode to the head of the table. Reaching past Devon, he pressed a button on a recessed panel. "See for yourself," he said as a rectangular section rose from the center of the table, revealing a cluster of television screens. Although the conference room monitors were usually used only for business presentations, they were also connected to a local cable provider. Exner adjusted the controls until he had the broadcast channels up on the screens. He flipped through the stations, settling on CNN.

"What is this?" Devon demanded.

"Just watch," Exner muttered.

Devon glanced at Menninger and Blaumpier. Both men ignored her, staring instead at the screens. Sighing in resignation, she sat back and waited. In less than a minute the familiar face of a CNN anchor began recapping the top stories of the day. Then another familiar face appeared, this time a face in a photograph.

Tyler.

Suddenly alert, Devon leaned forward. Exner turned up the volume.

". . . *Los Angeles Times* reported that members of the LAPD took Gregory Tyler into custody early this morning," said the commentator. "Tyler was wanted by the FBI in connection with a series of murders in Minnesota, Arkansas, Texas, and Alabama. After escaping federal custody, Tyler had eluded authorities for over thirteen years before resurfacing in Los Angeles. Sources in the police department revealed that photographs in their possession place Tyler at the Century City fundraiser at which California gubernatorial candidate Arthur Bellamy was murdered. Tyler, who has reportedly admitted complicity in that killing, was in the employ of the Elysian Foundation at the time. Representatives of the Elysian Foundation, a major contributor to the campaign of businessman Lyle Exner, Bellamy's main campaign rival, have thus far been unavailable for comment.

"In a subsequent development," the newscaster continued, "after confessing his involvement in Bellamy's murder, Tyler apparently committed suicide in his West Los Angeles prison cell, where he was awaiting transfer to federal authorities." Then, turning to a new camera angle, "In other news today—"

"Damn!" Exner snarled, thumbing a button that sent the screens to darkness. "I hadn't heard that last part."

Devon said nothing as the monitors descended back into the table. Feeling the eyes of the others on her, she contemplated this unexpected turn of events. Menninger interrupted her thoughts. "If I'm not mistaken," the German said, "this is the work of your recalcitrant latent. Mike Callahan, I believe he calls himself?"

"I worked with Tyler once," Blaumpier interjected. "He was one of our best. Not especially smart, but strong. Really strong. I can't believe he's dead."

"Believe it!" Exner shouted angrily, droplets of spittle spraying from his lips. "He's dead, and who knows *what* he told the cops first."

"Control yourself, Lyle," Devon cautioned. "Histrionics will accomplish nothing."

"I concur, Ms. Varkoff," said Menninger. "Nevertheless, Mr. Exner makes a good point. At this juncture our most prudent course would be to assume the worst and act accordingly. I would like to add, however, that a timely intervention on your part could have prevented all this."

"You're suggesting . . . ?"

"I'm suggesting that you demonstrated an unconscionable lack of caution by allowing this Callahan person to live. Like you, I find his ability to survive interesting, and under other circumstances he might have proved useful. But at present he's simply too dangerous. As a result of his actions we've lost several operatives, our network on the West Coast is in shambles, and now this."

"You're questioning my judgment?" Devon moved to stand behind the German, her knuckles whitening as she gripped the back of his chair. "May I remind you, Herr Doctor, of the blunders you and your *wunderkinder* made in Germany some years back? If you had listened to me, things would have been different, *nicht wahr*?"

Menninger squirmed uncomfortably. "I don't understand how bringing up past mistakes can help. We need to go forward."

"Correct. And let me spell out for you how we shall do that." Devon looked at Menninger for a long moment, then at Exner and Blaumpier in turn. "First of all, in the future none of you will ever again question my authority," she said quietly. "Ever. You will do exactly as I say, and you will do so without hesitation. Is that understood?"

The German nodded warily. "Yes. I understand."

"Oh, cut the crap," Exner blurted angrily. "Why don't you just admit that your game with the latent got out of control?"

Devon turned. "You go too far, Lyle. Perhaps a lesson in etiquette is required?"

"No! I—"

Devon's eyes flashed. Exner froze, an apoplectic grimace twisting his lips, his limbs shaking as though some terrible current were flowing through his body. As the others watched, he sank to his knees in agony. A thin flow of blood started from his nostrils, running down his chin onto his shirt.

"Do I make myself clear, Lyle?" Devon asked evenly.

Retching, Exner raised a hand in assent.

Devon glanced questioningly at Blaumpier.

"Perfectly clear, Ms. Varkoff," Blaumpier answered, his eyes scintillating with pleasure as he regarded Exner's bloodied face.

"Good," said Devon. Then, again regarding Exner, "You seem to be bleeding, Lyle. Please go clean up. We'll await your return."

Exner seemed about to speak. Thinking better of it, he rose shakily and made his way to a bathroom that adjoined the conference room.

After Exner staggered out, Devon strode to the window and stood with her back to the others. To the north she could make out a blue-gray shimmer that marked Conservatory Pond in Central Park; to the east, New York's spires of glass and steel ascended majestically into a clear blue sky.

Devon stared through the window until she heard Exner reseat himself at the table. Then turning, she again pinned each council member in her gaze. "This can all be ours," she said, indicating the world outside with a wave of her hand. "This, and more. Infinitely more. Once again, after so many years, we have it within our grasp to place one of our kind in a position of true political power. Although that is merely a first step, it is a step that will ultimately lead to others. Creating further inroads into the world power structure will require time, planning, and most of all—patience. Nevertheless, in the end we shall have all we desire, I promise you that. First, however, we need to attend to our immediate problems."

Devon turned to Exner. "Lyle, your position with regard to the media shall be one of absolute denial. You will steadfastly maintain that you've had no financial interest in the Elysian Foundation since your divestiture, and that you exert no control over Foundation activities. In addition, you will have no further contact with any of us until this situation is rectified. Is that understood?"

"Yes."

"Tyler is dead and therefore unable to recant his confession," Devon continued. "Nonetheless, we must nullify or at least minimize the effect of his revelations. And those infernal photographs must be destroyed once and for all, and all memory of them erased." She turned to Blaumpier. "I want you on one of our corporate jets to Los Angeles as soon as possible. Take whomever you need from your sector. Just make certain you have adequate resources to complete the job."

"Yes, Ms. Varkoff," said Blaumpier.

"Now, to our immediate concerns . . ." Devon's voice trailed off. Momentarily lost in thought, she returned to the window and gazed down at the plaza.

"What's wrong?" asked Menninger.

"Don't you feel him?" Devon replied, staring down at the street. "No, I don't suppose you do. Well, no matter. Suffice it to say that the question of Mike Callahan will soon be resolved." She turned. "Now, back to the work at hand. Doctor, you and I are going downstairs to talk with our friends in the media. Listen closely. Here's what we're going to say . . ."

Forty minutes later Devon climbed into the back of her limousine, her confidence restored. Following a few judicious *pushes*, the interview with the press had gone well, as expected. Her present efforts, however, would provide only a stopgap solution; much would hinge upon what Blaumpier and his team could accomplish in Los Angeles. If nothing else, however, she had bought them some time.

216

As her limo pulled from the curb at Rockefeller Plaza, Devon glanced back through the rear window, spotting a tall, dark-haired man crossing the promenade. He entered a waiting cab. When her driver turned north on Third Avenue, Devon looked back again. The man in the cab was five cars behind, following at a discreet distance.

"The heliport, Ms. Varkoff?" her driver inquired out of habit, already certain of their destination.

"Not this time," Devon replied. "Take the Queensboro Bridge to the expressway."

"You want to drive home?"

"Yes. Tonight we're going to drive."

Devon settled herself comfortably in the back of her limousine, satisfied that as she had told the others, the question of what to do about her errant latent would soon be resolved. In a few hours, Mike Callahan would cease to be a problem.

One way or another.

Chapter Twenty-eight

*H*ad the bolt twisted? Even a little?

Jamie groped in the darkness. Gritting her teeth, she yanked at the chain that bound her. Though she was certain the iron bar she'd been using as a lever had given slightly, the welded ring and the bolt securing it to the wall seemed as firmly fastened as ever. Carefully, she replaced the tip of the iron bar into the welded ring. Then, knees bent, hands flat against the wall for balance, she stood on the opposite end of the bar and began to bounce.

After many failed attempts, Jamie had abandoned efforts simply to lever the expansion bolt from the wall. The metal pin was anchored too firmly. Her main hope now lay in using her weight on the bar either to twist out the metal shaft or to break it off as it emerged from the concrete. Despite her best efforts, neither prospect appeared promising.

On her fourth bounce Jamie sprang too hard. One foot lost contact with the iron rod. The bar twisted, whacking her shin as she fell. Groaning, she sat on the floor and held her leg, waiting for the pain to abate. When the throb finally lessened, she ran her hands over the cold concrete floor, searching for the bar. She found it lying against the base of the back wall. After placing the tip of the bar back into the ring, she again stood on her lever. Again, she fell. She tried again, working the bolt from the other direction. She fell and tried again, and again . . .

The expansion bolt never budged. But like a wire repeatedly bent back upon itself, the weld joint in the ring unexpectedly gave way. In no time Jamie had the ring spread wide enough for her to unfasten her chain. She was free!

No, not yet, she thought grimly, gathering the length of galvanized chain still trailing from the shackle around her neck. *I'm not out of here yet.*

Holding the chain in one hand, Jamie quietly moved to her cell door. Left ajar by the old woman, the door creaked outward under cautious pressure from Jamie's hand. Peering out, she could make out vague shapes in the darkness beyond. Remembering the bulb she had seen dangling from the ceiling of her cell, she groped the wall outside, searching for a light switch. Finding one, she flipped it on. The bulb in her cell shined weakly, sending a thin shaft of illumination into the cavernous chamber beyond.

Hardly daring to breathe, Jamie moved to the table with leather restraints she had seen earlier. Across from it sat a sturdy, seatless chair, also equipped with leather straps. Tongs, pliers, and knives hung in a nearby rack. To the right, a bench held an assortment of metal boots, gloves, and iron masks.

Trembling, Jamie crept farther into the room, noting that the walls of the chamber appeared to have been cut from solid rock. Instinctively, she moved toward the light of the furnace. Silent now, the monstrous shape hulked in the gloom, a manual gas valve mounted on a wall nearby. The face of the furnace displayed a pair of stainless-steel doors. Below was what appeared to be a large access hatch with ventilation grillwork, which allowed a glow from the pilot light to seep into the room. As Jamie approached the furnace, she also noticed that the beams forming the ceiling of the rock chamber had abruptly ended. Craning her neck, she peered up.

An intermediate loft lay above her. Although barely visible in the darkness, Jamie could also make out the floor joists of another level higher up, probably the main floor of her captor's house. A staircase rose from the loft. Jamie's eyes followed the steps, also noting a second set of stairs accessing the rock chamber in which she now stood. Grasping her length of chain, Jamie crossed the chamber and ascended the stairs in a rush, ignoring the intermediate loft on the way. Seconds later she reached a landing at the top. There she found a locked door.

Jamie flipped on a wall switch at the top landing, inspecting the door in the light of a dim bulb. The door was constructed of rough-hewn oak, its surface broken by reinforcing straps and a heavy deadbolt. No door handle. Checking further, Jamie noted that each of the hinge pins had been welded to its respective hinge plate to prevent withdrawal.

Jamie focused her mind as she had before, probing the space beyond the door.

Nothing.

Her mouth set in a grim line of determination, Jamie retraced her steps to the lowest level, returning with the iron rod from her cell. Using the metal shaft as a pry bar, she worked at the oak door for thirty minutes without rest, unsuccessfully trying to force it open. Exhausted, she sank to her knees, her breath coming in ragged sobs.

It can't end like this. It can't!

Sure it can, came a perverse thought. This is the real world, where things don't always turn out as you want.

I'm not going to quit.

She'll be back. And when she discovers what you've been doing . . .

I'll fight. There are weapons downstairs. I'll hide, surprise her when she comes in.

Who are you kidding? Your only chance is to escape before she returns, and you know it.

"Yes, I know," Jamie said aloud. "And I also know that I'm going to get out. I am."

Abandoning her efforts at the door, Jamie descended to the intermediate landing, leaving the light on at the top of the staircase. Proceeding into the loft in the faint illumination from above, she stumbled through a maze of passageways and chambers filled with cruel, inhuman devices—searching for a window, a hatch, another stairway to the floors above.

She found nothing.

The space beneath the woman's house appeared to be sealed off from the floors above, with but a single point of entry. And that was locked. Jamie was about to head back up the stairs and resume her efforts at the oak door when she noticed something odd. A strange object hung suspended from a beam above her, dangling over a drop to the rock chamber below. It looked like a gigantic, elliptical ball—a cage of some sort with inward-pointing spikes lining the interior. Drawn by its peculiar shape, Jamie took a step closer. She brought her hand to her mouth in horror, suddenly realizing that the interior spines were actually blades, each a deadly sword thrusting into the center of the ball.

Jamie stumbled back. In the darkness she tripped on a table and almost tumbled over the edge of the loft to the stone chamber below. Barely catching herself in time, she teetered, heart in her throat. She looked down. Below, radiating outward from beneath the cage, a pattern of dark stains marked the concrete floor.

"Oh, God," Jamie whispered aloud, abruptly comprehending the origin of the stains. Though trembling with terror, she remained at the edge, struck by something else. Letting her gaze travel the floor, Jamie hunted for whatever had caught her eye but still eluded her mind. Then she saw it. The bloodstains beneath the cage weren't the only marks on the floor. Similar dark trails covered the concrete surface in other areas . . . all leading to the furnace.

She's burning the bodies, Jamie realized with a shudder. *She's using the furnace as her own private crematorium.* Then another thought occurred.

An oven that size needs a chimney to the outside. A big one.

But big enough for someone to crawl through?

Hoping against hope, Jamie rushed to the lower chamber, undid a catch on the furnace, and threw open the oven's stainless-steel doors. Bracing herself, she peered inside. The interior of the firebox measured about four feet wide and seven feet deep, easily large enough for a body. Several, in fact. Traversing the perimeter of the sooty chamber was a course of thick, perforated pipe. A grill lined the bottom. In the flickering light of the pilot flame, Jamie saw more burners beneath the grill, along with a sturdy metal pan.

Something to catch the dripping fat?

Sensing that time was running out, Jamie began to climb inside the firebox. Partway in she hesitated.

What if this comes on while I'm in here?

Jamie recalled seeing a gas valve on a wall near the furnace. She climbed from the firebox and hurried to the valve. Squinting at the brass regulator, she saw that it was in the "off" position.

She twisted the valve lever clockwise. An instant later the oven roared to life. Satisfied, Jamie turned the valve back to the "off" position and returned to the oven. The brief time the burners had been on hadn't heated the firebox significantly. Jamie gave it a few seconds to cool. Then, swallowing an almost overwhelming feeling of dread, she crawled inside.

Above her the refractory walls of the firebox constricted as they rose. Once inside, Jamie barely had room to kneel. Ignoring the grate cutting her knees, she ran her hands up the blackened brickwork, searching for the chimney opening. Soot showered down, stinging her eyes. Squeezing them shut, she groped blindly, finally locating a large hole high on the rear wall. Ignoring a growing sense of claustrophobia, she shoved her arm into the opening. Two feet back her fingers encountered an impassable cross of secondary burners.

Blinking back tears of frustration, Jamie crawled from the oven. There appeared to be no escape from her prison. No windows, hatches, or vents. A single door at the top of the stairs was the only way out, and that seemed impregnable. The chambers below the woman's house were as tightly sealed as a coffin. Still, a feeling she had overlooked something kept nagging. What had she missed? Something she remembered from chemistry class . . .

All at once she had it.

Combustion air.

Any gas-burning device requires a source of oxygen—especially one this big, Jamie reasoned. *Even with the vents on the access hatch, without a supply of air from the outside a huge furnace like this would choke like a candle in a closed jar. There has to be an air duct.*

But where?

Jamie had seen nothing resembling a duct to the outside except the chimney flue at the top of the firebox, and that was blocked.

The firebox . . .

Dropping to her knees, Jamie pried open the access hatch below the furnace doors, releasing an avalanche of ash. More ash followed as she scooped with her hands. Working feverishly, she raked back the gray dust, gradually clearing an eighteen-inch space beneath the lowest burners. As she reached the bottom layer of debris, she began dredging up shards of teeth and bone, portions of skull, and a grisly assortment of melted watches, buttons, dental work, eyeglass frames, and rings . . . dozens of rings. Fighting a sickening surge of revulsion, Jamie backed away, searching for a tool with which to complete her excavation. She found a small shovel beside the furnace. Swallowing against her rising gorge, she used it to finish clearing the opening.

There! Far in the back, behind convolutions of burner pipe, the mouth of a clay duct projected into the rear of the firebox. That had to be it. That had to be the air shaft to the outside . . . and her one hope of escape. But was it big enough for her to crawl through?

Lying on her stomach, Jamie began working her way under the burners, thankful that she was slim, even for a thirteen-year-old. Someone slightly larger couldn't have made it.

Jamie's efforts raised a cloud of dust, filling her nose and mouth with the chalky taste of death. Holding her breath as long as possible, she squirmed toward the rectangular opening of the duct. Finally, when she thought she could endure no more, she reached it. It was larger than she had first thought, but not by much. Still, it looked big enough for someone her size to crawl through. Gasping, she thrust in her head and shoulders.

Suddenly she could breathe! Fresh air was wafting down from above, cool and clean and smelling of newly mown grass. She had been right. The duct must lead to the outside.

The walls of the duct pressing in on all sides, Jamie inched forward. Farther in, her heart fell as it appeared that the air shaft had abruptly ended. Fighting panic, she rolled onto her back and felt above her, discovering that the tunnel had taken a vertical turn inside the brickwork, paralleling the chimney flue. Wriggling to a sitting position, Jamie worked herself up into the opening and struggled to her feet, letting her chain dangle between her legs.

Though grateful to be able to breathe, Jamie fought a renewed wave of claustrophobia. She had first experienced it in the sooty confines of the firebox, but this was worse. Although she knew she had to proceed, she doubted she would be able to retreat if she got stuck. For that matter, Jamie realized she might have already passed the point of no return. Her shoulders and hips were tightly pressed against the narrow confines of the pipe, and in the smothering blackness the duct seemed to be closing around her like a fist, squeezing . . .

Don't think about getting stuck. There are worse things than being trapped in here. Move.

Taking a deep breath, Jamie began to climb. Elbows, back, and feet pressing against the clay surface behind, knees and palms in front, she wormed her way upward—opposite pressures locking her in. Gradually she fought her way higher inside the duct, now moving her hands, now drawing up her feet and knees for another move, then hands again . . .

Slowly, Jamie ascended. Though she could pause, she couldn't rest. Remaining stationary in the vertical pipe required nearly as much effort as moving upward, and moving upward was becoming progressively more difficult. She had to stop.

Don't quit. You've come too far. Besides, your only option now is falling, and there's a twenty-foot drop below you. Move.

Jamie hesitated, peering up the shaft. Fifteen feet higher she could make out a hint of light.

The opening?

Yes!

Her legs and arms were exhausted, but Jamie willed herself to continue, moving faster but trying to conserve her remaining strength. In her rush toward the light, she almost slipped.

Careful. Don't fall.

Forcing herself to move more cautiously, she proceeded. Agonizing minutes passed. At last Jamie reached a branch in the duct. She groped with her hands. Directly above she felt what seemed to be the blades of a fan; to the left, the tunnel continued upward at an angle before turning vertical once more. And flooding down this lateral shaft was light.

Using a combination of opposing pressures, Jamie turned her body in the duct. Keeping her back pressed against the upper wall, she squirmed around the bend. After passing the turn, she climbed another six-foot vertical section. She was almost there.

Her heart soaring, Jamie scrambled to the top. Her fingers closed over the edge of the pipe. But as she pulled herself up the final few feet, hope once again turned to bitter disappointment. Six inches above the opening of the duct, a conical metal cap was bolted to the chimney-step, making escape impossible.

"No," Jamie sobbed, alternately clinging to the edge of the pipe with one hand and pounding on the steel cover with the other, continuing until both fists were bleeding. Then, exhaustion finally taking her, she simply clung to the edge and shouted for help, praying someone would hear.

No one did.

The sun was setting, illuminating the grounds surrounding Devon's mansion in muted hues of red and gold. Across acres of rolling landscape Jamie could see a knoll of maples flanking a tall hedge; to the right, a silvery mist rose from the surface of a lovely saltwater inlet.

So near, and yet . . .

Day gradually faded to dusk. Jamie held on to the edge of the duct as long as she could, drinking in the beauty of the world outside, trying to imprint one last vision of it on her mind. She knew it would be her last. In the end her hands finally gave out. Though she lacked the strength to keep from falling, she fought to brake her descent, pressing against the inside of the duct to slow herself as she skidded down, down . . .

A sickening impact shocked through her body as she slammed into the first bend. Slowed by the change of direction, she clawed at the wall of the angled pipe, trying to arrest her fall. She almost succeeded.

An instant later her momentum carried her past the bend, and again she was accelerating down the vertical shaft, dropping blindly through the darkness. Screaming, flesh tearing from her elbows and knees, hands now slippery with blood, she fell . . .

Hours later Jamie's mind slowly spiraled to consciousness. Someone was talking. A strong voice, rich and full. Steely fingers closed on her leg, dragging her into the light.

Her!

"No need to rush things," Devon said. "You'll be back in the furnace soon enough. Until then it seems you'll need a better cage. I think I have just the thing." Grabbing the chain dangling from Jamie's neck, she pulled her to her feet. "By the way, we're about to have a visitor, so we'll need to hurry," Devon added. "There's much to do in preparation, and we don't want to keep your father waiting."

Chapter Twenty-nine

Night.

I sat in the back of the taxi, my mind churning. Fifty yards down the road, a massive iron gate guarded Devon's estate. A half hour earlier Devon's limo had driven through that gate, emerging shortly afterward without its passenger. No one had come or gone since, but from inside the grounds I felt the unmistakable chill of danger.

A trap? I wondered.

Probably. Nevertheless, I had to go in. From my pillage of Tyler's mind I knew that Jamie had been brought here, and she might still be alive. I refused to believe she was dead. Somehow, I would have known.

As I studied the gate, I wondered once again whether involving the police had been a mistake. The warning left for me at Susan's house had been explicit, and in forcing Tyler's confession to authorities I had taken a mortal risk. On the other hand, in addition to removing Tyler as a dangerous adversary, I had hoped to create a diversion that might help me reach Jamie in time. But in doing so, had I increased the danger to her as well?

With a feeling bordering on despair, I had begun to suspect that every move I'd made for the past week had been orchestrated by the hand of another. Was my presence here the final installment?

Even if it is, I thought, there's nothing I can do about it now. With a mix of both resignation and dread, I opened the taxi door and stepped to the street.

The cabby rolled down his window. "Sir? Want me to wait?"

"No," I answered, passing him a handful of money. *Leave. And forget you ever saw me.*

A raw wind pierced the night. I stood with my hands deep in my pockets, waiting until the taxi's taillights vanished into the darkness. Then I walked slowly toward Devon's gate. As I approached, I noticed a guard exiting a blockhouse concealed behind a clump of bushes on the other side. When I arrived, I found the uniformed man watching me through the iron bars. "Mr. Callahan?" he asked.

Taken aback, I didn't reply.

The guard entered some numbers on a gate keypad inside the barrier. "Ms. Varkoff is expecting you," he continued, construing my silence for assent. The gate swung inward. "Follow the driveway to the main house," he added.

I passed through the gate, pausing in front of the guard. Nervously, he backed away.

Don't move.

The guard froze. I took his weapon, a Smith & Wesson Combat Masterpiece with a four-inch barrel.

Leave, and never return.

I watched as the guard exited the gate and started down the road on foot. Then, shoving his gun into my belt, I proceeded down a long, cobbled driveway, passing thick stands of trees and hedges on either side. Several minutes of steady walking brought me to a broad promontory. Several hundred yards farther down the driveway I could see Devon's huge mansion looming like a stone citadel, dominating a knoll overlooking a saltwater cove. Giant firs flanked it on one side; on the other side a winding path descended to a boathouse at the water's edge. I studied the mansion carefully. With the exception of a single light burning in a lower window, the gigantic structure appeared deserted. I knew it was not.

With a dreamlike sense of déjà vu, I stepped off the road and crossed the remaining distance in the trees, branches and undergrowth clawing at my clothes. I approached the house from the side. Moments later I stood in shadow outside the front door. I listened. I heard nothing but a whispering of wind in the pines. But somewhere inside the mansion I sensed Devon's presence, stronger now than ever. She was near, very near.

I withdrew the revolver I had taken from the guard. I flipped open the cylinder. Six .38-caliber hollow-point cartridges nestled in the chambers. I rotated the cylinder and snapped it shut. But as I started for the door, I recalled another pistol, the pistol in

228

Arthur Bellamy's hand. Against Devon a weapon could cut both ways. Regretfully, I tossed the gun into the bushes. Trembling, I walked the final steps to the door.

As I placed my hand on the doorknob, I was seized by an overwhelming premonition of death. I hesitated. Then, taking a deep breath, I steadied my hand and turned the knob.

The door was unlocked. It swung inward, revealing a dimly lit entry beyond—slate floor, high ceiling, and a broad, sweeping staircase ascending to an upper level. To my left lay an enormous living room, illuminated by a faint glimmer filtering through a pair of carved oak doors to my right. Moving quietly, I crossed the stone floor and threw open the oak doors.

Inside, Devon was standing behind an ornate marble bar, casually mixing a drink. She looked up, her dark hair loose on her shoulders, framing her lovely face.

I froze in the doorway. I had forgotten how truly beautiful she was. In the lambent light of the room, she appeared almost radiant. I was reminded of something that Jamie, while in an uncharacteristically cynical mood, had once said about love. "Relationships usually go like this, Dad," she had cautioned. "I love you; I love you; I love you . . . I HATE you!"

After what had happened, I was having trouble believing that Devon was the same woman with whom I had spent time in Mexico. Either she was a consummate actress, or she was so consumed with herself and her egotistical, sociopathic lack of any sort of conventional morality that she couldn't distinguish good from evil. Maybe both. In any case, I had no intention of trusting her.

I entered without speaking, never taking my eyes from the stunning woman before me. She was beautiful, yes . . . but deadly.

Devon regarded me solemnly. "Hello, Mike."

"Where is she?"

"Jamie is safe and unharmed. Care for a drink?"

Tell me where she is.

Although I had *pushed* with all my strength, Devon easily parried my thrust.

"You've grown strong, Mike," she said, as though speaking to a child. "But over the centuries I have learned things you can't yet imagine. Don't try my patience. Now, how about that drink?" She held up a bottle in her left hand. "It's an extremely good Scotch, one of the single-malt whiskeys so in favor nowadays."

When I didn't answer, Devon set the bottle on the bar. "Relax, Mike. I have no intention of harming Jamie."

"You're lying. I saw what you did to Susan."

"Who? Oh, Jamie's mother." Drink in hand, Devon stepped from behind the bar. I noticed she had changed clothes since I'd last seen her outside Rockefeller Center, exchanging the wool suit she'd been wearing for a short black skirt and an embroidered silk blouse. Warily, I watched as she settled herself onto a leather stool at one end of the bar, revealing a smooth expanse of thigh as she crossed her legs.

"I never laid a hand on this . . . Susan," Devon said slowly, smiling as she saw my eyes drawn to her body. "But if you recall, I told you that others would try to harm you. I removed your daughter from Los Angeles to protect her."

"I don't believe you. Remember your friend Tyler? Before I took him, I picked through his mind. I know everything."

"Ah, Mike," Devon sighed. "You think you know everything. In truth, you know nothing. Tyler was a good operative, but he was never privy to the inner workings of our organization." She thought a moment. "Speaking of Tyler, you certainly stirred up a hornet's nest with that stunt of yours, forcing him to confess to the police like that. Very naughty, Mike. It's going to take considerable effort to straighten things out." She took a sip of Scotch and added reproachfully, "Had I known you were going to be so spiteful, I might not have allowed you to have him."

"You *allowed* me to have Tyler?"

"Of course. Tyler, and his helper Carlos, and the others, too—the picador at the bullring, the two operatives in our hotel room in Mexico, the agent outside your blond reporter friend's condo. They were my gifts to you—a small enough price to pay in the furtherance of your education."

"What are you talking about?"

"Don't be obtuse, Mike. After your first taste of death in the bullring, I knew you wanted more. I also knew that you needed to be prodded, coaxed like a reluctant virgin to the wedding bed. Sometimes even the strongest bull requires training."

I hesitated, stunned by her revelation. "I'm not a bull. I'm a man," I said numbly.

"No. You're more than that. Much, much more."

Devon crossed the room and took my injured hand. "Is this the hand of a man?" she asked, forcing me to look. "Can a man regrow a finger, a hand, a limb? Can a man send his mind into that of another, bending him to his will as easily as a child crushes an insect?"

Over the past twenty-four hours my maimed hand had almost completed its regeneration. I flexed my newly grown fingers, a physical embodiment of the changes that had enveloped me. Ignoring Devon's question, I pulled my hand from her grasp. "How did you know about my hand?" I demanded.

Devon smiled mysteriously. "Perhaps we'll talk about that later," she said. "Regardless of how I know about your lost fingers, their regeneration is a sign you're becoming more," she continued. "Don't you feel it? You've made immeasurable progress, and it's just the beginning." She drew closer and placed her palms on my chest, barely touching. Then, gradually circling me with her arms, she held my gaze and moved closer still, lightly pressing her body to mine.

Against my will, I felt myself responding. "This has just been a game for you, hasn't it?" I said harshly, shoving her away.

"Of course," Devon replied. "A game, a trial by fire, a fight to the death. I knew you would understand. We're alike, you and I. Don't you see that?"

"No!"

"Ah, Mike. Now who's lying?"

"I'm not like you. You're . . ."

231

"Insane? A psychopath?" Devon finished the rest of her drink in one quick toss. "Or is the word you're searching for . . . monster? Well, you might be right, were I to allow myself to be measured against the standards of ordinary men. And *that* will never happen again."

As if shaking off a distasteful memory, Devon strode to the bar, added ice to her glass, and poured another generous portion of Scotch. "Am I so different from you? What do *you* feel for those around you?" she demanded. "Love? Compassion? Hate? When you're with them, do you feel anything at all?"

I turned, refusing to meet her gaze.

"Of course you don't," Devon answered for me. "You and I and others like us have no need of the passions so treasured by ordinary people. You have survived in their midst by displaying a face they wanted to see, perhaps at times even deceiving yourself. Now it's time for the truth. Have you never asked yourself why human emotion has always eluded you? The answer is simple, Mike. It's because you're not like them. You're like me."

"That was you in Century City. You killed Bellamy."

Devon stirred her freshened drink with an index finger, then brought her finger to her lips and gently sucked the tip. "Bellamy was in our way. I removed him."

"And you feel no remorse, no—"

"You speak of remorse?" interrupted Devon. "What a hypocrite. Was it guilt *you* felt when you took those two at the hotel, or the sentry at your reporter friend's house, or Tyler and his assistant?"

"That wasn't the same. I had no choice."

"Oh, you had a choice, Mike. You had a choice, and you chose to kill. It's your nature. It's *our* nature. Now, answer truthfully. What do you feel when you take a life?"

Once more I looked away.

"I know exactly what you feel," Devon answered for me again. "It's not remorse. No, what you feel is a ravenous craving pounding in your veins, driving all thought from your mind save one. And then, in that glorious instant when you take a life and make it your own, you feel an immense, indescribable ecstasy. You feel the same hunger as I. And that's all you ever *truly* feel, isn't it? Everything else pales in comparison. You ask whether I experience guilt at taking a life? Don't be foolish. I've taken hundreds! Ordinary people are nothing compared with us. Nothing."

"You're wrong."

"Are you so sure? You are just beginning to realize your true nature. You can't deny it, Mike. It's too strong. Give in to it and join me."

When I didn't respond, Devon continued. "Look, I know it may seem a lot for you to renounce your values, your life, your job, your friends—even your daughter. But is it really so much to ask? What we could share is so much more. Remember our joining in the shower, and our lovemaking later, and the ecstasy we shared in the bullring? That's just the beginning. I have incredible things to show you, Mike, things that will shake the very foundation of your beliefs. In return I ask one small proof of your commitment, a step from which there will be no turning back."

"What?" I asked, certain I wouldn't like the answer.

"You'll see," Devon said with a mysterious smile. Then, her smile fading," Claim your birthright, Mike. You can be a god on Earth. Join me."

In taking the lives of others, first with Devon's help and afterward on my own, I had succumbed to the craving that had plagued me for years, not understanding it at the time. Now that I did, I realized with a surge of shame that if I continued to submit to it, I could very well become like Devon. Maybe worse. Never again, I thought, coming to a decision that was long overdue. Raising my eyes to meet Devon's, I said, "That will never happen."

"I tire of this charade," Devon sighed. "You disappoint me, Mike," she continued, her voice shifting subtly, taking on the aspect of a language long dead. "You seem destined to repeat your mistakes throughout eternity. You still don't remember, do you?"

"Remember what?"

Devon studied me curiously. "Who you are, what you once were. Death is often not the end for our kind. You have lived before. I can see it in you clearly. Don't you remember?"

Shaken, I crossed to the window, my mind reeling. Shining like a beacon through the trees, a sliver of moon hung low on the horizon, tolling an ancient chord within me. And from somewhere came the strains of the unsettling nocturne that had haunted my dreams, beckoning softly at first, then becoming louder, louder . . .

With a shudder, I turned from my demons. "Where is Jamie?" I demanded again. "I know she's here. I'll find her, even if I have to tear this place apart to do it."

"That won't be necessary. You seem to have made your choice. Let's see whether you can live with it."

Without another word, Devon strode from the room.

Startled by her abrupt departure, I hesitated, then followed. I arrived in the entry just in time to see her stepping into a closet beneath the staircase. When she didn't reappear, I looked inside.

A section of paneling had been moved aside in the back, exposing a thick, reinforced door. No sign of Devon. I entered the closet and pressed my hand on the heavy door. The massive slab of oak creaked inward. On the other side was a stairway leading down. Light shined up weakly from below.

Cautiously, I descended to a landing about fifteen feet below the main floor. Once there I could make out what appeared to be an intermediate loft to my right. Ahead, the flight of stairs continued downward.

Which way? I wondered.

From somewhere on the right came a whimper.

Jamie.

And I sensed another presence there as well.

Devon.

Stealthily, I moved into the loft. From ahead came a flickering glow that seemed to be growing steadily stronger . . .

There! I saw that the light was coming from a metal brazier with several iron bars laid across the top of the pan, their tips heated red-hot in the coals. As I proceeded forward, another shape began to emerge. At first it looked like a huge egg. I drew closer, realizing it was actually an elliptical cage. The metal ball hung suspended from a beam, its interior laced with gleaming blades. And pinned like a moth in the center, blades biting into her flesh, was—

Jamie!

I rushed forward, almost stumbling over an abrupt drop to another chamber below. Skidding to a stop at the edge of the loft, I peered into the cage. It dangled above the abyss, just out of reach. Jamie was trapped inside, and yet . . . somehow it wasn't her.

Jamie's eyes were open. Burning with unearthly fire, they glared at me across the space between us. And in that instant, I knew. It wasn't Jamie in the body I saw.

It was Devon.

"What do you think of my device?" she murmured. "Impressive, no? The blades are strategically placed—eyes, torso, legs. Even the slightest movement will cause our young subject the most excruciating pain."

Jamie's voice, but Devon's words. To my dismay, I saw reflected now in my daughter's face the expressions I had grown to know in Devon—the arch of her eyebrow, the tilt of her head, the twist of her lip. "Come out, Devon," I ordered, searching the darkness behind me.

"Not yet," said the girl in the cage, Devon's taunting tones sounding alien on Jamie's lips. "First, an experiment," she continued. "Faced with fire in front and an open window behind, people will invariably choose the window—even though it means certain death. We shall offer our subject a similar choice: the caress of a heated prod, or retreat into the arms of the cage's steel blades. The result should provide a fascinating insight into human nature."

As Jamie spoke, my eyes traveled to the top of the cage. A suspension cable joined the cage to a metal track. From there, pulleys descended to a winch mounted on the wall, providing a means of moving the metal orb over the drop. I raced to the winch, grabbed the handle, and started turning. The cage jerked, moving farther over the drop. I reversed direction. The cage swung dangerously for a moment, then began inching back toward the loft.

"Stop. I'll take her now if you force me."

I paused midstroke, watching in horror as Jamie raised her hands and placed each palm on the tip of a sharpened spike. Showing no emotion, she slowly forced her hands onto the blades. Able to do nothing to stop her, I watched in horror as the wicked knives entered her palms, grotesquely raising the skin on the backs of her hands as they pushed through. Spurting red, each of the sharpened points sliced all the way through—emerging wet and glistening from her flesh.

I released the winch. "Don't! I'll . . . I'll stop."

"That's better." Jamie smiled, seeming unaware of the bloody rivulets now coursing down her arms. "Taste her pain, Mike," she whispered, her voice husky with exhilaration. "Drink it in. Let me show you how to—"

Stop.

Again, it felt as if I had encountered a granite wall around Devon's mind. "You're hungry," Jamie's voice crooned. "I sense it in you. Bring one of the heated prods."

I didn't move.

Jamie's eyes found mine. "Together we could accomplish anything, Mike," she said. "The world around us, with its banquet of riches and pleasures, can be ours. All of it. Forever. The only thing I ask is proof of your commitment. It's a small matter, compared with what I'm offering, something that will be soon forgotten." She paused, her eyes hardening. "Your daughter is all that remains to tie you to your previous existence. Break that bond and join me, Mike. It's time to choose. And choose you must—one way or another. Take the life of your daughter, or die."

When I didn't respond, Devon continued. "My patience grows thin," she warned. "Bring one of the heated irons."

With a lurch of revulsion, I realized that this was what Devon had intended from the very beginning. As it had been for the matador in Mexico, this was to be my moment of truth.

I shook my head. "No."

Do as I command.

It was my turn to block Devon's thrust, and I did it easily. "This is between you and me, Devon. Let her go."

"Never," Jamie replied.

And then suddenly Devon was gone.

Jamie's body collapsed, becoming further impaled on the cage's spikes as she slumped. She hung briefly. Then the blades in her hands began cutting through her palms, causing her to drop even farther onto the steel knives lining the cage. Blood soaked her clothes, drizzling like crimson rain to the chamber below.

"Don't move, Jamie," I cried, frantically turning the winch. "Please, please don't move."

Careful in my haste not to start the cage swinging too violently, I reeled Devon's cruel device back over the loft. After fumbling with an unfamiliar catch, I managed to split open the orb, all the while praying that Jamie would still be alive. Grimacing as I saw how deeply the blades had cut into her, I cradled her in my arms and gently lifted her from the spikes. After freeing her hands, I laid her on the floor. Placing my fingers on her throat, I felt a pulse beating weakly. Her chest rose and fell, and again . . .

Quickly, I examined her wounds. Most were deep, but none appeared fatal. And to my surprise, I saw that her bleeding was already slowing. "Jamie," I whispered. "Can you hear me?"

Slowly, Jamie opened her eyes. She appeared disoriented, as though emerging from a deep sleep. "What . . . what happened?" she mumbled, attempting to rise. Her eyes widened. Glancing wildly around her, she struggled to a sitting position, smearing the floor with bloodied palms. "Where is she?"

"She's gone," I answered.

Jamie turned, noticing me for the first time. "Oh, Dad. I . . . I knew you would come," she choked, placing her arms around my neck and burying her face in my chest.

I held her tightly, her sobs tearing into me like daggers. "Shhh," I whispered, smoothing her hair. "Everything's going to be all right."

Abruptly, Jamie stiffened. With almost inhuman strength she shoved me away, sending me sprawling. She rose to her feet and in two swift strides stood over me. My heart plummeted as I looked up again into her eyes.

Once more they burned with Devon's demonic fire.

Jamie's lips curled in Devon's malevolent grin. "How sweet," she mocked. "'Everything's going to be all right.' Well, that remains to be seen, doesn't it?"

Scrambling backward, I rose to my feet. "Come out, Devon," I yelled, searching the darkness. "Come out!"

"Not yet," Jamie said. Leaving me, she moved to a nearby weapons rack and withdrew a short-handled ax. She hefted it, turning it over in her bloody palms. Though the ax appeared heavy, she handled it easily—wielding it with the familiarity of a lumberjack. "This is it, Mike," she said, starting back across the room. "Kill her. Kill or be killed."

My heart fell as I realized that Devon intended to force me to kill Jamie, or to be killed by Jamie's hand. Fighting panic, I focused my mind.

Stop.

My daughter shook her head, continuing her advance. "I thought you understood by now. That doesn't work on a *Deus*."

Suddenly I knew why I hadn't been able to control the picador in the bullring, or my assailants at the Meliá. Devon had been the puppet master behind their actions, the one pulling the strings. It had been Devon from the very beginning. But on the same token, how had I been able to block Devon's mental commands, unless . . .

Unsure of what to do, I retreated, carefully backing toward the drop behind me. I reached the edge of the loft. Jamie came in rapidly, ax in both hands. Realizing I couldn't retreat further, I glanced to the left. The metal cage blocked escape in that direction. On the right lay the brazier with the heated irons.

Jamie rapidly closed the distance. She noticed my glance toward the brazier. "Looking for a weapon? Good. You may yet live."

I feinted to the right. Jamie cut me off. I reversed left. Swerving, Jamie swung the ax. She missed. Quickly, she readied for another stroke.

I skidded to a stop, slipping in a smear of blood beside the cage. I fell hard, arms and legs splayed, the back of my head slamming into the wooden floor. I lay stunned, fighting for breath. Jamie moved to stand above me.

"Good-bye, Mike."

At the last instant I rolled away from Jamie's blow. Her ax cleaved the flooring planks, narrowly missing my shoulder. Scrambling to my knees, I made a grab for the weapon. Too late.

Jamie levered the ax from the floor. I was trapped. The cage blocked escape on one side; Jamie on the other. The ax rose again in Jamie's hands. A moment later it began its downward arc.

In a final act of desperation, I threw myself backward off the loft. I fell for what seemed forever. I felt a sickening crunch as I crashed to the concrete floor below, followed by an excruciating stab of pain.

Then nothing . . .

*   *   *

Devon stepped from the shadows, inspecting the crumpled figure at her feet. "You fool," she spat. Grabbing a fistful of hair, she dragged the limp body to a heavy table in the center of the chamber. She effortlessly lifted the unconscious form, placing it supine on the table's blood-stained surface. After securing restraining straps across chest and thighs, she quickly bound the hands and feet to the table corners with leather thongs.

Then she waited.

Though barely able to control her hunger, Devon understood herself well, and she knew how best to take her pleasure.

Anticipation played an important part, but above all the subject had to be conscious.

Shortly afterward, to her immense satisfaction, her vigil ended.

*   *   *

My eyes opened, narrowing as I saw Devon leaning over me. I tried to sit. Leather restraints held me fast. I struggled to free my hands. I couldn't. Fighting a wave of panic, I focused my mind.

Release me.

"Don't waste your strength, Mike," Devon advised. "You'll need it later." She leaned closer, her silky hair spilling over her shoulders, almost touching my face. "You could have had everything," she said softly. "Now you'll have nothing. Nothing but this."

Reaching beneath the table, she withdrew a long, curved blade—a knife suitable for gutting a fish. She rotated the blade before my eyes, then moved it down, slicing open the buttons of my shirt. Gently, she moved back the fabric.

I turned away, repelled by the hunger I saw in her face.

"Oh, no, you'll look at me," Devon said, grabbing my chin. Passing her tongue over her lips, she placed the tip of the knife in the hollow of my throat. Slowly, she drew the blade down to my navel, tracing the midline of my body, careful not to cut too deeply . . . at least not yet. A trail of red welled up behind her blade, like paint flowing from a brush.

"You could have lived forever," Devon mused, as though speaking to herself. "Even that could have been yours. I know the secret of life eternal. In time I might have shared it with you. But now . . ."

Devon laid the knife on my chest, tip pointing toward my groin. Stepping from the table, she began removing her clothes. "To be honest, ever since our trip to Mexico part of me has hoped it would come to this," she continued. Her blouse came off with a shrug, exposing her breasts. Next she unbelted her skirt and slid it down her legs, finally kicking off her shoes.

Nude except for a black thong, she returned to the table, her eyes glowing with cold, ravenous luminescence. She placed a hand on the knife. "This will be a singular experience for us both, Mike," she said. "Unfortunately, when it's over, you won't be around to remember it."

A noise came from somewhere behind us. Devon stiffened, turning toward its source. "Oh, it's you," she said dismissively.

Straining to turn my head, I saw that Jamie had descended from the loft and was standing at the foot of the stairs, silent and servile—eyes lowered, ax trailing loosely in one hand.

"She's quite an assistant," Devon went on, readdressing me. "Did you know she has the power? No? Well, she does. That apple certainly didn't fall far from the tree. Unlike *you*, however, she might have had the will to use her strength."

"Let her go," I begged. "She's only a child. She can't possibly harm you."

"She can't harm me—yet. But later, when she learns to use her power . . ." Devon thought a moment, then shook her head. "No. I can't take that risk. But before she dies, perhaps I'll let her assist in your death, as she assisted in her mother's." Devon glanced behind her. Jamie had moved a few steps closer, still dragging the ax.

Bring a heated iron.

"It was touching," Devon continued, again turning back to me, her eyes glittering. "Near the end, her mother's final words were: 'I love you, Jamie.'"

Jamie shuffled several more steps toward the table, her face still hidden, ax in both hands now.

Devon turned, anger darkening her features. "I told you to bring a heated rod."

Fetch it.

The ax suddenly rose. And in that instant I caught a glimpse of Jamie's face. To my shock, I saw that her eyes were burning with a radiance of their own.

A split second later I sensed Devon lashing out in terror.

Stop.

Devon's mental command had no effect.

"No!" she screamed. She threw herself to one side, raising her hands in an attempt to deflect the ax.

Jamie's blow missed Devon's upper torso, but the weapon bit deeply into the flesh of her thigh. With a howl of pain, Devon staggered back, gaping incredulously at the ax buried in her leg.

Jamie jerked out the weapon, cleaving a slab of flesh from Devon's thigh. She raised the ax for another blow.

With shocking speed, Devon dropped to her knees and scrabbled across the blood-slicked floor. Before Jamie could swing again, Devon crabbed beneath the table and clawed to her feet on the other side. Fury flooded her face, twisting her aristocratic features into a mask of rage. Brandishing her knife, she swiftly hobbled back, melting into the darkness.

Still gripping the ax in one hand, Jamie began fumbling at my bonds. Her fingers shook as she ripped at the leather restraints. In seconds she had the knots securing one of my hands partially loosened.

"Go," I said, struggling to finish freeing my hand. "If she makes it to the door, she'll lock us in."

Realization flooded Jamie's face. Lips set in a grim line of determination, she grabbed the ax and ran to the stairs, mounting the steps two at a time.

*   *   *

Jamie raced up the stairs to the loft, her heart pounding in terror. Praying that she would be in time, she bolted up the final treads to the top landing. The heavy oak door there stood partially open, a wash of light seeping past its frame. She checked the planks beneath her feet. No blood. Devon hadn't made it that far. She had to be somewhere below.

Jamie inspected the door. There seemed to be no way to block it, or to prevent it from being locked.

Wait for Devon here? she wondered.

No. She's still down below. And so is Dad.

242

With a sense of foreboding, Jamie returned to the middle landing. She saw a smear of red leading into the loft.

She's in there. I can feel her . . .

Jamie took a deep, shuddering breath.

I can't let her get up the stairs. I have to keep between her and the door.

Jamie hesitated. *I can't do this alone*, she thought. *I can't.*

But I can't risk going down to release Dad. She'll lock us in, like he said. And we'll die down here.

Tightening her grip on the ax, Jamie crept slowly into the loft.

*   *   *

Devon waited in the darkness, furious she hadn't been able to reach the upper door in time. Instead, she had been forced to take refuge in the loft, hiding in a concealed alcove near the feeble glow of the coals in the brazier. Seconds later she had heard the girl mounting the stairs to the top landing. Once there the girl had hesitated, then descended again to the loft.

Unconsciously, Devon's hand went to the gold chain around her neck, taking comfort from the key it held. It was a possession that gave her an immeasurable advantage. Because of it, the girl couldn't risk returning to the lower chamber to release her father. If she did, Devon would simply climb the stairs and lock them in. And if the girl fled, Devon would dispose of Mike and deal with Jamie later.

Devon felt a flicker of doubt. Had the girl already freed her father? But if that were true, Mike would already be here, she reasoned. No, Mike still lay strapped to the table below. The girl would have to come to her alone. And then this fiasco would end.

Moments later Devon sensed the girl creeping into the loft. With a surge of satisfaction, she followed the girl's approach, waiting patiently as the child moved toward the glow of the brazier.

Remaining as still as death, Devon tracked the child's progress with a perception more ancient than sight. She might have found the girl's stealthy approach amusing were it not for the horrible burning in her leg. The girl will pay for that, she promised herself. As will her father.

With an effort of will, Devon slowed her breathing. Despite her injury, she almost regretted that things were coming to such an abrupt end. She would have enjoyed toying with the child. Now she couldn't afford that luxury. She tightened her grip on the knife. No, when the girl passed Devon's alcove, she would quickly end the child's life, spilling her essence in one glorious spurt.

And so she waited, feeling Jamie moving closer, closer . . .

At precisely the right instant, Devon stepped from hiding, her knife slipping unerringly through the darkness. A delicious shock ran up her arm as the blade entered flesh. Then the knife lost its bite. Somehow, the girl had shifted away from her attack!

How had she known?

A split second later, against all reason, Devon felt a crushing blow tearing into her ribs. The knife clattered from her fingers. She fell, the hard planks of the floor rising to meet her.

And then the girl was above her, ax in both hands.

The girl's arms rose.

And as the bloodied ax began its descent, Devon heard her speak these words: "This is for my mother."

*   *   *

Jamie took a deep breath, trying to still her trembling. Using an ability she didn't understand, she sensed her captor's form beneath her on the floor, ax blade buried deep in the woman's chest, her partially severed head lolling to one side. In attempting to roll away from Jamie's blow, the woman's weight had wrenched the weapon from Jamie's grasp, trapping the handle under her lifeless body.

Heart racing, Jamie attempted to retrieve her weapon. She couldn't.

"Jamie?" Mike called from below. "Jamie?"

"Yeah, Dad," Jamie called back, touching her face where Devon's knife had caught her. Her fingers came away sticky with blood.

"Where is she?"

"She's dead," Jamie replied shakily.

But is she?

Suddenly unsure, Jamie leaned closer, staring down at the woman's body. As her eyes adjusted to the lambent light of the brazier, she could make out more of the body. With a sickening lurch, she saw that Devon's eyes were still open.

They were glowing. *Alive!*

Unable to retrieve her ax, Jamie backed toward the brazier, searching for another weapon. As she approached the edge of the loft, in the illumination filtering up from the furnace—

The furnace!

Do it fast. Don't give her time to stop me.

Trying not to think about what she was doing, Jamie ran to the woman, grabbed her ankles, and dragged her a short distance to the edge of the loft. In one quick motion she shoved her over the precipice. A sickening thump sounded as Devon's body slammed to the concrete floor below.

Breath coming in ragged sobs, Jamie raced down the stairs. As she started toward the furnace, she spotted Devon's body sprawled beneath the edge of the loft above. She also saw her father on the far side of the room, struggling to free himself from Devon's table.

Should I help Dad?

Later, Jamie decided. *Don't take any chances. Finish the woman first.*

Cautiously, Jamie approached the woman. Though Devon wasn't moving, her eyes were still open, watching Jamie's approach with undisguised rage. The fall had dislodged the ax, which was now nowhere to be seen.

Jamie considered searching for the ax, then decided to stick with her original plan. Leaning down, she grabbed Devon's ankles and dragged her to the furnace. Once there she tripped a latch and threw open the furnace doors. Inside, the old woman who had been Devon's assistant lay facedown on the grate. A spike had been driven into her temple.

Oh, God, that's my fault, Jamie thought, reeling in shock.

Not now. Think about it later . . .

Straddling Devon's body, Jamie began struggling to lift her into the oven. One of Devon's arms caught on the grate. As Jamie fought to free the arm, a bolt of terror slammed through her. Devon's wounds were closing!

Dumfounded, Jamie watched as the gash in Devon's neck began pulling together, sealing without a mark. Summoning a final burst of energy, she raised her captor's legs, attempting to shove her all the way into the furnace. Instead, Devon's limp form slid to the side, sprawling once more to the concrete floor.

Jamie leaned down for another attempt.

Quick as a snake, Devon's left hand shot up, closing on Jamie's throat.

Jamie gagged, clawing at the iron fingers encircling her neck. To her horror, she found she couldn't free herself. Then she felt Devon beginning to thrust herself deep inside her, initiating a mental transfer that Jamie sensed could never be reversed, a transfer she was powerless to resist.

*   *   *

I sensed a desperate struggle taking place, and I knew that Devon still lived. By then I'd freed the hand Jamie had started to untie. Straining at my bonds, I redoubled my efforts to release my other hand. An instant later I succeeded. Quickly I unbuckled the leather straps that held me, then sat to free my feet. As I did, I heard Jamie calling from across the room.

"Oh, God," Jamie screamed, her voice filled with terror. "Dad, she's still alive. She's trying to force herself inside me. I can't keep her out!"

"Hold on, Jamie," I called back, hurriedly freeing myself from the last of my restraints.

"She's too strong, Dad. I can't stop her. Oh, please God, don't let her in don't let her in don't let her in . . ."

246

I rolled from the table and raced to the furnace. With a feeling of horror, I ripped Devon's hand from Jamie's throat, praying I was in time.

Choking, Jamie stumbled back.

Before Devon could resume her mental attack, I scooped up her bloodied torso and thrust it into the furnace, jamming it in beside the body of an old woman. *Another victim of Devon's?*

Quickly, I latched the doors. Jamie raced to a gas valve mounted on the back wall.

Hand on the gas control, Jamie turned to me. Her eyes found mine.

I nodded grimly.

Jamie twisted open the valve. Seconds passed, seeming an eternity.

An instant later the furnace roared to life.

It took several minutes. A wordless, demonic howling raged from the oven, a satanic flood of invective spewing from Devon's mind—imploring, threatening, damning—and in the end, delivering a chilling promise.

I'll see you again, her final words sounded in our minds. *Both of you.*

And then came another voice, momentarily filling the silence of Devon's passing. It was a small voice, the voice of a child, the same voice Jamie had heard on the plane. Speaking without words, it sounded at rest now, peaceful . . . as it too faded away.

Thank you . . .

Epilogue

The telephone in our hotel room rang at precisely 5:45 A.M. Groaning, I reached across the bed to the nightstand. Fumbling in the darkness, I picked up the receiver on the fifth ring.

"Front desk, sir. You requested a wake-up call?"

"Uh, right," I yawned.

"Complimentary rolls and coffee will be served in the lobby starting at six," the voice continued politely. "Room service is also available if you prefer, along with a breakfast buffet in the dining room from seven to ten."

"Room service will be fine," I said, replacing the receiver.

"Who was that?" Jamie murmured from the adjacent bed.

"Wake-up call."

"Jeez, why so early? It's still dark out."

"Seemed like a good idea last night, remember?" I replied, turning on a light. "You know, get an early start and put as many miles between us and New York as possible." I rubbed my eyes, stretched, and picked up the TV remote control. "Want to check the news?"

"No, thanks," Jamie mumbled, pulling the covers over her head.

Still half asleep, I watched with the volume down until the Channel Two News came on at six. The report of Lyle Exner's death was the lead story. As I turned up the sound, Jamie dug out from under her covers to listen.

". . . discovery of Lyle Exner, victim of an apparent suicide, again throwing the California governor's race into turmoil just weeks before the election," the commentator said soberly. "Political aide Christine Adams discovered Mr. Exner's body late last evening in his Park Avenue residence. A spokesperson for the campaign revealed that Exner had been under extreme pressure in the wake of allegations tying him to the death of political rival Arthur Bellamy.

"In a related story," the newscaster continued, "U.S. Attorney General Carol Spelius recently filed charges against the Elysian Foundation's Board of Directors, indicting them as co-conspirators in the murder of Arthur Bellamy. Authorities are presently searching for Ms. Devon Varkoff, the foundation's CEO, missing from her East Hampton estate since last Thursday. Also sought are board members Hans Menninger and Copeland Blaumpier. To date, attorneys for the foundation have been unavailable for comment."

I raised the remote control and thumbed off the TV. Neither Jamie nor I spoke as the screen faded to darkness, each of us knowing that like Devon, Menninger and Blaumpier would never be found.

"It's over," Jamie said at last. "It's finally over."

"Is it?" I replied, wishing I could agree. "Those associates of hers said there were others, remember?"

"At least now there are fewer to worry about." Jamie was silent for a long moment. "Dad, what we did . . . I mean, did we do the right thing?"

"Getting rid of Devon and the others?"

"Yes."

Detecting a note of uncertainty in her voice, I carefully considered my next words. "Jamie, I once heard that those who do the hard things in life are those who can," I said. "Someone had to stop those people. No one else could. We did what we had to. And if we hadn't, they would have come after us. Of that I'm certain."

Jamie pressed her temples, as if to banish the memory from her mind. "Well, I suppose what's done is done," she sighed. As I turned the other way, she rolled out of bed and pulled on a clean T-shirt, jeans, a cable-knit sweater, and a new pair of Adidas high-tops that we had bought for her the previous afternoon.

"Feel like breakfast?" I asked when she finished dressing.

"Sure." Jamie crossed to an adjoining bathroom and squeezed a glob of toothpaste onto her toothbrush. "Downstairs or room service?"

"Room service," I answered.

As I lifted the phone to order, I studied Jamie's reflection in the bathroom mirror, watching as she brushed her teeth. Though it had been only days since we had escaped death in Devon's mansion, Jamie's wounds, like mine, had almost totally healed. The slash on her face and the lacerations she had received in the cage were gone. Even her hands, which had been horribly wounded, were miraculously whole. Little more than a small white scar showed on the back of the hand she was using to brush her teeth.

Abruptly, something caught my eye. With a hollow feeling, I replaced the telephone receiver. Jamie was right-handed . . .

. . . but she was holding the toothbrush in her *left*.

Noticing that I had hung up the phone without ordering, Jamie turned. "Couldn't get through?" she asked. "I know it's early, but—" She stopped midsentence, noticing the stunned expression on my face. Then, with sudden understanding, she saw that I was staring at the toothbrush in her left hand. Slowly, she smiled.

All at once I couldn't breathe. Heart pounding, I sat frozen as Jamie moved toward me, her eyes fixed unwaveringly on mine. Once again I recognized the same raised eyebrow I had first seen in Mexico, the same mocking tilt of her head. How could I have missed it? Then it all came back. The way Devon had used her left hand to eat, to pour her Scotch, to force the patrol officer to shoot Bellamy . . .

"Fool!" Jamie laughed. "Did you really think you could be rid of me so easily?"

I gaped in disbelief. Around me the room began to spin. "No!" I choked, a sheen of sweat suddenly glistening on my brow. "You're dead! You can't be alive! You can't!"

Shocked by my reaction, Jamie raised her hands. "Easy, Dad. Just kidding."

"Damn it, Jamie!" I shouted. "That wasn't funny!"

Jamie crumpled. "I . . . I'm sorry," she stammered, abruptly close to tears. "I . . . when I figured out why you were staring, I thought I'd make a joke of it, lighten things up. I guess I can't even do that right anymore. I'm really, really sorry."

"Maybe I overreacted," I said uncertainly, my heart still racing. "Why were you brushing with your left hand?"

"I started when I broke my wrist in the seventh grade," Jamie answered. "I still switch off once in a while. I can write with my left hand, too."

"You broke your wrist? I didn't know that."

Jamie shook her head sadly. "You weren't around much then, Dad."

"No, I wasn't." I took a deep breath, then let it out. "Well, that's going to change. A lot of things are going to change."

Jamie's expression brightened slightly. "Good. I'd like that," she said.

"Me, too," I replied. "Me, too."

Later, in the car, Jamie and I rode in comfortable silence as the white Tahoe we had purchased that morning steadily ate up the miles, I doing the driving, Jamie watching the countryside spin past her window. We had been traveling for several hours when Jamie posed a question that had been on both our minds. "Do you think Devon was telling the truth when she said she would see us again?" she asked. "Is she really dead? Or can she come back somehow, like she said?"

"I don't see how," I replied, praying I was right.

"Do you think there are others like her? Others who will know what we did?"

"I can't be sure," I said. "But it's a good bet the answer is yes."

"Will they come after us?"

"I don't know, Jamie. I hope not. We'll just have to stay alert and take one day at a time."

Jamie glanced at a leather suitcase sitting in the back. "Think anyone will miss the money we took from her house? There has to be several million there, not counting the jewelry."

"For Devon, it was probably nothing," I said. "I'm not going to worry about that now."

"You're right. I suppose that's the least of our problems," Jamie conceded. Then, changing the subject, "Hey, I forgot to ask. Are we going anyplace special?"

"Montana. A cabin on Flathead Lake."

"Cool. I've never been to Montana. But why didn't we just fly? It would have been a lot faster."

"I thought some time on the road might give us a chance to, you know, get things back together," I answered. "Besides, I enjoy driving."

"I'm enjoying this, too. Are we meeting anyone at this cabin?"

"Someone from the newspaper."

"Taryn?"

I nodded.

"Great." Jamie smiled. "I like her. You like her too, don't you?"

I nodded again. "I do. She's a good friend."

"I'm glad, Dad." Then Jamie's smile faltered. "Does she know about you . . . about us?"

I shook my head. "Not everything. For that matter, Jamie, neither do you."

"I know more than you think," Jamie replied. "When Devon was trying to force herself inside my head, I got a good look around the inside of hers, too. Among other things, I know about the hunger . . . and what it did to her."

"You don't know what the hunger is like," I said grimly. "Not really. Believe me, it could do the same to us that it did to her. I'm worried, Jamie."

"So am I." Jamie hesitated. "Do you believe in God, Dad?"

"What does that have to do with anything?"

"I'm serious. Do you?"

I turned. I found Jamie studying me intently. "I'd like to believe," I said, deciding to try to answer her question seriously, even though it was a subject I hadn't thought about in a long, long time. "In some ways it would be a comfort, but . . . ."

"But you don't?"

"I didn't say that."

252

"Then what *are* you saying?"

It took me a while to reply. When I did, it was to pose a question of my own. "How many stars do you think you can see on a clear night, Jamie?"

"Please, Dad—"

"I'm trying to answer. How many?"

"I don't know. A jillion. No—say, fifty thousand, maybe."

I smiled. "On a good night, only a few thousand stars are visible to the naked eye," I said. "But there *are* 'jillions' of them, as you put it, out there—a hundred billion in our galaxy alone. And there are billions of galaxies, tremendous swirling spirals of stars spread throughout the universe. The star we call our sun is just an insignificant point of light, one of many like it, shining in some forgotten corner of the cosmos."

"If you're trying to make me feel small, you're succeeding."

"Just the opposite," I said. "Don't you see? Life can't be unique to our own tiny planet. It has to be everywhere out there, everywhere you look. Otherwise, what a colossal waste of space. No, the universe must be crammed with life, and we're a part of it. I can't help but think there must be a reason, a force behind it all—*something.*"

"But what about us?" Jamie demanded bitterly. "Where do we fit in?"

"I don't understand what you mean."

"I can't forget what Devon said about us," Jamie explained, her voice trembling. She turned, her eyes again searching mine. "About us being killers. If there is a God, then why did He make us . . . the way we are?"

"You mean evil, don't you?"

Jamie turned away.

"Listen to me," I said gently. "Devon was wrong about a lot of things. For one, she was wrong about us. We're more than flesh and blood, more than the things with which we were born. The powers we posses may turn out to be a gift, or they may be a curse, or perhaps both. Either way, one thing I do know. If it ever happens that we stand in judgment to speak the truth of our lives, I want us to be able to do so without guilt or shame or regret. We have a choice to be whatever we want to be, Jamie. Despite all that's happened, we will always have that choice."

"I hope you're right."

"I know I am," I said firmly, wanting more than anything for my words to be true.

Jamie wiped her eyes. "Thanks, Dad," she said. "I . . . I guess I just needed to hear it."

Following an uncomfortable silence, I reached into my pocket and pulled out a pack of photographs. "I have something for you," I said, forcing a lightness to my tone. "I've been carrying these around for the past week," I added, passing her the packet. "I was going to save them for later, but I suppose now is as good a time as any."

"My pictures? The ones on my memory card?"

"Uh-huh. It's a long story, but Taryn had some prints made."

Jamie flipped through the photos we had taken on our motorcycle ride up the coast, pausing on the shot she had taken of us at the picnic table. The picture was framed slightly off-center, but it still clearly showed us both, the remnants of our lunch at Neptune's Net strewn on the table before us.

Jamie continued shuffling through the photos. "That was a fun day, wasn't it?" she said. "Remember that little kid who . . ." Her voice trailed off.

I turned, finding Jamie staring at a picture of her mother. The photo showed Susan kneeling in a flower garden behind her house, squinting up into the lens. She had on a bright-yellow sundress, and although a straw hat partially obscured her face, I could see she looked surprised, a smile just beginning to touch her eyes. "I forgot that was in there," I said, my voice breaking. "I'm sorry."

"No," Jamie replied woodenly. "I'm glad you left it in. This is how I want to remember her. Not like . . ."

An abysmal, ineffable sadness gripped me as a series of sobs wracked Jamie's body. Blinking back tears, I drove without speaking, helpless in the face of my daughter's despair. I realized from having lost both my parents that the deepest pain of Susan's death would come later for me, when enough time had passed for my loss to become real. For Jamie, though, the hurt had come now. I knew I would do everything in my power to ease her grief, but I also knew that nothing I could do or say would ever make things right.

Later that afternoon Jamie found a small digital camera stuffed beneath some maps in the glove compartment. "You brought my camera, too?" she said, her mouth dropping open in astonishment.

"Actually, yours got lost," I replied. "I bought another one for you just like it. Here, let me see it a minute."

Jamie handed me the camera. After rolling down my window, I extended my arm and held the camera outside, pointing it back into the interior of the car. "Say cheese."

Jamie ducked. "Don't take it yet," she pleaded. "I must look awful." Flipping down her visor, she surveyed her face in a mirror mounted on the back.

"You look fine," I insisted, pressing the shutter.

"I didn't think you liked photos," Jamie observed, regarding me curiously.

"Me?" I said. "No way. A girl I know set me straight on that. She told me that pictures are moments we can look back on and remember. You know—remind ourselves of the good things, the things that matter."

"Like time spent with people you love?"

"Exactly."

Once more Jamie stared out her window. "She must be a pretty smart girl."

"She is, Jamie. She sure is."

"I love you, Dad."

Glancing over, I saw the need in my daughter's face. Turning my thoughts inward, I searched deep within myself, and with a sense of both wonder and surprise, I discovered that something elemental inside me had changed. Without my knowing it, without my even realizing it had happened, the burden of self-loathing and guilt I had carried for so long had somehow lifted, leaving me whole for the first time in my life. And for the first time in as long as I could remember, I spoke the words that would free me, knowing I meant them with all my heart.

"I love you, too," I said softly.

Outside, the landscape flowed silently past, billboards and buildings gradually surrendering to farmland and rolling hills—distant, receding, unable to touch us. Jamie turned from the window and smiled, her eyes bright with tears. In those eyes, the eyes of a child who had grown up long before her time, I saw a heartrending amalgam of desolation and loss and fear and hope.

And at that moment, with a swell of unshakable conviction, I grew certain of one thing. Though I couldn't predict what the future would bring, I knew we would face that future together.

No matter what.

Acknowledgments

Authoring a novel is never a solitary endeavor, and I would like to express my appreciation to a number of people who provided their assistance while I was writing *Glow*. Although this is clearly a work of fiction, I try to stick to reality whenever possible, so any errors, exaggerations, or just plain bending of facts to suit the story are attributable to me alone.

To Susan Gannon, my wife, editor, best friend, and muse with a sharp eye for detail, to friends and family for their encouragement and support, to my eBook editor Karen Oswalt, to Karen Waters for her help on the cover, to Mike Dunning for his back-cover photo, and especially to my core group of readers—many of whom made critical suggestions for improvements—my sincere thanks.

If you enjoyed *Glow*, please leave a review on *Amazon* or your favorite retail site. A word-of-mouth recommendation is the best endorsement possible. As such, your review would be truly appreciated and will help friends and others like you look for books. Thanks for reading!

~ Steve Gannon

About the Author

STEVE GANNON is the author of numerous bestselling novels including *A Song for the Asking*, first published by Bantam Books. Gannon divides his time between Italy and Idaho, living in two of the most beautiful places on earth. In Idaho he spends his days skiing, whitewater kayaking, and writing. In Italy Gannon also continues to write, while enjoying the Italian people, food, history, and culture, and learning the Italian language. He is married to concert pianist Susan Spelius Gannon.

To contact Steve Gannon, purchase books, receive updates on new releases, or to check out his blog, please visit his website at: stevegannonauthor.com